Perils Past
S.J. Cunningham

A Ramsay Castle Mystery—Book 1

PERILS PAST: A RAMSAY CASTLE MYSTERY BOOK 1
by S. J. Cunningham

© Copyright 2024 S. J. Cunningham

ISBN 978-1-7368136-7-6
Paperback Edition

All rights reserved. No part of this publication may be reproduced, stored in a retrieval system, or transmitted in any form or by any means—electronic, mechanical, photocopy, recording, or any other—except for brief quotations in printed reviews, without the prior written permission of the author. To request permission, contact the author at sarah@sjcunningham.net.

This is a work of fiction. All the characters in this book are fictitious, and any resemblance to actual persons, living or dead, is purely coincidental. The names, incidents, dialogue, and opinions expressed are products of the author's imagination and are not to be construed as real.

This edition published by S.J. Cunningham:
www.sjcunningham.net.

To James, a true Scottish laird. Thank you for the adventure. Thank you for everything.

For the ghosts that never leave us. May we continue to honor your history and your stories.

So! now, the danger dared at last,
Look back, and smile at perils past!

From *The Bridal of Triermain*
—Sir Walter Scott

Chapter 1

Thick words fell through the mist of Liza's unconscious, and whispers wrapped themselves around the pictures of her dreams. She drifted up through the fog of slumber.

"No, of course not. I promise," said the voice.

Owen's voice, Liza realized as she emerged from the depths of sleep. "It's going to take more time than I thought it would," he said quietly. "I told you that."

Liza breathed in and blinked her eyes open. The bedroom was dark.

"I know," Owen was saying from somewhere. "Believe me, I know. But I'm not sure what else I can do right now." He sounded perturbed.

Liza shifted on the mattress. She reached out a hand, placing it flat on the empty bed beside her. Her eyes searched for her significant other and the source of his voice.

He was sitting at the desk in the corner of their bedroom, his shadowed silhouette hunched forward as he held the mobile against his ear. It took her a minute to process the image.

Why was Owen taking a phone call in the middle of the night?

She immediately assumed the worst.

"Owen?"

His spine straightened and he turned toward her. "I have to go," he said quickly, and hung up, putting the device down. He was plunged into darkness, but she sensed him moving toward her. "I thought you were out like a light. You took a sleeping pill."

"Is everything okay?" She pushed herself into a seated position on the pillows.

"Yeah, yeah. Of course." She felt his body sink into the mattress. "Go back to sleep. You're groggy." He reached over and patted her elbow.

She had not taken a sleeping pill before bed. She was trying to wean herself off that particular crutch. Now that her last, stressful work assignment was over, she didn't think she should need a pill to help her sleep. But the residual anxiety continued to lick at her heels, like flames at the edge of a fire always on the verge of devouring her. This time, it was a new anxiety. Thoughts, unease, and apprehension about life and being in the place that, at thirty-two years old, Liza had somehow found herself—unmarried, childless, and a little rudderless.

"Who was that?"

Owen didn't answer right away. He stretched out his long legs. "That was just Amy. You know how she is." He sighed, the signal that he was readying himself for sleep.

Amy, Owen's errant sister, disappeared from and returned to his life without warning. She was what Owen's mother liked to call a 'free spirit'. Liza had many other, far less complimentary, nicknames for her. Liza dreaded Amy's reappearance in their lives, though she'd never say as much to Owen.

"Does she want money?"

He had closed his eyes. "You know Amy," he said on an exhale, without answering the question.

A slow simmer of anger began to bubble deep within Liza's chest. Owen had been laid off from his job just a few months earlier, and he didn't seem to be in a hurry to find another source of steady income. Instead, he preferred to work on a podcast about fitness, gym life, and the best workouts for different body types. He swore it would take off any day, and he'd begun spending nearly all his time at the gym or in the studio space that was costing them—costing *her*—a small fortune.

Liza was trying her best to be supportive. But she knew the podcast market was already oversaturated, particularly with fitness feeds. And Owen couldn't articulate what made his podcast any different from the others.

All of that meant that any money Owen had promised his sister would come from Liza, and Liza was not willing to fund, through her own hard work, Amy's bad habits. Liza's last assignment had been lucrative but brutal, and she'd earned every penny working with a difficult client, and navigating the competing and territorial personalities in their dysfunctional corporate culture. Amy didn't deserve a cent of her hard-earned cash.

Owen's breath deepened, and Liza looked over in the dark. She could just make out his profile in the dim light. Even softened by sleep, his features were rugged and masculine. But he had other attributes that balanced out that masculinity, giving him an arresting and intriguing appearance. Most people—especially women—found it hard to look away from him. Now his heavy-lidded eyes were closed, the long dark lashes almost touching his high cheekbones. His lips were parted slightly, breath escaping in small, audible puffs.

She watched him for another minute, but he gave no indication of consciousness.

Liza sighed, slid back under the sheets, and stared at the ceiling. Her mind began to churn.

Her boss, Raj, had emailed her that afternoon about a new assignment for a large corporate tech client in San Francisco—a client that had just gone through a round of layoffs and was working to restructure its organization and culture. The CEO of the company had a reputation for his intensity as well as his arrogance, which meant Liza would be in a no-win situation if her advice ran afoul of the whims of this man's ego.

She hadn't yet responded to Raj's email, and she felt conflicted. She really needed a break—personally, mentally. She also knew how much money this particular client was willing to pay the firm for its services. Liza didn't want to let the firm down, but more accurately perhaps, she didn't want to turn down lucrative and visible assignments.

She felt as if she were already over the hill and being chased down by the young, ambitious graduates who were just at the onset of their careers. This new generation was hungry, and they were willing to do anything to show their loyalty to the business. If Liza faltered, there would be another high-achiever willing to take her place, sacrificing much more than she'd been willing to offer.

She eased herself out of the bed and padded to the desk where she opened the top right drawer. Underneath a stack of statements and receipts rested two manila folders in a thick cream-colored envelope. She pulled it out.

It was dark, but she didn't need light to know the wording on the front of the envelope. *Attn: Ms. Elizabeth Ramsay.*

Elizabeth was the name on her birth certificate, an appellation she rarely used. Not since her father had left her mother when she was five years old. She had one very distinct memory of the man—tall and ramrod straight, imposing.

When the envelope had arrived and Liza had seen her full name in bold printed letters, it had given her pause.

And then there was the return label. *Douglas, Burns, and Bruce: Solicitors and Estate Agents; Fountainbridge, Edinburgh, UK.*

Liza had searched the internet for the firm before she'd opened the envelope and read the contents of the letter. She'd discovered a rudimentary and static website for a small law firm housed in a small stone building that very well could have been built in the sixteenth century. The 'About Us' page featured three men, well past middle age, smiling awkwardly in bad lighting.

She'd been perplexed. Other than a few passing classmates from college, and a few current coworkers she'd encountered in random virtual meetings, she knew very few people who lived in the United Kingdom. She knew exactly *no one* in Edinburgh.

The letter itself, though…That had been a shock of a different sort. Liza was, she discovered, a descendant of a very influential and illustrious Scottish clan. An unknown relative on her father's side, who was not named in the letter, had tracked her down through a DNA and genealogy investigation, and her presence was requested at a family estate near Edinburgh to determine if she might be a suitable heir, should she choose to assume the responsibility. The letter hadn't been entirely clear, and Liza hadn't carefully studied the pages of genealogical data that had been included in the envelope.

It all sounded ridiculous. Scammy and suspicious. She'd been given a deadline by which to contact Misters Douglas, Burns and Bruce, and that deadline was tomorrow. She had fully intended to ignore the envelope, but she couldn't stop thinking about it. And now that the deadline was approaching, her heart thrummed a slow beat in her chest when she considered its contents.

It's probably a scam, she assured herself for the thousandth time.

But in the shadowy room, she traced the indentation of the lettering on the envelope.

Still, even if the offer turned out to be legitimate, she wanted nothing to do with anything related to her father. Her mother had rarely spoken of the man, but it had been clear he'd been a disappointment at best. Wouldn't exploring this opportunity be disloyal to her mother's memory? She hated the thought of hurting the kind and gentle soul who'd given up every hope and dream for Liza's future.

And maybe more than that, the thought of traveling to another country to sort out the mess of an estate matter was overwhelming. What would she do with property in Scotland? She'd never been there, had no interest in the place, and had no time to figure out a path forward. Better to let the bank assume the property and do with it what it would. She certainly didn't have the energy for the hassle, especially if she were going to call Raj back and accept the latest corporate strategy assignment.

She slipped the envelope to the back of the drawer again. The matter was settled. She hadn't told Owen about any of this, which in her mind was a sign that it wasn't meant to be. If she'd been excited by the prospect of the inheritance in any way, wouldn't she have been excited to tell her significant other—the man who'd been by her side for the past decade?

As she closed the drawer, Owen's phone, which he'd left on top of the desk, buzzed. The screen lit up with a notification. A text message from 'Mitchell From Work' popped up. Liza frowned. She couldn't remember anyone named Mitchell from Owen's last job.

She shrugged it off, and was about to walk back to bed when the screen lit up again. This time, Liza caught sight of the first line of the message.

Is the bitch sleeping yet?

Liza's extremities went cold as the words sunk in. Was this Mitchell guy talking about her? She wracked her brain, trying to remember who he was and what she could have done to offend him.

Just as the phone dimmed, another notification popped onto the screen.

Owen, you need to call me back. We need to settle this, baby.

Liza's stomach lurched as the reality of the string of messages hit her. There was no Mitchell. This was a woman. A woman who called her boyfriend 'baby' and called her *bitch*.

Another buzz and notification.

Are you there? Call me. I need to talk to you.

Even as her head knew the truth of what she was reading, her heart was searching for a logical explanation. Could this possibly be Amy? But…no. Owen's sister might call her a bitch, but she definitely wouldn't call Owen 'baby'. Could it be some misunderstanding? A wrong number, maybe?

No. The notification had addressed Owen by name.

Liza stood staring at the phone. It went dark. Her heart pounded in her chest as she waited for another notification to light the screen. None came.

She wasn't sure what any of this meant or what she should do.

Part of her felt numb and wanted to ignore what she'd just seen, hoping it had all been a bad dream. Part of her wanted to take the phone and throw it as hard as she could at the sleeping form of the man who was supposed to be her partner.

Could she really have been such a fool?

Tears pricked her eyes, but didn't fall. Instead, they

pooled at the back of her throat in a painful lump.

She wasn't sure how long she stood there before hearing Owen's voice.

"Come to bed, sweetheart."

Still stunned, she turned and looked at him. Sleep shadowed his face, and his sandy brown hair was adorably mussed.

Liza stared at the hand he'd stretched out toward her.

The phone stayed quiet. She glanced toward the bedroom door. The third-story Back Bay apartment only had one bedroom since she'd converted the spare room to her office. The couch in the sitting room was more for sitting than for sleeping, though she supposed she could curl up there and sob herself to sleep.

Another burst of anger washed over her. Why should *she* have to leave the bed? Owen was the one who was apparently being unfaithful. Owen was the one without a job, without an income, without ambition. He needed to get out. Now.

But when she looked back at the bed, ready to scream demands that he vacate immediately, he'd drifted off again, as if there were nothing at all wrong between them. She felt drained. She would not solve this tonight. She needed time to think and plan. She needed time to figure out how she wanted to approach Owen and what would happen next.

Because what she'd seen on that phone screen had just changed everything.

Chapter 2

Between grief, anger, sorrow, and self-pity, she agonized well into the night as she lay on the firm cushions of the sofa. At some point she must have worn herself out and fallen asleep. Now, the warm New England summer sun was streaming through the windows. She sat up and rubbed her face with her hands. Her head throbbed with a dull headache, and her eyes were so swollen she could barely see.

Her long brown waves of hair wound around her head and her face in a matted, tangled curtain. She pushed the hair from her eyes.

She listened, but heard no sounds coming from the back of the apartment. From the living room, she could see the small kitchen. Owen wasn't there. She wondered if he'd bothered to look at her when he'd left. Had he noticed the tears, or her mottled face? Had he wondered why she'd been sleeping on the sofa?

She wanted him to feel guilty. To feel some sense of shame or remorse for his actions.

Then she remembered that he didn't know she knew about 'Mitchell From Work'. In his mind, everything was just as it had always been. Their lives hadn't shifted at all.

On the end table, beside the couch, her phone trilled. She glanced over and noticed two things simultaneously: Firstly, it was nearly nine thirty in the morning, and secondly, that it was Raj calling her, most likely for an answer regarding the assignment. Reflexively, she picked up the phone.

"Raj," she said, her voice hoarse and nasal to her own ears.

"Liza?" He paused, reacting to her altered voice. "What's wrong? Are you ill?"

Liza ran a hand through her hair. Her fingers snagged in the knots. "Yes," she lied. "Head cold."

"Well, get some soup in you and get well soon because we need you back as soon as possible. Any chance of you coming into the office tomorrow? I know you're technically using your vacation hours, but I'd like to brief you on this assignment. It's already in progress, and the Dallas office has been having some challenges. As I outlined in my email, you're just the person to get the work back on track." He went on to say that he'd already committed to the egotistical CEO and that Liza was his secret weapon for getting his company to where it needed to be.

Liza leaned forward and pinched the bridge of her nose between her thumb and forefinger. There was no way she could take this assignment before attempting to straighten things out with Owen.

"We'll need you in California by Thursday, latest. Unfortunately, Dallas let the situation fester far too long, and the client is losing faith in us."

"Raj, I appreciate the confidence. But unfortunately, I'm dealing with a bit of a personal situation."

The silence on the other end stretched out.

"Raj, are you there?"

A beat, and then, "I'm here."

"Did you hear what I said?" She knew he had.

Another pause. He was weighing his words. And then, "Look, Liza. We're really relying on you here."

"I know, Raj. And I appreciate that. It's just—"

"I shouldn't need to remind you that you just made partner a few months ago."

Her face flushed at the implied threat.

Neither of them spoke.

Finally, Raj cleared his throat. "So, can I expect you in the office tomorrow morning?"

Liza swallowed hard. She looked up at the textured white ceiling and blinked hard. Tears rolled down her cheeks, and she struggled to keep them out of her voice. "Of course," she said, her voice little more than a whisper.

"Okay, good," Raj said, his voice softer. "Liza, this is a tough role, and you've done a great job for us. We all recognize your capabilities and determination. And believe me, if you can sort this assignment out, the sky's the limit for you."

She nodded, but she was unable to make the words come out.

He continued. "Sometimes when we have personal issues, the best thing is to just push forward. No sense in wallowing, right?"

Liza picked up the hem of her nightshirt and wiped her face. Raj had no idea what her personal issues were. What if she'd received some disturbing medical news, or a family member was sick? Those are certainly not things you *just push forward* through.

But that was not her case. She only had a cheating boyfriend. So, maybe Raj was right. Maybe work was what she needed.

But she was so very tired, and she didn't know if she had the energy to give to a client right now. Especially a demanding client.

"I'll be sending you some information about the project throughout the day. If you can study the business cases, their list of key performance indicators and the biographies of the executive leadership team, that should be enough of a start. We can talk about their financials tomorrow, but I'll send you their board decks so you have an idea of what was promised to shareholders. I'll also attach the org charts. I have a vague sense their organization needs to be reexamined, but they're not going to accept that as a root cause. Likely, you'll need to put some temporary fixes in place before you can dig deeper. You're going to need a quick win to sway this CEO." Raj whistled lightly. "He's a…challenge."

Raj kept talking, about culture shifts, employee experience, strategic transformation, and low-hanging fruit, but Liza's head had begun to pound. She stopped listening. As he spoke, her phone began to simultaneously chime with the incoming emails he was forwarding. The rest of her day would be spent sorting through hundreds of email strings that were indicative of whatever problems this company was facing. Raj would expect her to be well-versed about the problems by tomorrow, and he'd likely want her to identify some sort of initial path to success.

"Do you have any immediate questions?"

"No," she answered weakly.

He paused, probably wondering if she'd been listening. She'd heard enough.

"Okay, great," he finally said. "I'll see you at nine tomorrow morning?"

"Yes."

"Perfect." He drew out the 'r' as if he were purring. "And Liza, if you need any support at all, you just let me know."

She didn't answer.

"Okay?"

"Sure, Raj."

"Don't forget to look over those materials today."

Liza felt numb. Her tears had dried up, and her body had shut down. "Sure, Raj," she said again.

"Fantastic. See you tomorrow, Liza. You're going to be great."

She ended the call. Her phone pinged with another incoming email. She glanced at her inbox. Six new message strings, and that wouldn't be the last of them. She set the phone down on the coffee table and went to the kitchen to brew a pot of coffee before showering and getting started with her day. So much for a break.

She set the coffee maker to brew. As she did, her mind shifted back to Owen. They needed to have a conversation. She would not stay with someone who was unfaithful. She was still fairly young, and moderately attractive. When she'd been a teenager, someone had described her looks as 'timeless', though at the time she'd no idea what it meant. Now, she realized they'd been trying to say that she'd look in her thirties like she'd looked in her teenage years. She was tall for her age, and willowy, but she'd always held herself with a confidence that she never really felt.

Her dark hair was long and thick, and her amber eyes were eerily piercing.

But none of that had ever mattered to her. What mattered was her intelligence. She was educated at Harvard. She'd worked with CEOs and executive leaders, and they valued her insights and opinions. She didn't need a man to be happy or fulfilled.

Yet, she couldn't see herself alone. She'd been with Owen for nearly a decade. She wasn't sure she knew how to exist without him.

She poured a mug of coffee and sipped it as she stood in front of the bay window of the brownstone. Through the trees, she could see the Charles River glinting in the distance.

The front door opened, and Owen barreled through, his earbuds in place. "Yeah, no," he said, laughing before catching sight of her standing at the window. "Hey, can I call you back?" He caught her eye then looked away quickly. "Definitely…Okay, later."

He walked over to her as if to kiss her. She backed away.

He stepped back with a frown on his face. "Everything okay?" Without waiting for an answer, he said, "You slept out here last night."

She braced herself for the conversation. Her heart had begun a steady thumping in her chest, and she looked out the window again. "We need to talk."

Owen straightened. The good-naturedness disappeared. "So, talk."

He sounded angry. She felt her resolve waning.

"I'm going to need to go out of town in a few days."

This wasn't unusual, and his posture relaxed. He nodded. "Where?"

"San Francisco."

"Okay. Anything you need from me?"

She shook her head and turned to stare back out the window.

He stood there a second longer. She could feel him staring at her. When she didn't answer, he gave a little scoff. "I'm going to take a shower. I was at the gym."

He started into the bedroom.

"Who is Mitchell?" The question burst out of her mouth without her conscious cooperation.

There was silence. She was still staring out the window, her coffee growing cold in the mug.

The energy shifted, and she knew he'd come close behind her.

"What did you say?" he asked, his voice low.

She didn't respond, but she did turn to look at him. His face was screwed into a scowl, his playful, good-natured gaze gone, replaced by a hard icy stare.

"I said, 'Who is Mitchell'?" She enunciated each word slowly.

"Did you go through my phone?"

Her mouth was dry and her pulse raced. "No, but maybe I need to."

"This is bullshit, Liza," he said, taking a step toward her. "Why would you ask me that?"

She set her jaw and planted her feet. She would not back away.

"I'm going to ask you one more time. Did you go through my phone?"

"No, Owen. I did not go through your phone." She

hitched her chin higher. "I didn't need to, since your notifications pop up for the world to see."

He narrowed his eyes and she glared at him. Then he changed tack. "Look, I don't know what you think you saw—"

"What I *know* I saw was someone identified as 'Mitchell from work' calling you *baby*." She held up a finger. "First of all, you don't work. And second, I find it highly unlikely that a man named Mitchell would call you 'baby'."

His mouth dropped open as if in shock. "That's what this is about?" he asked, his tone incredulous. "This is about me not working."

It took a second for Liza to process the change in subject. "What? No, Owen. This is about the fact that you're cheating on me!" She couldn't help it. Her voice rose.

He put both hands up in front of his chest, palms facing her. "Easy," he said. "No need to get hysterical."

She wanted to scream. "Are you kidding me?" she yelled.

He shook his head. "I can't talk to you when you're like this." He walked away. "I'm getting a shower, and when you've calmed down and feel like you can speak like an adult, I'll have a conversation with you."

Liza stared at his back as he walked into the bedroom and disappeared. It was all she could do to keep from running after him and pounding his shoulders with her fists. She wasn't even sure what had just happened.

Her phone chimed with an incoming text message. She looked at it. Her whole body was shaking with tension and anger. She shut her eyes and took three deep breaths. When she felt like she was grounded again, she poured the coffee. She could hear the water of the shower start on the other side of the wall, and she glared daggers at the bedroom door. She noticed Owen hadn't left his phone lying around like he normally did.

The text message was from Raj.

I know we said 9 tmrw, but really need you here today. Erly aftn if possible. Thx.

Liza began typing, then stopped. She put the phone down and walked into the bedroom. Owen's sweaty gym clothes lay in a pile outside the bathroom door.

She slid the top right drawer of the desk open and pulled out the envelope that had haunted her for two weeks, took it into the living room, and dialed the number at the top of the stationary, using country code +44.

"Douglas, Burns and Bruce. How can I help ye this afternoon?" a heavily accented female voice asked in a lilting Scottish burr.

Liza paused. What did she think she was doing?

"Ha-looo?" the voice sang out.

"Hi," Liza said. "I, uh—" She took a breath. "I received a letter a few weeks ago from your firm." She shuffled through the pages. "It was signed by an, um…" She searched. "Robert Douglas."

"Ah, aye, Mr. Douglas. He's just in his office. Hold on a wee minute while I fetch him for ye."

Liza heard the water of the shower stop. She took the letter and her phone and walked into the office. Owen's microphones and sound-mixing equipment were strewn on a desk under the window. Her own desk was nearly bare. Since she'd found herself traveling for work more and more lately, she rarely had the need for an at-home office like she'd had only a few years earlier during the shutdown.

She heard a shuffling on the other end of the line, and she shut the door of the office behind her.

"Robert Douglas here," said the voice, Scottish and all business. Liza noticed that the 'r' sound was a slight trill, as if the man's tongue was just tapping the front of the roof of his mouth.

"My name is Liza Ramsay, and I've received a letter," she began. "It's related to a potential inheritance, I think."

There was a silence. Liza thought the connection may have been lost. "Hello?" she asked tentatively.

"Aye, Ms. Ramsay," the man responded. "I wasn't expecting yer call. Give me just a second, would ye?"

There was a loud bang as if the phone had been dropped, and Liza held the phone away from her ear.

She heard muttering and what she imagined were papers being moved around.

"Okay, I've got it now. Callum was so excited to find ye. It took a wee bit of work, even with your DNA. There are a few thousand Elizabeth Ramsays in America, if ye didn't know."

"I, uh—It's *Liza*, actually."

"What's that now?"

"I don't call myself Elizabeth. It's Liza."

A pause. "I see. Well, okay then. I take it ye had time to review the correspondence ye were sent a few weeks back?"

"Yes," she answered.

When she didn't elaborate, the man on the other end of the phone continued. "So ye understand why Mr. Ramsay would like to meet ye before moving forward with additional paperwork."

It wasn't a question, but Liza answered in the affirmative again.

"Right. So then…When are ye comin' to Edinburgh?"

Liza heard Owen moving forcefully around in the other room. She'd swear he was banging drawers and closet doors. Could he be packing?

"Ms. Ramsay?"

"Yes, I'm here." She tried to concentrate on the conversation while listening for Owen's movements. "I'm not sure I can come anytime soon. I was hoping we could just have a conversation, and I could decide the next course of action."

The man made a clicking sound with his tongue. "A condition of the inheritance is that ye be physically present at the estate. At least until the details are finalized. It's all outlined in the paperwork I sent along. Did ye read it?"

Despite the musicality of the words, Liza could hear the censure in his voice. She grimaced as she spoke. "I skimmed it," she admitted. "But, Mr. Douglas, I'm not sure it'll be possible for me to come. At least for a few weeks."

"Well, that's disappointing. Callum has been keen to meet ye. But I'm afraid if ye can't come, we'll need to move forward with other options."

Liza didn't think he sounded particularly disappointed, but she supposed this type of work was business as usual for the lawyer.

She didn't remember seeing the name Callum in the paperwork, but when she flipped through the addendum pages with the DNA results, her eyes caught the reference. 'Callum Ramsay'. The current chief of Clan Ramsay. Whatever that meant.

He was still alive, she thought with a start, wishing she'd spent some more time with the paperwork before making this phone call. But then again, she hadn't planned on calling at all. If the current owner were still alive, why was she being summoned? She asked the question to Mr. Douglas.

"Callum is not in good health, and his mind isn't as sharp as it used to be. But he wants to know that the estate is in the best hands before he departs this world. He thinks that those hands might be yours."

Liza's phone chimed with an incoming text. She moved it away from her face so she could read the notification. Raj. *Still waiting for your reply. Expecting you at 1.*

Liza's stomach clenched, and she ran her tongue over her teeth. It was already past eleven, and she hadn't eaten, showered, or even brushed her teeth yet.

"Ms. Ramsay?" Mr. Douglas asked.

"I'm here," she answered. "I'm just—can you give me just a minute?"

"Ms. Ramsay, if ye're not interested in the estate, we really need to know now. Yer bloodline is strong, but there are likely other ancestors we could consider. However, we're running out of time."

Her phone chimed again. She exhaled. She glanced at the notification, fully expecting another demand from Raj. But it wasn't her boss. It was Owen. Texting her from the bedroom.

Liza, I'm staying with a friend for a few days until you've had a chance to cool down and think about what you're accusing me of.

Another chime.

I've done nothing but support you, and your accusa-

tions are insulting and hurtful. We can talk when you're ready to apologize.

Liza stared at the phone, dumbfounded. Had she read those messages from the previous night incorrectly? Surely Owen wouldn't be so offended if he hadn't done anything wrong? She started to question what she'd even read the night before. Perhaps in her sleep-clouded brain, she'd seen something other than what had actually been there. Was it possible?

"Shall I take yer lack of response as an indication ye're not interested?"

She heard the words come out of her own mouth before she could process what she was saying. "I'll be there tomorrow."

Mr. Douglas sounded as shocked as she was. "Oh." There was a pause while the mutual surprise hung across the ocean between them. "Okay, Ms. Ramsay. Callum will be excited to meet ye, God willin'."

The magnitude of the decision hit Liza immediately, and she had to stop herself from doing a on-eight. She supposed she had the day to think it over, and any number of factors could keep her from traveling: flight delays, lack of accommodation. Raj. Owen.

"Do I need to book a hotel?"

"I'll take care of the accommodation and text ye any updates to this number, if this is yer mobile."

"Yes," Liza said. Her phone chimed again with an incoming text. She didn't look at it. "I need to book a flight."

Mr. Douglas read off the digits of his own mobile number and told her to text him her flight number and said someone would be waiting for her when she came through customs. She thanked him and disconnected the call, wondering what she'd just done, agreeing to travel to Edinburgh on a fool's errand. She had no idea how long she'd be gone, or what was in store for her. The only thing she did know was that when she returned, she'd likely have no job and no significant other.

Her pulse raced at the realization, and she realized with surprise that her quickening heartbeat wasn't wholly due to anxiety. Some of it was anticipation.

Chapter 3

A thin fog blanketed the ground as Liza looked out of the plane's window upon descent into Edinburgh International Airport. She could make out the green mountains in the near distance; the landscape reminded her of flying into the small airport near what had once been her grandmother's home in the hills of western Pennsylvania.

The sky was a steely gray, and she thought it might be raining, or misted. It looked cold outside. Much colder than the humid summer heat of Boston.

The overnight flight had been uneventful, even if the hours leading up to her travel had not gone as smoothly. Turning down the new work assignment had first been received with flat-out denial. When Raj finally realized Liza wasn't asking his opinion or permission to reject the assignment, his tone had shifted from persistence to cold acknowledgment. She was probably lucky he hadn't fired her on the spot, but she wasn't sure it mattered; when she'd told him she didn't know when she'd be returning to the States, he hadn't said a word.

It may have been the most difficult conversation she'd ever had, knowing she was actively sabotaging her own career on a lark. Liza could feel her mother's disappointment—almost as if the woman were sitting beside her—as the plane shuddered down the runway.

Liza hadn't bothered to tell Owen she was leaving. She'd heard him banging around outside her office door; she thought maybe he was waiting for her to emerge and beg his forgiveness. But she hadn't, and he'd simply left.

If and when he returned to their apartment, he would assume she was in San Francisco. Eventually, they'd need to talk. In her heart, she was already feeling his absence—the ghost of his crooked smile, the steadying warmth of his body beside her. She turned to jelly next to him. She molded to his presence. She hated to admit that, even to herself.

The plane turned toward the terminal building. As they approached the gate, Liza switched on her phone. The incoming text messages that buzzed their appearance were all from Mr. Douglas, giving her very detailed instructions about where to meet him when she emerged from baggage claim.

She navigated immigration and passport control easily, and, as always, was happy when her suitcase emerged on the baggage carousel. With her frequent travel and delayed and canceled flights, she'd had to file more than her fair share of baggage claims. At least the trip was starting off smoothly, she thought, as she pulled the checked bag off the belt.

As she exited the final gates and found herself landside, she spotted a short balding man of about sixty, dressed in a pair of business trousers and a black sports jacket, holding a white sign that read 'Elizabeth Ramsay'. She realized that here, people would assume her name was Elizabeth. She exhaled.

But she was here. She'd made the decision, and she would live with it for the next few days.

She walked up to the man.

"Ms. Ramsay?" His voice had a lyrical Scottish brogue.

She nodded once. "Liza, yes."

"Lovely." He tucked the cardboard sign under his arm. "Wasn't sure exactly what ye'd look like." He took her suitcase from her hand as he openly studied her with an unreadable expression. "Can I take yer knapsack?" he asked, indicating her travel backpack.

"I've got this one," she said, shaking her head. Her life was in that bag: passport, identification, phone, laptop. She realized that if everything else disappeared, this backpack and its contents were really all she'd need to start over completely.

She gripped the strap a little tighter.

"Ye don't look like what I thought ye'd look like."

"And how is that?"

He lifted his shoulders. "I thought ye'd be a bit

dafty, to be honest."

Liza didn't bother to let him know that her behavior and looks were two different things, but she assumed he thought she'd act like a silly American, and look like one too. How that might manifest in actuality, she didn't know.

She looked at him levelly.

He cleared his throat and started toward the airport's entrance, walking quickly. Liza lengthened her stride to keep up. As they moved, he spoke over his shoulder and asked if she were hungry or if she'd like to use the facilities before heading to the Ramsay Estate. She declined on both counts, and he seemed pleased.

When the automatic doors slid open and they stepped outside, Liza shivered. She was dressed in yoga pants and a comfortable t-shirt, but even though it was June, it must have been below sixty. In her rush to make travel arrangements, pack, and prepare for the trip, she'd neglected to check the weather.

Mr. Douglas glanced over at her. "Did ye bring anything warmer to wear?"

"I think so," she answered. At least she *thought* she'd packed warmer clothing. Truthfully, with the lack of sleep, emotional turmoil, and utter shock at her own spontaneity, she had no idea what she'd thrown into the suitcase.

They walked to a busy parking area. Mr. Douglas

stopped at a Land Rover and opened the trunk, carefully placing her suitcase in the compartment. She moved to the right side of the car, and Mr. Douglas watched her, bemused, as he closed the trunk. "Would ye like to drive?" he finally asked.

Liza glanced in the window at the steering wheel and gave a weak laugh, realizing the driving style was reversed here. "Force of habit," she said sheepishly. She quickly crossed to the opposite side of the car.

"Everyone does it," he mumbled and climbed in.

Liza slid into the passenger seat. She held on as Mr. Douglas shot backward out of the parking space and maneuvered quickly around parked cars and pedestrians on the opposite side of the road. She wanted to squeeze her eyes shut, but she overcompensated by opening them too wide.

As they whipped around two roundabouts on the way out of the airport, he glanced over at her and chuckled. "Ye'll get used to it. The estate has a car ye can use. Maybe to go get yerself some new jumpers."

"Oh, I won't be driving over here." Liza gripped the door handle as a bus nearly merged into them.

"Absolute rocket," the man muttered, swerving into the other lane. "Lachlan can probably take ye out, I suppose, if ye ask the lad nicely." She thought she detected a scowl, but it could have been directed toward the drivers on the road.

"Who's Lachlan?"

"Ah, he's..." The man frowned. "Well, he works at the estate. Ye know, on second thought, maybe he shouldnae take ye out after all."

He tapped on his horn as a small car on yet another roundabout nearly drifted into them.

After a few minutes, they merged onto an expressway, where the traffic flowed easily. Liza let out the breath she'd been holding.

"Were ye able to get some sleep on the flight?" Mr. Douglas asked.

With the accent, it took Liza a moment to process his meaning, but he didn't seem to notice the delay. "A bit," she answered. The amount of travel required with her job had drawbacks, but she'd been able to upgrade her status with the airline to business class. Yet even though she'd dozed off frequently, the sleep hadn't been restful. As she was over the Atlantic Ocean, her mind had lurched back to Owen and Raj and forward to the unknowns of the Ramsay Estate.

"Well, we'll try and let ye have a kip after ye talk with Callum."

Liza frowned at the unfamiliar phrase, but she was too tired to engage, so she leaned her head back and watched the landscape pass her by. Just as she had upon the plane's arrival, she noticed the familiarity of the scenery. She'd spent so much of her childhood, particularly in the years after her father had first left them, in the rural countryside of Pennsylvania. She couldn't shake the strange feeling that she'd been to this place on the other side of the ocean before. She hadn't expected that.

Mr. Douglas took an exit to the left and emerged onto a country road with little traffic. The bucolic scenery—the landscape of rolling green hills dotted with white sheep—had begun to lull her to sleep, and she rested her eyes for just a moment.

As the edges of unconsciousness began to impinge on her awareness, she heard Mr. Douglas exclaim, "Oh, my…What have we here?"

A queue of black-and-white police cars stretched down the road along the tree line. At the end, an ambulance waited with red lights flashing. Four uniformed men stood around a stretcher, lifting it carefully into the back of the vehicle. Liza could make out the still shape of a figure under the white sheet. A small pale hand was just visible at the edge of the sheet.

An icy wave of dread washed over her, sending chills through her body.

She made eye contact with one of the uniformed men as they drove by. His face was grim.

"Oh, my, my my," Mr. Douglas said over and over again. He glanced over at Liza and caught a glimpse of the horror on her face. "I can assure ye, Ms. Ramsay, this sort of thing never happens here."

He sounded apologetic. Liza didn't know how to respond. She felt a profound sorrow for the figure under the sheet, but she also wanted to know what had befallen the poor soul. Even an accidental death might cause her to rethink this ill-advised adventure. She wasn't sure what Mr. Douglas had meant by 'this sort of thing', but she knew she wasn't interested in staying someplace where random deaths happened at all, however infrequently.

In silence, they traveled a short distance further along a narrow and winding road, before the vehicle made a sharp left turn and the tires crunched onto gravel.

"Nearly there…"

They drove up a small rise where a massive sycamore tree stood sentinel. The tree's powerful trunk splayed upward and split into huge branches, like a gnarled hand grasping toward the heavens. Liza thought the tree must be centuries old.

Then, as they came up over the hillock, an enormous castle constructed of a washed-out red stone seemed to rise from the horizon. An honest-to-goodness castle complete with a battlement and parapets, drum tower and what appeared to be the remnants of a moat. Liza nearly forgot the shock of the scene on the road behind them.

"What is this place?" she breathed as they pulled into a parking area at the front of the massive building. She could just make out where a drawbridge may have once been situated. This place must have been a recreation of an ancient fortress.

"This is the Ramsay Estate, Ms. Ramsay. Did ye not look it up?"

She shook her head, too stunned to even begin to feel silly. The word 'estate' had conjured images of a small cottage on a few acres of property. This was—well, she couldn't even begin to describe the architectural marvel in front of her.

Mr. Douglas cut the engine of the Land Rover. They both climbed from the car.

"I'll get yer bag," he said.

Liza grabbed her backpack from the back seat of the vehicle, her mouth agape. She tore her eyes away from the structure to look at the sprawling and manicured grounds that surrounded it. Through the trees, she could make out the glinting of water—a river or a wide stream.

"The Creagan River," said Mr. Douglas, following her gaze. "It's more of a burn than a full-fledged river right here. But it's likely one of the reasons the castle was built on this hillside centuries ago."

Liza had hundreds of questions, but she didn't know where to begin. She stared at Mr. Douglas who was hustling her along. "Let's get ye to yer room, then ye can meet Callum—the laird of the Ramsay Estate and chief of Clan Ramsay."

The gravel crunched under their feet as they walked toward the massive wooden front door. Before they could reach the entrance, the door burst open and a woman—middle-aged and plump, her reddish-gray hair escaping wildly from the messy updo—ran toward them. The apron she wore over her white blouse and blue trousers was covered in food smears.

"Robert, have ye heard the news? They just pulled the lad Charlie Campbell from the river not two miles from here!"

Liza was able to quickly decipher the words through the brogue. She thought of the small white hand uncovered by the sheet. The body had a name. Charlie Campbell.

"Och!" Mr. Douglas said with a shake of his head. "Charlie was a wee scoundrel, but he didn't deserve to die."

"He was a child?" Liza asked, alarmed. It was one thing to see a body. It was quite another to see the body of a boy.

"He was also a thief," the woman said, raising her eyebrows at Liza.

Mr. Douglas seemed understandably flustered. He ignored Liza's question and said, "Margaret, this is Elizabeth Ramsay. She's the one who'll be staying with ye for a time. Elizabeth, this is Mrs. Boyle."

Mrs. Boyle's mood shifted as she turned to study Liza. "Ah, so ye're the one Callum's been blatherin' on about. Didnae think ye'd actually show up."

At a loss for a response to anything that'd happened thus far, Liza finally stepped forward and offered her hand. "Liza," she said, correcting Mr. Douglas's introduction. "To tell you the truth, I'm not really sure what I'm doing here."

"And how is Callum today?" Mr. Douglas asked.

Mrs. Boyle shrugged. "Hasn't said much of anything this morning, but he broke his fast with some haggis and tatties. That's somethin'."

"I'll just pop in for a wee minute, if ye can get Elizabeth settled in her room."

Mrs. Boyle took the luggage from Mr. Douglas's hand and pulled the suitcase violently across the stones toward the door. "Come on then," she said over her shoulder. Liza winced at the scraping of her bag on the gravel.

When they stepped through the doors, Liza's mouth fell open all over again. Inside the grand entrance was a sweeping double staircase leading up to a second-floor landing. An ornate antique chandelier hung from a deep recess in the sculptured ceiling. Ancient-looking tapestries adorned each wall as they climbed.

"We don't keep all the bedrooms open, but I've put ye in the nicest one we've got ready. Since ye're lookin' to assume the role of mistress, of course." Liza thought she detected a cattiness or sarcasm in that last statement.

"Any room will do just fine."

"I hope ye don't mind stairs."

Liza wanted to stop and stare at every portrait and framed document on the walls. She felt as if she were in a museum.

They reached the back of the second-floor landing and began to climb. Though Liza was in fairly good physical condition, the lack of sleep was catching up with her, and she was breathing heavily by the time they emerged four stories up onto the top floor. Mrs. Boyle turned to the right, still clutching the suitcase, and huffed and puffed as she continued down the corridor to a large room at the end of the hallway.

The walls were rounded, part of the castle's drum, and the room was decorated in deep purples and rich ivories, adorned with elaborate mahogany furniture. In the center of the room sat an imposing four-poster bed. A vintage desk was situated at one window of the room, and a love seat sat beneath the other. Even though the day was damp and gray, the room was filled with light from the massive windows. Liza also took note of the dim light emanating from the decorative wall sconces and small lamp at the bedside table. There did not seem to be a light affixed to the ceiling.

As Mrs. Boyle heaved Liza's suitcase onto a small bench at the foot of the bed, Liza studied a portrait of a young woman wearing a pale blue dress. Dark tendrils of hair skimmed the woman's cheeks, and though her lips curved up slightly, her brown eyes were unfocused and impossibly sad. Despite the apparent age of the portrait, Liza detected a resemblance in that face, mostly in the eyes and the curve of the cheek.

"Don't stare over hard at Lady Catherine. She's likely to attach herself to ye." Mrs. Boyle laughed at her own joke which Liza didn't understand.

"Ye're probably hungry. I've just started to fix the lunch and tea, if ye'd like."

"That would be wonderful, thank you."

"It'll be ready presently." She nodded once and looked around as if searching for someone or something. Then she sighed. "I wish Robert had told me ye were comin' a bit sooner. A little notice would've been nice."

Liza lifted a hand apologetically. "That's my fault. My plans were all very last-minute."

"Well, no matter. I'll ask Lachlan to show ye around. If I can find the keelie, that is."

Mr. Douglas had also mentioned Lachlan, but before Liza could ask who he was, Mrs. Boyle had bustled out of the room and shut the door behind her, leaving Liza alone in the alien space. After the other woman had gone, the air around her seemed heavier, more energized. Her nerves must have been sensitized by the unfamiliarity of the place and the situation.

She moved to the bed and ran her hand along the smooth poster frame, studying the intricate inlays on the headboard. *Who had slept in this bed before her?*

she wondered, imagining ghostly figures of times long past.

Even if filled with ghosts, the bed was inviting. Liza looked longingly at the mattress. But she knew if she lay down, she'd sleep the day away. She needed to stay awake and establish a normal sleep routine if she was going to understand what was being asked and expected of her here. She couldn't quite wrap her head around the fact that she might have the opportunity to assume ownership of this property. It was unthinkable. It was laughable.

She laughed out loud then.

It was also a pipe dream. She ran her hand along the curved brick of the wall as she walked to the window. This place would never be hers, but it felt nice to dream.

Out the window on the left side of the room, she discovered that from this height, she could see far down the road along which she and Mr. Douglas had driven. Two police cars were still parked by the side of the route, and she could just make out the movement of figures over the hillside where the river cut through the landscape. She hadn't realized it in passing, but the line of police cars had been parked along the tree line that ran parallel to the river.

She thought of that poor boy with the pale white hand. Had the young man drowned? From what she could see, the river didn't look deep or fast-moving enough for a drowning, but she didn't know the terrain, nor did she know the circumstances. An accidental death would be a relief. She couldn't handle the thought of a murder so close, and where she was so alone.

She turned from the window, and thought she saw movement in the corner of the room near the door. Her heart leapt into her throat.

But there was no one there. Just dust eddies that danced on the light.

Liza shook the cobwebs from her head and found the door to the bathroom. A small shower stall had been installed in the corner of the room, but the focal point was a white clawfoot bathtub. Did she have time for a quick soak before lunch? Her whole body yearned to melt into a pool of hot water, to ease some of her tension away.

She went to the door of the bedroom and poked her head out. The hallway was empty and silent.

She shut and latched the door behind her. If she missed lunch, she could surely find some leftovers or snacks in the kitchen. She was not picky.

She hurried back to the bathroom, closing the door. The bedroom was drafty, and the bathroom, with its updated white floors and granite fixtures, seemed even colder. She ran the water into the bathtub, adjusting the temperature so that swirls of mist rose into the chilled air. While the tub filled, Liza gathered her toiletry case from her suitcase. By the time she'd brushed her teeth, pulled her hair up, and found a towel, the water was close to the top of the tub. She turned the handle of the faucet; the water slowed then stopped.

Shedding her clothes in a pile on the floor, she shivered as she stepped into the steaming water. She lowered herself and sank slowly, feeling her muscles loosen as the hot water warmed her bones and dissolved her tension. She had to pause to remember the last time she'd taken a bath—two years ago on vacation with Owen in Vermont, in that luxury resort with its marble countertops and deep soaking bath.

She furrowed her brow and pushed thoughts of Owen aside. She wasn't ready to examine her feelings about him and their separation yet. The sense of betrayal still lingered, but here in the strange sanctuary of the Ramsay Castle, maybe she could momentarily forget.

She slid into the water, letting it cover her ears and muffle all sound except for her breathing and heartbeat. She felt as if she were in a cocoon, completely removed from the outside world. She stared up at a small chandelier hanging from the high ceiling. Its crystal pendants caught the light from the window above her and sparkled like stars.

The Ramsay Clan had clearly once been one of great wealth and influence; her own bloodline was entwined with this history. Liza felt the weight of her ancestors' legacy pressing down upon her.

She leaned back and closed her eyes, and within seconds, felt herself drifting into sleep. She was powerless to stop its sweet magnetic pull toward a time and space that wasn't entirely of this world.

Chapter 4

Liza opened her eyes.

A man's face hovered inches from hers, his green eyes peering intently. It took her less than half a second to come to her senses and let out a scream.

He jumped back. "Jesus Christ!" he yelled in a thick Scottish burr.

Liza sat up quickly, and in her haste to hide her nakedness, water sloshed out of the bathtub, soaking the floor and the man's jeans and work boots.

"Get out!" she ordered, her arm folded awkwardly over her breasts and her knees pulled up to her stomach and twisted to the left.

The man seemed confused, angry, and frozen all at once; Liza yelled the command louder, before he came back to life and fled the room.

"The door was open! I thought ye were dead!" he yelled from outside.

"I suppose a naked woman in the bath had nothing to do with your curiosity?" she yelled back. "Close the door behind you on your way out!" she ordered, and listened until she heard heavy retreating footsteps and the door to the bedroom shut with a bang.

Liza stayed in her hunched position, staring at the door and breathing heavily. Only when she was fairly certain the man was not going to return did she dare lift herself from the water to grab a towel. She dried herself quickly then wrapped herself up best she could, her long dark hair still dripping water down her back and onto the floor.

She opened the bathroom door just a crack. The bedroom beyond seemed empty. She crept out, the towel still cinched tightly by her fist at her breastbone. Quickly fishing out underwear, jeans, and a peach-colored button-down shirt from the luggage, she pulled the clothing on. She dried her hair with the towel then pulled it up into a damp, messy knot at the top of her head.

The towel she abandoned on a hook on the back of the bathroom door. The floor was a soggy mess, but she'd ask Mrs. Boyle for a mop when she managed to find her.

She slipped on her sneakers and opened the bedroom door.

Immediately greeted by the figure of the bathroom intruder, her hand flew to her chest. She glared at him fiercely, but she was also acutely aware that if this man wanted to cause her harm, he could do it in a second and there wasn't a damn thing she'd be able to do about it.

He wasn't that much taller than her five feet eight inches, but he was powerfully built, his muscular frame clearly visible underneath the blue work shirt. These muscles were different from Owen's carefully toned and sculpted physique. If she had to guess, she'd assume this build came from physical labor, not time spent at the gym. His hair was dark, with hints of red visible even in the darkened hallway. His eyes were deeply set under a prominent brow. With his scowling face, he reminded her of a younger version of a character from a Scottish movie she'd seen decades earlier.

She took a step back, her hand on the doorknob, ready to slam it shut at any hint of movement from him. "What do you want?" she demanded.

He didn't meet her gaze; she was reminded he'd gotten an unobstructed view of her naked body while she was dozing in the bathtub. In addition to embarrassment and fear, she was also infuriated.

"Mrs. Boyle said I'm meant to show ye around."

This was the Lachlan Mrs. Boyle and Mr. Douglas had referenced. Some of Liza's trepidation faded, making more room for anger. If the man worked here, he should know better than to go sneaking up on people. *Guests.* She told him as much.

He crossed his arms, revealing on his forearm a large tattoo of what looked like a lion's head. He responded with as much anger as her. "Well, why were ye sleepin' in the bathtub? That's a good way to drown. And we've had quite enough of that here today."

"I wasn't sleeping," Liza argued. Then she backtracked. "And even if I had been, what business is that of yours? You had no right to just…" She swept her arm dramatically around the room. "…to just let yourself in when the doors were locked."

"Yer door was wide open, lassie. Both of them. I don't even have a key." He held out empty palms.

Liza bristled at the word 'lassie'. What's more, she didn't believe a word that was coming out of his mouth. She distinctly remembered shutting and latching both doors.

She sighed. There was no use arguing with this man. Instead, she walked out of the room and pointedly pulled the door shut behind her, glancing at it for good measure.

He shook his head as he turned away from her, leading the way down the hall. "Lunch is about ready," he said. "I'll show ye around later, if ye like."

Liza knew the offer was empty. He didn't want to show her around any more than she wanted him to show her around. But at the very least, she was reasonably certain he was not planning to attack her. A small part of her relaxed as she followed him down the main passageway.

As they walked, she cast glances at the portraits, tartan tapestries, and framed documents hanging on the walls. At intervals down the hallway, small inlets in the walls enclosed antique side tables that held seemingly ancient treasures. She wanted to stop and study each one, but Lachlan kept moving.

He led her to another staircase, this one narrower and more rudimentary than the splendid flight by which Mrs. Boyle had brought her up. The walls and stairs themselves appeared to be constructed of the same red stone as the outside of the castle. At uneven levels along their descent, narrow and screened cutout windows let in slender streams of light.

Down and down they descended, passing low bolted doorways that ostensibly led to other floors of the castle. After four flights, Lachlan led them through an opening into a small anteroom that could have been a closet. He passed into a formal dining room, where a group of people were seated at a long and elaborately constructed table. Two crystal chandeliers hung from the high ceilings, and three large mirrors hung along one side of the room. On the other side, heavy silk curtains were drawn open, revealing an expansive meadow that ended in a tree line. Above a fireplace at the far end of the room was a yellowed tapestry depicting two unicorns rampant beside the silhouette of a red lion encased in a crest. The lion's tail forked out behind it, its claws outstretched, ready to strike.

Mrs. Boyle was a flurry of activity, her unruly hair flying around her head with each step, as she arranged platters on the sideboard. The silver dishes were filled to the brim with delicious-smelling food.

"Nice o' ye to join us," she said in her lowland accent, and directed a pointed glance at the man in front of Liza. "Lachlan, there are a few more plates in the kitchen. Go and fetch them, will ye?"

Without a glance in her direction, he left through another doorway. Mr. Douglas appeared at Liza's side, ushering her to the table, which had been laid out with fine bone china, linen napkins, and polished silver atop an elaborate ivory lace tablecloth.

"I apologize," Liza said with a glance and nod toward the guests at the table. "I didn't realize this was a formal affair."

Another man, older, much frailer but somehow statelier with a cloud of wispy white hair, pushed back his chair at the head of the table. He stood up and walked toward her, his hands outstretched. He wore a blue sweater, the color of a robin's egg, and a pair of gray trousers that were cinched tightly by a belt around his gaunt frame. "Ye came," he said, with something close to wonderment. "I knew ye wouldn't let us down."

Liza allowed this elderly man to enfold her in a surprisingly powerful embrace. Even so, she felt mostly bone as she hugged him back, and was gentle in her reciprocation.

"Callum," Mr. Douglas said. "This is Elizabeth

Ramsay. Remember? She's the one ye found."

Mr. Ramsay loosened his grip, taking her by the hands and staring into her eyes. "Catherine?" he asked. The name was a question, and his eyes were bright and hopeful.

"It's Liza, Mr. Ramsay."

Some of the light left his gaze. He looked confused.

Mr. Douglas placed a hand on Mr. Ramsay's elbow. "Elizabeth Ramsay," he clarified incorrectly.

The older man was frowning at her. "Aye," he said slowly, as if everything were coming back to him. He nodded. "Aye, of course. We invited ye here."

"Yes," Liza responded. "I wasn't sure I was going to be able to make it, but fate has a way of guiding our steps, doesn't it, Mr. Ramsay?"

He lifted his eyebrows at that. "Fate. Aye." He smiled, and his watery blue eyes crinkled at the corners. "Please, dear. Call me Callum." He leaned toward her as if they shared a secret.

Mrs. Boyle appeared beside them and led Callum back to the table. "Come on, now, my laird. Yer lunch'll be gettin' cold." She spoke gently as she helped the shuffling man back to his seat.

Mrs. Boyle shot Liza a look, but before Liza could puzzle on it, Mr. Douglas placed a hand on Liza's arm and gestured to the strangers at the table. "Ms. Ramsay, may I present Brodie Graham from the Royal Kingdom Trust, and Kenneth Morrison from Eliot Properties in Edinburgh?"

The men stood up. Kenneth Morrison, to her right, nodded his head. He was a large man and his jowls wobbled with the movement. His thinning gray hair was combed carefully over his shiny bald pate. Fleshy folds of skin hung under each of his eyes, making his eyes look small in comparison to his large face.

Brodie Graham, on the other side of the table, gave a slight bow. His dark hair, shot with gray at the temples, was cut short and neatly parted on one side, emphasizing a finely hewn profile and giving him an air of sophistication. His clear blue eyes sparkled when they met Liza's, prompting her to flush as her breath caught in her throat. He winked discreetly; she felt her face color even more deeply. She cleared her throat and looked away, trying to mask her very visible reaction.

"This is Ms. Elizabeth Ramsay," said Mr. Douglas. Liza didn't bother correcting him again.

She was about to take a seat across from Mr. Graham, when Mrs. Boyle announced to the group, "Come on and get yer lunch. What are ye waiting for?"

Liza was surprised, and embarrassed she had expected Mrs. Boyle to serve them. Instead, the meal was laid out buffet-style on the sideboard. When Liza turned, she noticed that Lachlan had quietly rejoined them and was standing off to the side, apart from the rest of the group.

Mr. Douglas gestured for Liza to serve herself first, and she took her plate and lifted a serving spoon. Under the cover of the first platter was a baked ham, next to it petite yellow potatoes and roasted carrots. Liza had been expecting sandwiches or something equally simple. Her stomach rumbled in anticipation. It had been days since she'd had a full meal, let alone one this elaborate.

She heard Mr. Douglas give a derisive snort. "Did ye take a dip in the loch, Mr. McClaren? Yer trousers are sodden." She glanced behind her to see Mr. Douglas eyeing Lachlan with a look of contempt. The younger man's gaze caught Liza's and held. She quickly turned back to the food, hoping to hide the new wave of heat spreading across her face.

"No, sir," Lachlan responded quietly. Mrs. Boyle drew in an exasperated breath. "Robert, quit giving the lad a hard time."

Brodie Graham leaned close to her. "You must feel a bit out of your element here, Elizabeth."

Liza looked at him and he smiled. His accent wasn't the same as the others, and she guessed he hadn't grown up in the same area. In fact, he sounded vaguely British with just the hint of a Scottish rhythm to his words.

She nodded. "A little. And it's 'Liza'," she corrected.

He looked stricken. "Forgive me. I thought Robert said—"

"He did. They all seem determined to rename me."

"Well, Elizabeth is a beautiful name," he said, the words lilting on his tongue. "So is Liza." He paused a beat. "So are you."

Before she had a chance to react, Mr. Douglas appeared at her other side. "Mr. Graham is here to talk about a potential partnership with the Ramsay Estate, isn't that right, Mr. Graham? The Royal Kingdom Trust is keen to understand our intentions for the property, and now perhaps *your* intentions."

"Please, call me Brodie," the man said smoothly. Liza took her seat across from him at the table. "And there will be plenty of time to talk business later."

"What is it that the Royal Kingdom Trust does?" Liza asked. She took a bite of the salty ham, savouring its smoky flavor.

"We do quite a lot actually," Brodie said, dabbing at the corner of his mouth with a linen napkin. "One of our primary purposes is to maintain the historic and architectural significance of the land and properties across the area. We do that through grants, consultancy, research, conservation efforts, and partnerships. In special cases, we even acquire entire buildings and properties, assuming all ownership and responsibilities."

Mr. Morrison gave a little snort as he sat down next to her. "Which is exactly why ye're here, is it not, Mr. Graham?"

Brodie took a slow sip of water before he answered. "At least we have the preservation of Clan Ramsay at heart, which is more than I can say for Eliot Properties."

Mr. Morrison started to respond, but Mr. Douglas

held up his hand. "Now, gentlemen, now's not the time. Elizabeth's just got here, and she hasn't even had a chance to talk with Callum or see the property."

Brodie caught Liza's eye and raised an eyebrow.

She smiled and shrugged, even though the blatant oversight of her name had started to become tiresome.

"I cannot believe how much ye look like her," Callum said. He sat back and stared at Liza. "It's truly fascinating."

Mrs. Boyle agreed. "With her hair up like that, she certainly does." The woman took a seat next to Callum. She patted his hand. "Lady Catherine," she explained to Liza, "the portrait ye were studying in the bedroom—we call her the Grey Lady."

An awkward silence fell over the table while everyone stared at Liza. She shifted under the scrutiny while she chewed her food. When she'd finished her bite, she asked, "Why do you call her that?"

"Because when she shows herself, she appears as a gray mist. Lachlan has seen her, isn't that right, lad?" Callum asked, his eyes sharp again.

Liza couldn't say she believed in ghosts appearing as apparitions. If she were honest with herself, she hadn't spent much time thinking about phantoms at all, though she believed in the spirit world and the afterlife. There were certainly times she would swear her mother was right next to her.

The thought of ghosts in this building, though, made all the sense in the world. So, she wasn't sure why she chose this particular time and this particular subject to poke fun. Perhaps it was to mask her discomfort or to take the attention off herself. Or maybe because Lachlan seemed like an easy target or to punish him for seeing her without her clothes on. She snorted lightly, looking at Lachlan. "You've seen this 'Grey Lady', then? I bet she visits you often in your dreams…"

Brodie Graham and Kenneth Morrison chucked.

Lachlan McClaren became very still. And when he spoke, it was thoughtful and deep. "Ye think the spirit world is a laughing matter, do ye, Ms. Ramsay? Are ye sayin' they're not here now, all around us, maybe even sighing at our foolishness? Or is it death ye find humorous? Perhaps it's with mirth that ye think of how Alexander Ramsay may've killed Lady Catherine, taking her one sweet babe from her arms?"

Liza's smile froze on her face. She shifted in her seat and opened her mouth to respond, to double down on her glib comment. Before she could get a word out, Lachlan continued. "And do ye laugh when ye think of peerie Charlie Campbell drownin' in the Creighton burn yesterday?"

That made Liza's smile fade. The lack of sleep must have been getting to her. Of course, she hadn't intended to speak ill of the dead, especially a recently deceased child.

Mrs. Boyle spoke quietly. "Ms. Ramsay was only having a bit of fun at yer expense. I'm sure she didn't mean anything by it. No need to go aff yer heid."

Another awkward silence settled over the table. Liza rushed to fill it. "I don't find any amusement in that boy's drowning. It's tragic. I was just trying to lighten the mood." She waved her hand ineffectually.

A muscle ticked in the side of Lachlan's jaw. His emerald-green eyes flashed, and she was once again struck by his appearance and the simmering intensity of his presence.

Brodie Graham spoke up then. "I think we might all agree that the Ramsay Castle has some ghosts in it, but we might have a moment of silence for Charlie Campbell, and pray for peace for his young soul."

Liza blinked at him gratefully. It should have been the right thing to say, but the words fell flat on the table in front of them.

And perhaps that was the difference between Lachlan and Brodie Graham. Where Brodie was all polish and carefully cultivated words, Lachlan seemed wilder, slightly feral. Yet beneath the rough exterior she sensed a calculating intelligence and an edge of danger that was both fascinating and disturbing.

Lachlan continued as if Brodie had not spoken at all. "Ye know, Ms. Ramsay, the spirits that appear in our lives do so for a reason. Sometimes, they're asking ye to help them, but more often than not, they're a *faileas*—a shadow of yer own thoughts and feelings. A reflection of yer own struggles. You'd do well to remember that here."

Liza didn't bother attempting to respond. She had nothing at all to say.

Mercifully, the rich, melodic chime of a doorbell reverberated through the room. It was so deep and resonant that it took a few seconds for the sound to die down. Mrs. Boyle popped up from her seat, muttering that she wasn't expecting any deliveries that afternoon.

The group around the table continued in hushed conversation, either unaware of any residual awkwardness or choosing to ignore it. Brodie said something to Callum that Liza wasn't sure Callum had heard, even though he smiled and laughed politely. Mr. Douglas leaned close to Mr. Morrison, speaking earnestly. She couldn't make out his words.

Lachlan had picked up his fork and resumed his meal, but he was glowering into his plate.

Liza considered apologizing, but she didn't want to make the situation more uncomfortable than it already was. What she really wanted was for the gathering to end so she could get on with her day. She wanted to talk to Callum or Mr. Douglas, or someone who could tell her exactly what she was doing here.

Mrs. Boyle reentered with a middle-aged woman in a rumpled pantsuit, and an incredibly tall man wearing a button-down shirt that ended too high on his wrists and with dark slacks that didn't quite cover the patterned socks which disappeared into worn brown loafers. The woman, though she looked worn and weary, carried an air of authority about her. Her curly dark hair was cropped close to her scalp. A pair of reading glasses perched high atop her head like a crown. She wore no makeup; Liza was sure she probably considered makeup to be frivolous and silly.

The man walked a few paces behind the woman, his eyes assessing each person in the room. Liza shuddered slightly when his gaze landed on her, but she didn't look away.

The woman spoke first. "So sorry to interrupt your lunch. I'm Detective Chief Inspector Dean from the Specialist Crime Division, and this is Detective Inspector Lawson." She paused for just a beat as if she were allowing their positions to sink in. "You may be aware that there's been an incident just down the road."

"The Specialist Crime Division?" Mr. Douglas exclaimed. "Detective Chief Inspector? Since when would a DCI be investigating an accidental death? And why aren't the local police handling the investigation?"

The tall man pulled a notepad from the breast pocket of his shirt and made a notation.

The woman trained her calm gaze on Mr. Douglas. "It may very well be an accident. And the local police *are* involved. As I said, we're just taking a look around, talking to the neighbors. Can't be too careful, especially given the victim's age and family connections."

Mrs. Boyle's voice shook slightly when she asked, "Is there any reason to think Charlie's death was anything *but* an accident?"

"We don't have enough information to have an opinion on that at this stage."

Callum looked around as if he'd just woken up. "Charlie? Charlie Campbell, the lad who worked here?"

No one answered him, but Detective Inspector Lawson scratched something else in his notepad.

Brodie Graham spoke up next. "Most of us arrived just a short time ago, Inspector."

"That's fine, that's fine," Chief Inspector Dean said agreeably. "We'll just want to be asking the lot of you a few questions. All very routine."

Liza felt the energy shift in the room. When no one answered, she felt compelled to speak up. She stood up, walked to the pair, and held out her hand. "I'm Liza Ramsay," she said. "I just arrived this morning to meet with Mr. Ramsay and Mr. Douglas regarding the Ramsay property. But I'm sure all of us will be happy to help out in any way we can."

The woman lifted her chin just a notch. Despite her conversational tone, Liza detected a glint in her eye. A suspicion. "An American Ramsay," Chief Inspector Dean murmured in her soft burr. "Something we don't see in these parts every day. Are you planning on staying a while?"

"For a short time, yes." She was only about an inch taller than the older woman, but she used the height difference to her full advantage, drawing herself up.

"Well, that's something you don't see every day," Dean said with a wide smile. "Isn't it, Lawson?"

The tall man nodded but didn't speak. Standing this close to him, Liza estimated him to be roughly a decade younger than his superior officer. He had a soft body and a round face. She could see where he'd missed some spots shaving his chin.

"About time we got some new blood around here," DCI Dean said, but something about the way she said it made Liza think she meant the exact opposite.

Dean glanced around the room then gave a businesslike nod as if everything were settled. "I'm glad you're all willing to suffer a few questions from us. We'll try not to blether on." She smiled, then just as quickly, her smile faded, and she tapped the heel of her hand to her forehead. "You know, we need to be down at the station for a meeting shortly, don't we, Detective Inspector?"

Lawson didn't respond.

She turned to the table. "Do you all think you can stay put for a while?"

"For how long?" Mr. Morrison asked. "I need to be headin' back to Edinburgh this afternoon."

"Shouldn't be terribly long. We'll be out of your hair by suppertime. Maybe just a wee bit later."

Liza heard Mrs. Boyle sigh. Mr. Morrison made a noise at the back of his throat, but didn't complain outwardly.

Callum spoke up. "Come for supper!" He held his hands out wide. "Yes, yes," he continued, warming up to the idea. "It'll be like old times. Like the parties we used to hold. A real *cèilidh*!" He clapped his hands together.

Dean smiled. This time it looked genuine. "Awfully kind of you, Mr. Ramsay. Excuse me. *Chief* Ramsay," she corrected.

Callum bowed his head slightly at the acknowledgment.

"Your parties back in the day were the stuff of legends. I remember hearing about them when I was just a lass up in Dalmally. But we'll have a bite to eat down at the station, won't we, Lawson?" Again, Lawson didn't answer, but the chief inspector didn't seem to expect him to. She raised a finger, as if something had just occurred to her. "That's a great idea. You fine people can dine together, then we'll be by to ask you some questions. Won't take but a few hours."

Callum nodded his head happily, seemingly thrilled by this prospect, but it was Liza's turn to sigh. So much for an early night.

She supposed they wouldn't have many questions to ask her. She had just arrived, after all, and didn't know the young dead boy nor the circumstances that could have led to his death.

The chief inspector looked around the table once more before bidding them a good day. DI Lawson remained silent, and Liza realized he hadn't said one word since he'd entered the room.

At the doorway, Dean turned back around. "I nearly forgot. Mr. McClaren, I'm so sorry for the loss of your cousin, Charlie. I know the lot of you weren't always on the best of terms. His mother told me about the recent row you'd had. Still, it's a shame, and you must be broken up about his passing. Especially so close to home and after all the other death and murder in your life."

Lachlan's face lost some of its color. He stared at the floor. While Dean had indicated that their questions were routine, the way she'd singled out Lachlan made Liza suspect otherwise. Was it possible they might consider him as a suspect? She shuddered. That feral quality she'd sensed... Perhaps her initial instincts about the man had been correct.

Dean nodded once more then the two inspectors disappeared with Mrs. Boyle in tow.

No one spoke, and they all listened as the front door shut. A minute later, Mrs. Boyle reentered the room as they heard gravel crunch beneath the wheels of the departing vehicle.

"Well," she said with a sigh as she began to gather up the plates. "I guess we'll all be getting to know each other really well."

Liza unwittingly glanced over at Brodie. His smile was innocent, but she couldn't ignore the gleam in his eye. He winked at her again and her pulse jumped. She forgot all about Lachlan McClaren.

Chapter 5

Mrs. Boyle had shooed everyone from the dining room after the visit from the detectives in order to make supper preparations. Since it was still early afternoon and Mr. Morrison had already poured himself a rather large tumbler of Inchmurrin whisky, Liza suspected there may also be overnight guests in the castle.

Callum Ramsay retired to his living quarters to rest from the excitement, and Mr. Douglas informed Liza that he would collect her at three in the afternoon to discuss a potential arrangement, whatever that might mean.

As Liza had walked out of the room, she noticed that Brodie Graham and Robert Douglas were standing off to one side in a seemingly intense conversation. She couldn't say that it looked particularly friendly, but nor had it appeared to be antagonistic. She may not have paid them any attention except for the fact that she was hoping to spend more time with Brodie. While she was well aware that she and Owen had some issues to address, she didn't see that there was any reason she shouldn't enjoy the company of an attractive man while she was away. This was a holiday of sorts, after all. At the very least, it was a respite from her normal existence.

She also didn't want to appear overly eager or aggressive, so with mild disappointment, Liza continued on toward the back staircase. In a room off to one side, she caught sight of Mrs. Boyle and Lachlan McClaren also standing together, heads bent close. Mrs. Boyle's plump hand was on Lachlan's arm, almost as if she'd been comforting the younger man.

Maybe that was not out of the ordinary, especially given the fact that Charlie Campbell had been related to Lachlan. And Mrs. Boyle, no matter how rough around the edges she appeared, worked with Lachlan every day. Perhaps they had a familial relationship. The gesture between the two of them softened her, and she felt a swell of empathy for Lachlan. She got the impression that Lachlan may not have had the easiest of lives.

After a few wrong turns she managed to navigate the dim passageways, first finding the staircase then traversing the empty hallway toward her bedroom on the fourth floor. The eyes of the portraits on the walls followed her as she walked.

When she entered the room, she caught sight of the portrait of Lady Catherine. She looked away quickly, thinking of how she'd made fun of Lachlan. She was ashamed of how she'd behaved.

To distract herself, she dug into her backpack and pulled out her mobile phone. She hadn't even glanced at it since Mr. Douglas had collected her from the airport that morning. She checked her email accounts first. Other than a few random messages about automatic bill payments withdrawn from her bank account, no one was trying to reach her. Her work account was another story, with plenty of documents and links being sent between the new client and a man named Andre Shafer who had apparently been assigned to take her place. It appeared as though Raj had directed all parties to keep Liza on copy to the correspondence.

Liza wasn't sure how she felt about that. On the one hand, her job must be safe and she was expected to return. On the other hand, she wasn't sure that's what she wanted anymore. She certainly wasn't convinced she wanted to stay in Scotland, and in fact, had no intention of staying at the Ramsay Castle. But it was very clear that there was a world beyond Boston, and there were people other than Owen. This world and these people had something to offer beyond the life she'd been living.

No text messages were waiting for her. She realized it was still early in the United States, but she was also aware that somehow, over the past few years, all of her old friendships had fallen away. She could usually attribute her lack of friends to general life growth and development. Many of the women with whom she'd graduated from university had married and had children. Others had relocated for family reasons or jobs. Liza had done the same.

But now she found herself very much alone. Her mother, who had been her best friend, was gone, and her grandparents were housed in a senior living community eight hours away from home. She didn't visit nearly as often as she should, but when she was able to see them, they seemed happy and healthy. They had friends and other relatives around. And they had each other.

Liza was not only alone; she was lonely.

She thought of Owen, and about the fact they hadn't yet married or had children of their own. They'd talked about it, but the timing had never been right. She'd been too busy with her career, or Owen had been too busy saving the vestiges of his youth. They'd fallen into their own comfortable rhythm, and now Liza wondered if that rhythm hadn't just been a funeral dirge in disguise. They certainly weren't getting any younger.

A sudden loud noise made her jump. It sounded as if something had fallen and hit the tiled floor of the bathroom. Frowning, she hesitated, listening to a faint, low whistling that she hadn't detected when she'd entered the room.

Despite her racing pulse, she tossed the phone on the mattress and moved cautiously toward the bathroom. She knew it was ridiculous, but in this old building, she was more afraid of ghosts than she was of real-life danger. This was payback for taunting Lachlan earlier.

When Liza pushed open the door, she saw her toiletry case lying sideways next to the sink, half of its contents spilled onto the ground. A breeze was blowing in and moaning mournfully through the high window above the bathtub. She looked up at it, frowning. She didn't remember the window being open when she'd been in the room earlier, though she supposed if there'd been no breeze she may not have noticed. Even so, had the breeze been powerful enough to cause her case to fall to the floor?

She stooped to gather the contents, and had just fastened the zipper when she heard another faint noise from the main room. She stopped.

The noise was soft and barely there. If the house hadn't been so empty and silent, she wouldn't have picked up on the sound at all.

She crept into the bedroom, listening to that faint and faraway murmur—a voice.

Liza dared to cast her gaze upon the portrait of Lady Catherine, and in that moment, those black eyes were watching her. She looked away quickly, but an icy finger of fear slithered down her spine.

"Liza," a small voice called from somewhere in the room, as if it were trapped.

She thought she might be losing her mind. Another murmur. Her heart raced. She was torn between searching for the source of the voice and running from the room. She felt paralyzed.

"Liza!" it called again, louder but still barely discernible.

She spun around her eyes searching. Her breath was coming in short, fast gasps.

"Liza!" came the call once more, both pleading and threatening in equal measure.

What kind of madhouse was this?

Then her gaze snagged on the phone at the corner of the mattress. The screen was bright, an active call in progress.

She sucked in a breath when she saw the name at the top of the screen. *Owen.*

Shit. She recovered quickly and lunged for the phone, pressing 'End' just as Owen said, "Liz—"

She threw the phone back onto the deep purple comforter as if it had burned her hands. She must have accidentally hit Owen's contact information when she'd heard the noise in the bathroom, she reasoned to herself. But she hadn't. She knew she hadn't. At no point had her contacts or recent calls been opened.

The phone vibrated again, and Owen's name appeared. She let it ring through. She wasn't ready to talk to him. Wasn't ready to hear more excuses or take more blame. Wasn't ready to explain why she was in Scotland. Didn't even *know* why she was in Scotland.

A heavy knock sounded on the door just as her phone started vibrating again. She picked it up gingerly and threw it in the front pocket of her backpack. Then she went to the door, avoiding Lady Catherine's eyes, and opened it just a crack.

Lachlan stood there, looking none too pleased to be back in this familiar position, right where he'd been before lunch.

"Yes?" she asked. She made sure her voice sounded friendlier than it had been upon their first meeting. But not too friendly, just in case he was a murderer. But she really did feel guilty about mocking him at lunch. Especially since his young cousin was dead. She managed an awkward smile she wasn't sure was appropriate, given the circumstances.

"Everything all right?" he asked. His accent seemed softer when he wasn't yelling or being defensive.

"Why wouldn't it be?"

"Thought I heard ye swearing."

Liza blinked. Had she sworn out loud when she'd seen Owen's name? She hadn't thought so.

After a moment, she said, "Yes, I'm fine."

Lachlan nodded and turned to leave, but Liza opened the door wider. "Can I ask—is the bathroom window sash broken?"

He turned back and grinned, giving his face a mischievous quality that overlaid his normally intense features. "It seems to have a tendency to blow open," he said. "Would ye like for me to close it?"

She hesitated just a beat before opening the door wide and gesturing him in.

He didn't say anything, but she could tell he was relieved by the invitation. "Yer bag's buzzin'," he said as he walked past the backpack at the foot of the bed.

Liza ignored it and followed him into the bathroom.

Though the window was high, Lachlan was able to reach it without too much trouble. He latched it and shook it for good measure. "That should hold for a bit. If it happens again, I'll bring a ladder up."

She nodded. "Thank you."

He nodded and their eyes caught.

Liza cleared her throat. "About what happened at lunch—the ghosts. I didn't mean to embarrass you."

"It's not me ye should be worried about offending." His gaze slid to the portrait. Liza didn't know if he was serious, but given the mysteriously open window and the accidental phone call, she couldn't help but wonder.

"Someone really wants to get ahold of ye," he said, pointing toward her bag, which had started vibrating again. "Don't ye think ye should answer?"

Liza sighed and pressed her lips together.

"Should I ask?"

Liza gave a humorless little laugh. "It's not a great story."

"They never are, in the moment."

She let her head fall forward, and tendrils of hair escaped the knot on top of her head and fell against her cheeks. "He doesn't even know I'm here."

"Think ye should tell him?"

"Eventually."

"He's probably worried," Lachlan said softly.

"He's probably with his other woman," Liza responded more vehemently than she'd intended. She immediately regretted saying anything at all.

"Ah." He nodded. "Do ye want to go for a walk? I could show you around the house at least. I was supposed to do that earlier. Before…" His face reddened, and Liza quickly diverted the conversation.

"I'm supposed to meet Callum and Mr. Douglas at three."

He glanced at a wristwatch, something Liza couldn't remember having seen in what seemed like forever. "We've got some time."

She hesitated again, weighing her options. Finally, she nodded. Anything was better than being shut up in this room. Or wandering the halls herself—a living, sad spirit. Maybe she and Lady Catherine would make a good pair after all.

Lachlan led Liza the opposite direction down the corridor. He pointed out various clan chiefs and their spouses from the framed documents and portraits on the wall, including numerous portraits of Sir Alexandar Ramsay, who had defended the castle multiple times during a period of heavy siege from the English. There was a handsome likeness of Sir Nicholas Ramsay who had not only supported but had been a great friend of Mary Queen of Scots and King James IV, both of whom had spent many nights in the castle. In a more modern portrait from the nineteenth century, a Ramsay earl sat atop a gallant steed, painted in his role as Governor General of India.

Lachlan told Liza about secret meetings that had taken place at the castle prior to William Wallace's battle for Scotland's freedom from British rule. He showed her the magnificent bedroom, decorated in rich burgundy and gold, that Mary Queen of Scots had occupied as she'd traveled across the land, and the hidden room where King Edward had rested for the night during a visit in the thirteenth century on his way to Falkirk to do battle with Sir William Wallace.

Liza marveled equally at the rich history of the estate and at Lachlan's knowledge. "How long have you worked here?"

He furrowed his brow. "I suppose it's been about

eight years now—I came just after I left uni." He made a face. "Don't know how that happened." He shook his head.

"Time does seem like it moves faster and faster." She sighed deeply.

"Ye all right?"

She gave him a weak smile. "Just wondering how I've landed here."

"Landed in a Scottish castle, preserved for centuries, complete with the ghosts of former inhabitants roaming the halls?" His eyes crinkled at the corners and flashed when he grinned. Liza had the feeling he was poking fun at himself and maybe his earlier reaction to her teasing at lunch.

As they descended the main staircase, Liza glanced up. She hadn't noticed it before because they'd used a different stairwell, but immediately above the door was a massive and intricate mural of a battle scene, with the unmistakable image of the castle in the distance.

Lachlan followed her gaze. "The Ramsay land changed hands many times, but this scene shows Sir Alexander Ramsay retaking the estate from English occupation in the fourteenth century."

There was a verse beneath the mural, but Liza couldn't quite make it out from where she stood. Lachlan had begun moving to the left, through a doorway. With one more quick glance up at the painting—the soldiers brandishing their swords and moving as if one toward the castle—Liza hurried after him. They emerged in a small alcove, a loft of sorts, atop another long room, with massive stained-glass windows adorning the far wall.

"Is this a church?" Liza asked.

"Aye, a chapel. But it's not been used in years." And indeed, it was filled with abandoned items—tables, chairs, objects covered in dust, ghostly drop cloths and sheets. She noticed that the ceiling in the far corner was yellowed from some hidden leak. "Callum had been meaning to have this room cleaned out and restored, but didn't get around to it before his diagnosis. It's one of my favorite rooms, anyhow. It can be right *oorlich* outside, enough to chill ye to the bone, but it'll still shine like the sun in here."

Liza only heard one word that Lachlan had said. "Diagnosis?"

Lachlan paused, then he looked at her, confusion on his face. "I'm sorry. I thought ye knew." He blew out a breath. "I shouldn't have said anything. It's not my place."

"He's sick?"

"Aye." His voice was soft, filled with regret. He didn't elaborate, and Liza couldn't bring herself to ask.

They stared across the room, the light shooting down like jeweled beams, refracted and distorted through the stained glass. Eddies of colored motes swirled and danced. Through the dusty, close smell in the space, Liza thought she could detect just the hint of incense—a sweet smokiness that was both mysterious and comforting.

She wasn't sure how long they'd stood there, but after a while, she started. "I'm supposed to meet Callum and Mr. Douglas," she reminded him.

He glanced at his watch. "One more adventure?" he asked.

She wasn't sure it was a question meant to be answered, so she followed him. He led her to a room at the bottom of the main staircase, beneath the mural. This space wasn't nearly as richly appointed. A side table held some papers, and a plain wooden filing cabinet sat off to one side.

He pointed toward the opposite wall. "The kitchen is that way," he remarked. "If Mrs. Boyle is in there, she'll shoo ye away, but ye should know in case the munchies hit ye at night."

"Do you live in the castle?"

"I live in the workers' cottage just over the rise toward the river. I'm happy there. It gives me a bit of privacy."

She wanted to ask more questions. For example, if he'd gone to university, what was he doing as the groundskeeper on the estate? Not that there was anything wrong with that path, but it wasn't one she would have expected a college graduate to take. And how did he envision his future, especially if a new owner were to assume the property?

They passed through an unassuming, brown-painted door at the back corner of the room and emerged in a narrow stone passageway. Lachlan touched a switch to his left, and a weak yellowish light emanated from a fixture high up on the stone façade.

"This part of the castle is original, constructed in the thirteenth century or thereabouts. Some of the other, newer parts were reconstructed after various raids in the fourteenth and fifteenth centuries."

Liza placed a palm flat against the cool, thick, reddish stone walls, the same color as the outside stone. "Why is it red?" she asked.

"The stone comes from the quarry, not a kilometer over the rise." He hitched his chin to his left. "Close to my cottage, in fact. That's why the old and new parts of the outside walls look similar and probably why the castle had been built on this hill in the first place—the proximity to the stone. That and the proximity to Edinburgh and the river. Good place to take up arms and defend the land. Sir Oliver Cromwell figured that for himself with the help of Sir George Ramsay when the English invaded in the seventeenth century."

Liza's head spun with the history she'd learned in just this short time. She didn't deserve to inherit this place and could not fathom her relation to these Ramsay warriors, no matter which side they'd been fighting on. She was unworthy of even being considered a potential heir.

They descended the staircase, and the stone became colder and felt almost damp. Though the wall sconces held weak electric lights, Liza could just as easily imagine flickering candles lighting the passage. The air smelled of dirt and decay, like earth soaked with rain.

Lachlan charged forward confidently, as if he'd been in this passageway many times before.

"Do you spend much time down here?" Liza asked.

"When I was a wee lad."

"You lived at the castle growing up then?"

He shook his head. "My grandmother was the head mistress here way back when Callum was a proper laird and had a staff, and entertained regularly. I believe she may have been the one who hired Mrs. Boyle. Those were lively times. I even got to meet the Queen. She tousled my hair." He looked back at her in the dim light and gave her a nostalgic smile. "Nice lady. She and Callum were friends."

Liza blinked. "And what did Callum do?"

"Do?" He seemed puzzled. "When the Queen tousled my hair?"

"For a job," Liza clarified. "How did he earn money?"

Lachlan seemed to think this was an odd question. "He never had a *job*," he answered, putting emphasis on the word. "His mother was a princess of Denmark. I can't remember which one, if I ever even knew. He had a trust," Lachlan said. "That's what he's used to take care of this place."

Liza glanced up at the walls then looked behind her at the staircase they were descending. She couldn't begin to imagine how much the maintenance of the estate would cost. The utilities alone must cost tens of thousands of dollars per year. Not to mention the maintenance of the grounds, the cost of a staff, general repairs, and household supplies. She thought of the leaking ceiling in the chapel. It would require wealth to keep up with the estate's sheer size.

Liza thought of her own bank account, her comparably small nest egg. While she was comfortable now, the Ramsay Castle would eat up her savings in a matter of months.

She felt a curious disappointment that surprised her. In no way had she thought of considering Callum's offer of the estate. But there it was—a niggling at the back of her mind. An annoying little *what if.*

They emerged on a sort of walkway or parapet that overlooked a deep, dark pit. Lachlan stopped. There were no lights in the pit, and even with the dim illumination projecting weakly from the sconces along the wall, Liza didn't think she could make out the bottom of the hole. She squinted. "What am I looking for?" she asked Lachlan.

"This is the dungeon," said Lachlan.

Liza looked down again and leaned forward. "How did people get in and out?"

"Ye only needed to go in most of the time. Not many were coming back out again. But to get in, they were lowered by rope." He pointed to a smooth groove along the side of the ledge by which they stood. "Ye can still see the markings."

Liza traced this indentation with her finger. For just a second, she felt as if she'd traveled back in time. The air around her felt heavy, and something tugged at her hair, at the strands that had worked themselves out of the chignon at the top of her head. She reached up and splayed her palm out against the back of her scalp.

Lachlan continued. "It's said that Sir Alexander Ramsay himself was thrown into his own dungeon, and survived for nearly three weeks before he died of dehydration." Lachlan's words sounded far away, even though Lachlan was standing right next to her. "He haunts this place, and loves to play with the women's hair."

Liza stared over the ledge. Through the gloom, it was almost as if she was looking into the haunted eyes of starving and desperate men below. "How horrible," she heard herself utter, the words distorted as if she were speaking underwater.

They were so far below the main floors of the castle and completely insulated. There would have been no one to hear the groans or screams of the prisoners below.

She leaned further forward. Her imagination conjured their mouths, open, pleading with her for something. She strained to hear what they were saying. One man reached out with his thin, white arm covered in welts and bruises. And someone else, a slender figure, feminine, haunted…

She reached her own hand toward those thin fingers and could have sworn she smelled the acrid scent of smoke. She felt herself sway, felt herself fall…

Chapter 6

In an instant, an arm was around Liza's waist, dragging her backward.

Her head felt fuzzy, and she blinked. She looked up into the wide intense eyes of Lachlan McClaren. She was supported by one arm wrapped around her shoulders, the other at her hips.

"Liza? Are ye all right?" He was breathing heavily.

She scrambled for footing and disentangled herself from his grasp.

"Yes. I-I don't know what happened." When she felt stable, she pressed her fingertips against her forehead.

Lachlan's hand hovered near her torso, but he didn't touch her again. "I thought ye were going over that wall." He gave a dry chuckle, but there was no humor in it. "Imagine trying to explain that to the detectives."

She still felt slightly woozy, and she placed a flat palm against the wall to her left.

He touched her gently on her upper arm.

Again, she felt the snag of her hair against the wall,

and she moved quickly to disentangle from the sandstone the tresses that had come loose.

Lachlan took a step forward, shepherding Liza out of the passageway. "Come on," he said, "or ye'll be late for yer meeting with Callum."

They moved more slowly going up the passageway than they had coming down, with Liza leading the way and Lachlan following closely behind. Neither of them spoke.

The higher they ascended, the clearer the air became, and by the time they were back at the top of the stairway, she was gulping clean air.

Before they'd made it out of the small room, Mrs. Boyle appeared. "Where have the two of ye been?" She arched a brow in Lachlan's direction. Lachlan looked sheepish. Guilty almost. "Callum is waitin' for ye," she said to Liza, and hurried her toward the grand staircase.

Lachlan started to follow, but Mrs. Boyle turned back. "The wind has blown down some branches of the old sycamore in the yard. Ye need to clean them up."

"Yes, ma'am," he said, hunching his shoulders. He walked out the front door.

"I swear, that lad'll be the death of me."

"He's not a child," Liza said. She felt the need to defend Lachlan as repayment for rescuing her, even though he was the reason she'd been there in the first place. She tried to work out how old he was. If he'd been working at the castle for eight years and been out of university for the same amount of time, that would make him close to thirty at least. Nearly her own age.

Mrs. Boyle turned and gave her a shrewd look. "And here I thought ye were sweet on Mr. Graham."

Liza's mouth fell open. "I'm not sweet on anyone."

But Mrs. Boyle had already moved on, and talked right over Liza as they reached the top of the grand staircase. "Ye're right, Lachlan isn't a lad anymore. She was out of breath. "But when I look at him, it's hard not to see that ornery boy who used to catch snakes and let them loose at the laird's suppers. I remember one time Dame Mary screamed at the top of her lungs and knocked over four full wine glasses. Callum was irritated, but Her Majesty was tickled with it."

Liza was a bit mystified by this causal talk of the late Queen, but she was more curious about Lachlan and his decision to remain in one place for his entire life. "He must really love it here," she murmured.

They crossed the hallway and headed toward the back of the castle behind the stairway that led to the upper floors.

"After all that's happened, Lachlan doesn't feel like he's able to leave." Her voice was grim, but before Liza could inquire further, Mrs. Boyle knocked on an imposing mahogany door and pushed it open without waiting for an answer.

They entered into a tastefully decorated sitting

room, the entire back wall of which was constructed of alternating sections of red brick and floor-to-ceiling windows that showed the entire sweeping green grounds of the estate down to the tree line of the Creagan River. The lone figure of Lachlan walked through the grass toward the thick towering sycamore tree in the middle of the lawn. Liza's mind wandered back to the mural above the castle's entrance, and she thought about what that tree must have stood witness to.

Though the sky was still steel gray, the day was bright enough to light the room, and Callum, who was seated in a corner armchair, started to rise, a thick tartan blanket slipping off of his lap.

"Please, don't get up on my account." She thought of Lachlan's mention of the diagnosis, and pressed her lips together. If Callum were ill, the haste to name an heir made even more sense.

Mr. Douglas stood instead and guided her to a loveseat that had been arranged to face the windows. "Thank you for joining us, Elizabeth," he said and sat back down in an armchair to her right.

She opened her mouth and then shut it again. She suspected he was mis-naming her purposely at this point, and she had no idea why. But she would not give him the satisfaction of her response.

"May I get ye some tea?" Mrs. Boyle asked from the doorway.

"Tea would be most lovely," Callum said, at the same time Mr. Douglas said, "No, that'll be all, thank you."

They all looked at Liza as if she were the tiebreaker. She twisted around to face Mrs. Boyle. "I would love some tea," she said. The castle was a lot of things, but it could not be called cozy. Even in the height of summer, a cold draft glided through the walls.

Callum smiled warmly at her, but Mr. Douglas broke in. "Let's get down to business, shall we?" He leaned forward and shuffled some papers on the coffee table in front of him. "As I explained in my correspondence to ye, Ms. Ramsay, it's been determined that ye are a member of Clan Ramsay, and as such, eligible to inherit the estate upon Chief Ramsay's passing."

Liza glanced at Callum, who nodded.

"I have some questions about that."

"Of course," said Callum. Mr. Douglas sighed.

Liza shifted her body so that she was more directly facing Callum. "I find it hard to believe that I'm the last surviving Ramsay heir." She gestured toward the door to his apartment. "I've seen the impressive collection of portraits along the walls, as well as the old family tree. This was an incredibly large family."

"'Twas," said Callum. "And there are plenty of others. But our forensic genealogist determined that you are of the direct Ramsay line. Not only that, he's traced you back to Lady Catherine."

She thought she caught Mr. Douglas rolling his eyes slightly.

"Traced through DNA testing?" she asked, confirming what she already knew.

"If you would have just read the report—" Mr. Douglas began, but Callum interrupted. "Through a combination of ancestry research, genetic testing results, and old-fashioned private investigation," he said. "And...we had some help from—"

"*Callum*," Mr. Douglas said, in a warning voice.

Liza thought back to her mother's illness, and how she herself had made the decision to submit DNA for genetic testing because of the lack of information about her absent father. Had that decision and a drop of blood led her here?

Another thought that hadn't occurred to her before suddenly made itself front and center in her mind. She hesitated to vocalize this particular thought for a moment, savoring her ignorance for just a second longer. After a pause, she asked, "Can I assume then, since you contacted me and not my father, that he is dead?"

Callum opened his mouth, then shut it again. He looked at Mr. Douglas.

"It's okay," Liza said. "I didn't know him." That she didn't know her father was a fact. That she hated him was also a fact. But deep down, she knew that if she'd had the opportunity to meet him, even if just to ask him why he'd left, she would take it.

"Yes, he is deceased," confirmed Callum gently.

A heavy weight settled in her chest. A finality. She wouldn't have described it as sorrow or grief. It was regret, she supposed.

She cleared her throat, wanting to move on. She would need time to process these emotions on her own. Though she hadn't seen her father in years, the confirmation that he was gone hit her harder than expected.

"And Lady Catherine," she said, forcing a strength in her voice that she didn't feel. "How do you know I'm her descendant? I don't believe genetic testing is advanced enough to give such specific results. Especially to connect to an ancestor *that many* years ago." She wasn't even sure when Lady Catherine had lived in the castle, but in her short time here, the eighteenth century was starting to feel contemporary.

Callum leaned forward, his rheumy blue eyes bright. This is what excited him, Liza realized—family, history, and his connection to it all.

"There have been many stories about Lady Catherine, and her relation to the Ramsays. But over the years, many in the Ramsay line have done their research. The original story was that her father, Sir Alexander, found her with a stableboy and banished her to her room where she starved herself and died. But we have good reason to believe that she was exiled to her room when it was discovered she was with child. We also think she died in childbirth and the starvation story was likely spread to protect her reputation."

As he finished his sentence, Mrs. Boyle reentered the room with a small silver cart.

"I've brought you some fresh baked biscuits and tablet."

As she poured the tea from an elegant silver pot, Liza examined the tray that held the sweets, trying to determine what exactly *tablet* might be. To her, it looked like bite-sized morsels of a pale, textured fudge.

Mrs. Boyle noticed her curiosity. "Well, go on. Take one."

Liza took a tentative bite of the small square. A rush of buttery sugar filled then quickly melted in her mouth. She cupped her left hand beneath her chin to catch the small crumbles that broke off of the larger piece.

"Eat the whole thing, silly lass," said Mrs. Boyle.

Liza popped the rest of the sugary square into her mouth.

The texture was gritty, and she was reminded of the maple sugar candies her grandfather used to buy her during autumn in Pennsylvania when she was a child.

As the confection dissolved on her tongue, Mrs. Boyle handed her a milky tea in a matching cup and saucer. Liza was charmed by the delicate floral pattern that snaked its way around the rim of the porcelain.

She wasn't much of a tea drinker at home, preferring coffee, but when she sipped the hot creamy liquid combined with the sweetness still on her tongue, she was warmed through and comforted. Maybe it could be cozy here after all.

Mrs. Boyle finished serving the tea and left the cart with the plate of sweets before excusing herself. Though Liza was tempted by another piece of tablet, she resisted. Mr. Douglas, on the other hand, helped himself to both the tablet and the cookies.

"We were discussing Lady Catherine," Callum continued.

With his eyes sharp and his voice bright, Liza found it hard to believe that his memory had been failing him.

"For years, the rumor about Lady Catherine's secret baby persisted, and it was assumed her baby must have died along with her. But what was curious to the family was that there was no indication of the baby on her gravestone in the old kirkyard."

He waved his hand toward the window, and Liza's eyes went to the grounds, where she caught sight of Lachlan near the top of a ladder sawing at a branch that was hanging down from the massive sycamore. He reached up, seemingly unconcerned that one misstep would cause him to fall to the ground.

As if he could sense he was being watched, he looked up toward the window. Liza blinked. There was no way he could possibly see her in the daylight.

She brought her attention back to the conversation. "Wouldn't the family have wanted to deny the baby's existence, living or dead?"

Mr. Douglas took another cookie and sat back in the armchair, brushing crumbs off his belly.

Callum was shaking his head. "The family was very religious. And superstitious. They would have wanted to memorialize the babe somehow. There would have been a marking—a cross or an angel somewhere near Lady Catherine's headstone. But there's nothing there so far as we can tell. The headstone is worn now, but there would have been some record."

Liza made a mental note to ask Lachlan about the family burial plot.

"There were other whispers that perhaps, if the rumors were true about a secret child, a relative might have been given the child to raise as their own. Or even that the family of the stableboy might have absconded with the child."

The story was certainly an interesting one, and Callum's words were so animated that it was impossible not to share his excitement.

"That's a lot of rumor and speculation in order to make the leap that I could be a long-lost progeny of Lady Catherine."

Callum puffed his chest out in an exaggerated manner. "I have the DNA to prove it."

"I'm fairly certain my DNA just proves that I could be related to a particular group of people." Liza had done her homework before she'd submitted her own DNA to the testing site.

Callum shook his head. "Not *your* DNA. I submitted Lady Catherine's DNA."

Chapter 7

Liza stared at Callum. Lady Catherine had lived centuries ago—would it have been possible to extract DNA from a source so ancient? She pictured a hairbrush, or a cloth, perhaps covered in postpartum blood, of Lady Catherine's. But given the crazed intensity that shone in the man's eyes, she considered the fact that he may have had the woman's body exhumed.

"We found her teeth," he said excitedly. "Or, I should say, my grandmother did back in the early part of the century when they were cleaning out one of the rooms." He went on to describe the bracelet made of baby teeth found in a small velvet pouch marked with her name and enclosed in a compartment in the back of a bureau drawer. The family suspected it was a memento mori trinket, and it had been saved and passed down, then tucked away and forgotten.

"Genetic testing has advanced, so I figured the teeth were worth a try." He beamed at Liza.

She found the conversation difficult to process. Suppose she *could* be related to Lady Catherine? But it was so long ago. Why should DNA matter now? Surely connection and heritage mattered more than just blood. Aside from that, the talk of bracelets made of teeth and DNA processing was making her queasy.

She held out her hands. "If there are other relatives, why bother looking for me in the first place? Surely the inheritance of this estate would have been determined before all of these scientific and technological advancements." What she left unspoken was Callum's advanced age and failing health, even though he seemed sharp and healthy enough despite whatever diagnosis he'd been given. For all Liza knew, he may well be around for another ten years.

"Hamish Ramsay," Mr. Douglas said flatly, without further explanation.

Liza looked between the men, and found that some of the enthusiasm in Callum had dulled.

"The estate would have been passed down through my own kin," Callum explained. "When it became evident that marriage and children were not in the stars for me, the family and I determined that young Hamish would be the best of my cousin's children to inherit."

There was an awkward silence.

"And what happened to Hamish?" Liza finally asked. She drained the last of her cooling tea and set her cup and saucer back on the cart. She noticed that all of the cookies and the tablet had disappeared.

"I discovered that Hamish had signed an agreement with a developer to demolish the castle and develop the land upon my death," said Callum, the anger still evident in his voice. "An apartment complex—can you believe that? He stood to make millions on top of the inheritance. Obviously, after I was in the ground, I couldn't have stopped him, but I damn sure was going to stop him while there was still breath in my lungs."

"And there was no one else?" Liza asked.

Another long pause. A look passed between the two men.

"It wasn't long after that I decided to have the forensic investigation done. To see if there were others out there. That's how I eventually found ye." He beamed at Liza and his eyes went a little cloudy. "Ye really do look like her," he said, his voice distant.

Liza shifted on the sofa and glanced over at Mr. Douglas. "And they could determine my relation to Lady Catherine from the teeth?"

Mr. Douglas lifted a round shoulder. "I was as shocked as anyone when the results came back," he said. "The investigative team had found ye and others through genealogic research first."

"But ye didn't belong with the others," Callum added. The sharp eyes were gone, and he seemed elsewhere, as if he were communicating with them through a fog.

Mr. Douglas stared at Callum for a moment, then he looked at Liza. "When the team traced you back, they found that the official birth records of yer great, great, great, great, et cetera…" he waved his hand, "grandfather, in 1695, did not coincide with the birth records kept by his parents. In other words, that line of the family had five children and five birth records in the family files. Yer direct ancestor was not a part of those records."

"So, the theory was that my direct-line ancestor was the child of Lady Catherine Ramsay?"

Mr. Douglas nodded. "It was just a theory, of course. But when Callum asked them to test the DNA in the teeth, and they compared it to yours, there were unmistakable genetic markers. Truly fascinating stuff." He seemed as though he didn't want to be as impressed as he was.

Callum leaned forward and touched her hand. "This estate belongs to ye, my dear, after what he did to ye."

It took a minute for Liza to untangle that Callum was referring to what Sir Alexander had done to Lady Catherine, but a part of her interpreted it as what her father, Simon Ramsay, had done to *Liza* by leaving. Of course, Simon Ramsay would have had no idea he'd been a descendant of Clan Ramsay.

Mr. Douglas sighed and pursed his lips. "Come on, my laird. Let's get ye in bed to take a little rest. We've had too much excitement today, and unfortunately the day's not over yet."

When Mr. Douglas had shuffled Callum off to the bedroom behind them, Liza stood and looked out the windows at the far-reaching greenery of the lawn. To her right, she could make out a large patch of overgrowth that looked like it might have once been a garden. Just below the castle walls, the land dipped in a circle around the building. This would have been the remnants of the moat. As crazy as it felt to her, she understood Callum's vacillation between this world and another, more ancient one. She felt the pull of history—of memory—everywhere she looked.

She watched as Lachlan folded up the stepladder. She felt a tug of emotion toward him too.

He hoisted the ladder under one arm and gathered a pile of branches and leaves under the other. Then he walked purposefully across the grounds, away from the castle, toward the river. He disappeared on a narrow pathway that Liza hadn't noticed before. It was camouflaged by the wildflowers and vegetation at the tree line.

Mr. Douglas appeared silently beside her, startling her. She wasn't sure how such a large man managed to move so stealthily.

"Best to steer clear of that one," he said, staring in the direction Lachlan had disappeared.

"Why?"

"Despite his connections, Lachlan McClaren has always been bad news."

Liza frowned. "Lachlan said his grandmother worked here when he was a boy."

"Been a McClaren working here for years, according to Mrs. Boyle. Neither the Ramsay Estate, nor the country can seem to get rid of them. They're like lice." He chuckled at his own perceived joke that went over Liza's head. "But that one in particular…" He jerked his chin in the direction Lachlan had gone. "…everybody thought he had some promise." Mr. Douglas shook his head. "That poor girl. And his kin Charlie Campbell was heading the same way. I'm not saying the lad deserved to die, mind ye." He shook his head again. "I'm just saying, those apples are rotten to the core."

Mrs. Boyle bustled in then, and began clearing the cups and plates Mr. Douglas and Callum had left on the side tables next to their armchairs.

"How is he?" Mrs. Boyle asked.

"Tired," Mr. Douglas responded. "He started to get a bit confused."

"Dr. Patel will be in tomorrow." Mrs. Boyle's words were somber. Heavy.

Liza hated to have to ask the question, but with the lack of explanation, they hadn't given her a choice. "What exactly is wrong with Callum?" she asked.

Mrs. Boyle looked surprised, and then looked at

Mr. Douglas. "Ye didn't tell her?"

Mr. Douglas looked just as surprised. "I suppose I didn't." He cleared his throat. "Laird Ramsay has pancreatic cancer."

The weight of that hit Liza. Advanced pancreatic cancer, particularly in elderly patients, did not have a high survival rate. "When was he diagnosed?" Her voice was hushed, in case Callum could hear her from the other room.

"Six months ago," Mrs. Boyle said.

"It's why we expedited the search for an heir and the genetic testing process," Mr. Douglas added. "We contacted ye as soon as we found ye."

Liza thought she had time to make an informed decision about what the best course of action might be. Now she realized she might not have as much time as she thought. "And if I decide to decline the offer?" she asked.

"Callum can appoint another beneficiary, but he must be of sound mind."

"And if it's determined he's not of sound mind?"

"The Crown will take ownership, and the relatives will have to fight it out."

"Why can't Callum leave the estate to you?" she asked Mr. Douglas.

He shrugged. "I'm not a Ramsay, my dear. Though I could probably make a good case for it myself with the right judge. But," he added, "Callum has decided the estate belongs to *you*, his long-lost Lady Catherine. Changing his mind will take something of a miracle."

⸸

Liza made her way back to her room. She was officially exhausted and had every intention of climbing atop the bed and falling into a deep sleep. But curiosity got the better of her, and instead, she reached into her bag and pulled out her phone.

When she turned on the home screen, she saw two things—notification of twenty-eight missed calls and a battery indicator on red. She swiped up to unlock the device and opened up her text messages. She hesitated for just a second before she pressed Owen's name.

A string of gray boxes appeared. Liza swiped up so that she could read them in successive order.

Liza, did you mean to dial me?

Liza, are you there?

What was that noise?

Are you okay?

Liza?

This isn't funny.

Liza, I'm serious, pick up the phone.

I'm coming over.

Okay, you've made your point. I get it—you're angry. I'll give you space. Just let me know you're okay.

I assume you've left for your business trip, but you

need to tell me where you are.

Liza, I just called your office. Raj called me back and said you quit? WTF????

Seriously, you need to tell me what's going on!

I called your grandmother, and she says you're not in PA. She's worried about you.

If you don't call me back, I'm going to call the police.

Liza sighed. Eight percent battery left. Closing her eyes, she pressed Owen's name in her contacts.

The phone barely trilled before he picked up. "Liza, what is going on?" His words came out on a breath of relief and anger. "Where are you?"

"I don't want to talk. I'm only calling to tell you that I'm alive, I'm safe, and you don't need to call the police."

"You quit your job?"

"I didn't quit," she said, straining to remain calm. "I'm taking a break. Not that it's any of your business."

"We *live* together, Liza. We have a home together. It damn well *is* my business."

"Maybe you should have thought of that before you had an affair with *Mitchell From Work*."

"Oh, for God's sake. I can explain all of that. Just come home."

"I'll be away for a few days. Stay wherever you want, with whomever you want. If I have anything to say to you when I get back, I'll let you know."

"Don't be like that, Liza. You know how much I

love you."

She was silent.

"Ten years," he said. "We've been together for ten years."

"I'm aware," she responded. "Which is why I was so upset when I found out you were willing to throw them away so carelessly."

"Jesus, Liza, who do you think I am?" he yelled. "As usual, this is you overreacting! I swear to God—"

The connection abruptly went silent, leaving Liza with the deafening sound of her own erratic pulse echoing in her ears. She clenched her trembling hand into a fist around the mobile. Tears blurred her vision as she struggled to contain the overwhelming knowledge that Owen might be right. Maybe she was overreacting.

She sat on the edge of the bed, taking deep breaths. It had begun to rain again, and the drops hissed against the windows. When her pulse returned to normal, she reached into her bag and took out her charger, realizing immediately she couldn't use it without a travel adapter, which she hadn't thought to pack.

She looked at the door, debating whether to find Mrs. Boyle and ask if one was available, then she glanced down at the dead phone and thought about what new words, revelations, and accusations might await her with access to electricity.

She set the phone down on the bedside table,

kicked off her shoes, and climbed onto the bed. She sank into the soft mattress, which felt as if it were forming to her body, sucking her gently into its depths.

With the rain tapping softly against the window, and the pillow cradling her head, the cobweb of sleep spun fast across her consciousness. She had one last thought before she succumbed to the darkness.

I wonder if this is the bed upon which Lady Catherine Ramsay died giving birth to my distant grandfather.

Chapter 8

Liza woke to a soft knocking on her door. It was Mrs. Boyle, summoning her to dinner. She sighed, stretched, and entered the bathroom to brush her teeth and splash cold water on her face. She noted that the floor near the bathtub was wet and could see that the high window was once again open.

She would ask Lachlan to bring his ladder to latch the window properly after dinner, she thought, as she wiped up the floor with the towel she'd used earlier in the day.

When she'd completed the task, she glanced in the mirror, noting the dark smudges beneath her eyes and her pale pallor. She knew she needed a good night's sleep and maybe a bit of fresh air, but until then, she pulled out the toiletry case that held her rarely used cosmetics.

She smoothed some foundation over her skin, dotted concealer beneath her eyes, and applied eye shadow, a thin line of eyeliner, and a swipe of mascara on each eye. She then applied a cream blush on each cheek and rubbed some of the color over her lips.

She considered her reflection in the mirror, before brushing out her hair, which had dried in long dark waves that fell around her shoulders. No one could accuse of her looking like Lady Catherine with her loose hair and smoky makeup.

With some sleep and a bit of color on her face, she felt better than she had earlier. Reentering the bedroom, she opened her suitcase and pulled out a long blue dress, cinched at the waist, and a pair of brown high-heeled sandals for which she'd paid way too much. They had been self-gifted as a splurge for making partner a few months earlier. While she'd been proud of herself, the shoes had been an insubstantial and frivolous reward. She only ended up feeling guilty when she looked at them.

Liza walked out of the room, pulling the door shut behind her. Despite her angst about the conversation with Owen, she felt surprisingly free. As if she were in a different reality where her relationship with him didn't even exist. She searched for guilt about that, but none came.

When she walked into the dining room, she found the room occupied by Brodie Graham and Kenneth Morrison. They held tumblers of golden-colored liquid. Mr. Morrison's face looked flushed and his eyes glassy.

Brodie's eyes traveled up and down her body. Instead of being outraged by the attention, she flushed with pleasure. Here, in this different life, it was nice to be noticed. "Ms. Ramsay, you look absolutely ravishing," he said. Liza couldn't remember being so delighted by flattery.

Instead of waving away the compliment, as she was apt to do, she simply said, "Thank you very much, Mr. Graham."

He tipped his head toward a bottle of wine on the table. She nodded. He poured a glass, and as he handed it to her, his fingers brushed hers and lingered. At her ear, he whispered, "You are most welcome, Liza." His voice was very nearly a purr. Liza shivered.

Lachlan walked in then, wearing a clean pair of trousers and a slightly more formal shirt. His hair was combed neatly to one side, the edges just starting to curl over his ears. He gave a quick nod to Brodie and Mr. Morrison before smiling widely at Liza. "Ye look much better," he said.

Brodie made a noise from the back of his throat, something near to a snort of derision.

Although it didn't rise to the level of Brodie's 'ravishing' comment, Liza was nonetheless just as charmed by Lachlan. "I *feel* much better," she agreed.

She noticed that he shook his head when Brodie offered him the bottle of whisky and instead poured himself a glass of water from the table.

"Let's get this over with and go home already," said Kenneth Morrison. "I've been wandering around this dreadful prison all day long."

Brodie raised a wry eyebrow. "I hardly think an ancient fortress, site of countless events of historical significance, can be described as dreadful."

"It's not doin' anyone a bit of good sittin' here as it is. This is prime real estate. Close tae the city, near tae the airport. This land is just wastin' away." His words were sloppy, slurred, like his tongue was too big for his mouth.

"Is that why you're here, Mr. Morrison? To convince Chief Ramsay the land needs to be developed?"

"O' course no'," he said, his words slurring. "Robert invited me here tae take a look at the place and meet Ms. Ramsay."

Liza looked up. "Me?"

"Ye might be the next owner," he said. He took another long swallow of his whisky then wiped his mouth with the back of his hand. "Robert just wants ye tae ha' all yer options."

Lachlan glared at the man, his mouth set in a thin line and his arms crossed over his chest. He shifted his weight to one foot. "Developing this land is not an option," he said firmly.

Mr. Morrison snorted. "I don't think that's up to you, lad." He started to raise the glass to his lips, but paused before it made it. "Come to think of it, why don't ye go on back to the servants' quarters where ye belong?"

Mr. Douglas walked into the room before Lachlan could respond. "Now, Kenneth, ye know the detectives would like to have a word with Mr. McClaren. Let's see what comes of that before we send the lad away."

Liza was puzzled. If Callum Ramsay had disinherited the previously identified heir for making a deal to sell the Ramsay land to a developer, why on earth had Robert Douglas invited this man to talk with her? Before she could ask for a moment of Mr. Douglas's time, he had pulled Mr. Morrison to the side, while Mrs. Boyle bustled in with a large tray of what looked like steaming pies. Instead of smelling of sweet pastry, however, a savory fragrance wafted in Liza's direction.

The two inspectors—Dean and Lawson—walked into the room behind her.

Mrs. Boyle set the pies on the sideboard, and said to no one in particular, "The inspectors have decided to join us after all." She did not sound particularly happy about this news. She wiped her hands on her apron. "I'll just go and whip up another pie."

DCI Dean bowed her head slightly in thanks. "It turns out the station didn't have much in the way of dinner, so we thought we'd take you up on your offer," she said with a wide smile. If Dean noticed Mrs. Boyle's perturbed expression or the fact that Callum—the person who had invited her in the first place—wasn't in the room, she didn't let on. DI Lawson wandered over to sniff at the pies Mrs. Boyle had just laid out.

Mrs. Boyle's nostrils flared. "I'll get some extra plates too," she said with a huff of breath and left the room.

The rest of the guests had stopped talking and looked at the newcomers with hesitant gazes.

DCI Dean waved her hand in front of her. "Pretend we aren't even here. Isn't that right, Lawson?"

DI Lawson gave a grunt that could have meant anything. Dean raised her eyebrows as if the noise her companion had made settled the matter.

Mrs. Boyle came back with the plates. "Laird Ramsay will be along presently," she announced. Then, when she saw no one had begun to eat, she directed them all toward the sideboard. Liza discovered that the pastry was filled with chunks of rich meat, mushrooms, and potatoes swimming in a thick gravy. She took a healthy slice then looked around her. Unlike their earlier lunch, no one seemed to be seated at the formal dining table, and instead had taken their plates to random side tables in the adjacent sitting room.

She caught the eye of Brodie Graham; he inclined his head to a small table in the corner of the room. She moved toward him, admiring the elaborate tapestries along the walls of the room. Upon closer examination, the tapestries seemed to depict the history of Scotland, beginning in the 1200s.

Brodie saw her eyes widen and he smiled. "Fascinating, isn't it?" he said, his gaze traveling around the room. He pointed to the edge of one wall. "That's Simundus de Ramesie, the founder of the Ramsay Clan. He built the original structure."

"Simundus?" Liza asked.

"What we would now translate to 'Simon'," Brodie said. "He was of Norman descent."

She sat down and turned her attention to the man across from her. "You know quite a bit about this place." She was silently comparing him to Lachlan.

He shrugged. "I'm an historian. It's my job."

"And your passion."

He held her gaze a beat too long. "My passion," he responded, drawing out the word. "You could say that, yes."

She felt the heat rise to her cheeks. She looked away. They didn't speak for a few minutes as they ate, a dinner which was as rich and flavorful as it smelled. She wasn't sure where she'd gotten the impression that Scottish food was bland, but so far that had not been her experience.

When they'd finished their meals, Brodie dabbed the corner of his mouth with a napkin. "Can I get you something to drink?" he asked.

She shook her head, acutely aware of her altered sleep pattern. She'd traveled enough to know that more alcohol would not help her.

He took her plate and returned with a fresh glass of whisky. Though he didn't appear nearly as inebriated as Mr. Morrison, she couldn't help but wonder if he was just better at holding his liquor.

He took a sip, seemed to hold the liquid in his mouth for a minute and then swallowed. His lips were wet from the drink, and Liza had a brief inappropriate vision of tasting the moisture with her tongue. She shivered, then shook her head slightly. What had gotten into her? She silently chided herself.

"Are you cold?" he asked. She realized he'd noticed her tremor.

"I'm fine." She was in a mind to walk away, leaving the temptation right where it was, but she didn't want to be rude. She wasn't interested in this man romantically. But it was nice to feel admired for a change. It had been a while since that had happened. And even if it *had*, she wasn't sure she'd have noticed. She and Owen had not been in a romantic place for quite some time, and a part of her had assumed that phase in her life might be over. She'd been so busy with work she hadn't had much time to care.

Right now, in this castle in a foreign land, all she had was time. "So, tell me. What are you doing here, Mr. Graham?"

Maybe it was the way she said his name, but he gave her a devilish grin. "Why don't you tell me?"

Her lips curved into a smile, and her intent to be restrained again threatened to flee. "I'm serious," she said, forcing the smile away. She leaned forward.

"Ah, no fun," he responded. But he took a deep breath. "I've kept in touch with Mr. Ramsay since I took this post five years ago. I've always hoped there might be a way that the Royal Kingdom Trust might partner with the owner of the castle and estate in some way. We want to preserve this monument and its place in history."

Liza furrowed her brow. "Isn't that what Callum has done?"

"Aye. He has." Brodie opened his hands in front of him. "But Mr. Ramsay isn't getting any younger, and there are others…" His words trailed off, and he shot a look in the direction of Kenneth Morrison who was seated with Mr. Douglas. "There are others who might have different motivations."

She turned, and was surprised to find that both Mr. Morrison and Mr. Douglas seemed to be staring right back at them. Their expressions did not look pleased or kind.

Lachlan was standing off to the side alone, also glancing in her direction. Something about his posture made him look wounded, betrayed.

She looked back at Brodie to find he was studying her with a serious expression on his face. Gone was the flirtatiousness of just a few moments ago. "The Trust could partner with the owner in any number of ways, from full takeover, to investor, to consultant. We have funds available, and I could guarantee that grant money would be provided to ensure this place is around for another few centuries."

Not that she'd seriously considered Callum's offer, but if she were to contemplate the possibilities, she might be able to see a potential path forward if financial support were available. "Would I retain ownership?" she asked, startling herself with the way the question had emerged from her lips. As if she were already in a position to claim ownership.

"We could work something out where you'd be either owner or trustee. It would depend on the arrangement."

She frowned. "And how would Callum feel about that?"

Brodie chuckled. "It depends. I've been a thorn in his side, but I think he knows I mean well." His laughter faded. "Or at least he used to know that. I'm not sure what he knows anymore."

"Does that mean Mr. Ramsay invited you here?" Chief Inspector Dean emerged from behind Liza's chair, startling them both.

Dean held up a hand. "Apologies, Miss Ramsay. I thought you knew I was behind you."

"Inspector, is there any way we can speed up whatever protocol you might be following? I'd like to go home at some point." Brodie didn't bother to try to hide his annoyance.

"You're certainly looking comfortable with Ms. Ramsay."

He gave a tight smile. "Ms. Ramsay is lovely, but I still would like to leave."

She gave a nod. "You probably want to get back to…" She stopped abruptly and frowned. "What's her name? Emma?"

Liza's eyebrows shot up. Brodie's mouth fell open.

She felt the blood drain from her face.

They'd had nothing but a nice meal together and a harmless flirtation. If Brodie was attached, it was of no consequence or concern to her. But the truth was, the flirtation had felt nice, and to know that's all it was—a flirtation and nothing more—was a blow to her ego she didn't need, not after having read the text messages on Owen's phone. After realizing she could be replaced so quickly and easily.

Liza stood abruptly. "If you'll excuse me," she said to DCI Dean. "I think I'll get some water." She couldn't bring herself to make eye contact with Brodie.

As she walked toward the dining room, she heard Brodie say, "Liza, wait," just as Dean said, "We can talk in the library now if that suits you, Mr. Graham."

Something inside of Liza closed off as a realization opened up: There was something wrong with her. It was why everyone left her. Her father. Mother. Grandparents. Owen. Brodie. Not that Brodie was even remotely hers to begin with, but still…she attracted these situations or these people who felt compelled to lie and then leave. Even her mother. Her beautiful mother who had withheld her diagnosis from Liza until the disease was wasting her from the inside out. Until it was too late to do anything but say goodbye and grieve.

Liza realized she was doomed to repeat the same patterns over and over again.

A cool breeze seemed to brush past her, and she thought of Lady Catherine who may have given birth to a child which was then taken from her. Liza wondered what had happened first—the loss of Catherine's child or the loss of Catherine's life.

Mrs. Boyle reentered the dining room with Callum holding onto her crooked arm. "There ye go," she murmured softly, walking slowly in time to Callum's shuffling.

What would become of Mrs. Boyle when Callum passed on? she wondered.

Callum's hazy eyes landed on Liza and he frowned, before recognition crossed his face. "Yer hair," he said. "It's down."

But the way he said it, it was as if he wasn't sure he were talking to her or his ghost.

Mrs. Boyle patted his arm as she sat him down at the table. "I'll get ye a plate."

He didn't respond but instead motioned to Liza. She walked over to him.

"Have ye decided, Liza?" he asked. She was surprised. He did know her after all. He also knew her name.

"I'm still thinking about it." She gave him a smile.

"Don't think too hard. I don't have that much time."

She was about to argue, but something about the way he said it made her believe it was true. Instead, she asked, "Did you invite Brodie Graham here?"

He frowned again, his mind working.

"The man from the Royal Kingdom Trust," she prompted.

"Aye, the young rake."

The description nearly made Liza laugh out loud, and she was glad for her grandmother's penchant for historical romance novels. A *rake* was exactly the right word for Brodie Graham.

"He has a habit of just turnin' up," Callum quipped. "Whether ye want him to or not."

"So you didn't invite him here to meet me?"

"Why would I do that?" Callum asked as Mrs. Boyle set a plate in front of him.

"Eat yer supper before it gets cold," she said. She caught Liza's eye, seeming to give her a warning look, but Liza didn't know what she was warning her of, or against.

Liza poured herself a glass of water and sat with Callum as he pushed the steak pie around on his plate taking half-hearted bites. She wanted to ask him more—about Brodie, about Kenneth Morrison, about Mr. Douglas. About Lachlan.

She wanted to ask him about Charlie Campbell and if anyone was sad the young boy was dead. But she didn't do any of that. She just sat with him in silence, and he periodically gazed up at her and smiled, seemingly happy just to have some quiet company.

After a while, Brodie reentered the room, and walked slowly up to the table. Liza had seen him out of the corner of her eye, acutely aware of the energy of his presence, though she avoided looking directly at him. It wasn't fair, she knew. He had done nothing wrong, and he owed her not a thing.

"I'll be heading out," he said. He addressed Callum, but she knew his words were meant for her.

Callum waved his fork in Brodie's direction.

He cleared his throat. "Ms. Ramsay, would you be so kind as to walk me out?"

Liza looked up at him then. His dark eyes were baleful with regret. "I'd love to explain," he said, his words trailing off.

Her resolve faltered. Perhaps there really was an explanation, she thought. Perhaps Emma was his mother or his sister. Their relationship hadn't been explained. And Liza doubted that DCI Dean had anyone's best interests at heart in her quest for information.

The least Liza could do was hear the man out.

She was half a movement away from rising, when an icy breeze rushed past her, over her, through her.

Another tremor racked her body, this one not pleasurable. Instead, the shiver felt like a silent warning.

"No," she found herself saying, her voice surprisingly firm. "I don't think I will."

He held his hands out in front of him and pitched forward as if he were ready to plead his case.

"Best be getting' on then," interjected Mrs. Boyle, her voice ominous. "And be careful out there, Mr. Graham." Brodie Graham pursed his lips and studied her before he turned without another word and walked out the door.

"We don't need the ilk o' him around here," she mumbled under her breath. Liza smiled. She wasn't sure why Mrs. Boyle didn't like Brodie Graham, but she was pleased to have an ally.

Liza was vaguely aware of someone leaving the room immediately after Brodie Graham, but she was too distracted by the towering DI Lawson entering the room to pay much attention to who it had been. One by one, Inspector Lawson called the residents and guests across the grand hallway to a room on the opposite side of the stairwell.

Liza's gaze searched for Lachlan as she waited her turn with the detectives, but he seemed to have disappeared. She remembered the look on his face as she'd flirted shamelessly with the 'rake', as Callum had called him. She felt a sense of regret. She certainly didn't owe either of these men any explanations regarding her mildly flirtatious behavior, nor did she owe either of them her loyalty. But Lachlan had been a perfect gentleman in each of their interactions. Even—she reminded herself facing the embarrassment directly—the encounter during which he'd seen her without any clothes on.

She sat at the long dining room table, resting her forehead in her palm. This is how DI Lawson found her. "Ms. Ramsay?" he asked. "Are ye all right?"

She looked up sharply, realizing this was the first time she'd heard Lawson speak. His voice was a deep rumble from his chest, and kinder than she'd imagined.

"Yes," she said. "Still a bit jet-lagged, I suppose."

He nodded and gestured for her to follow him. "And ye came in when?"

She trailed after him across the grand hallway toward a wing of the castle she hadn't yet had a chance to explore. Her eyes darted to more paintings and documents on the walls.

"Uh…" she said distractedly, "I came in this morning." They walked into a dark room, decorated in earthy forest greens and deep rosewood. Every wall was shelved from floor to ceiling with books. When DI Lawson shut the door behind her, the back side of the door blended seamlessly into the bookshelf.

The furniture in the room—leather armchairs and

sofas—was soft and smooth as butter, and the only artificial light came from the soft glow of tableside lamps and a dancing fire that had been lit in the hearth. The room had a definite masculine feel. She glanced up at the head of a large buck above the mantle.

On a small antique table between two armchairs was a chess board with sculpted ivory pieces, each a few inches tall. Liza stared at the little human figures with their spherical eyes and somber expressions. There was something creepy about the figures, their dead gazes staring back at her.

Inspector Lawson led her to a straight-backed chair placed across from a sofa, upon which perched DCI Dean. "Hello, Ms. Ramsay," the detective said, gesturing toward a carafe of water on the low marble coffee table between them.

Liza waved away the water. "I'm not sure what I can tell you about that poor boy's death. It had already happened by the time I arrived this morning."

"Oh, that's all right." Beside the water, Dean set down a notepad that she had been holding. "Nice to have a bit of a break and just have a relaxed conversation, anyhow." With her pen, she pointed at the table behind them, the one that held the odd chessboard. "Did they tell you then?"

Liza's gaze followed the direction of Dean's pen. "Tell me what?"

"About the chess set."

The dead eyes of the pieces stared at her accusingly. Liza looked away and shook her head.

"Apparently Charlie Campbell had stolen a few pieces from the set a few days ago. His mother found them and called Lachlan, who returned them to Callum and made Charlie apologize. Then Lachlan fired the boy."

"That seems a bit harsh." *For a creepy, ugly game,* Liza thought, but didn't verbalize it.

"What did you say they were called, Lawson?"

"Lewis chessmen," Lawson said in his deep droning monotone. "Each piece worth over eight hundred thousand pounds, roughly a million dollars."

Liza coughed. "Pardon me?"

"Exactly," Dean said. "Millions of dollars sitting right there on that table. Out in the open."

"They may be the oldest thing in this castle," Lawson added. "Estimated to have originated in Norway or Scandinavia in the twelfth century."

"And Charlie Campbell stole them?"

Dean held up two fingers. "Just two of them, but it's hard to say who else might know about the theft and now the value of the pieces."

"Do you think this has something to do with his death?"

Dean shrugged. "Rather coincidental that the scoundrel stole nearly two million pounds worth of ancient artifacts then ended up with his head bashed in, face-down in the river, wouldn't you say?"

"Didn't you say he returned the pieces?"

"And who else might he have told?"

Liza looked back again at the smooth white figures and their bulging eyes. "These should be in a museum," she muttered, then turned back around, even more on edge than she'd been when she entered the room.

DI Lawson stood beside the sofa, looming over them both. Liza looked at him nervously.

Dean smiled. "Don't mind Lawson. He gets a bit twitchy when he sits."

They both stared at her; Liza shifted in the uncomfortable chair.

"So," Dean continued, and this felt anything like a relaxed conversation, "from what I understand, you might be inheriting this place. Is that right?"

Liza gave the briefest of nods. The last thing she wanted to do was rehash her emotional quandary for this detective whom she one hundred percent did not trust.

"Will you be relocating to Scotland full-time then?"

"Honestly, I haven't had much time to consider the offer. It was a spontaneous decision to travel over here, and…" She let her words trail off and looked around her. "What would I possibly do with a place like this? How could I maintain it?"

Dean looked around the room too. "I'm sure Mrs.

Boyle and Mr. McClaren would be happy to stay on. Mr. McClaren, in particular, seems quite taken with you."

Liza's gaze snapped back to Dean, who looked back at her with an innocent expression. But Liza had not spoken to Lachlan in the presence of either of the inspectors. Had Lachlan said something which had given DCI Dean that impression? Perhaps someone else had mentioned it to them. She hated knowing she may have been a topic of conversation with the police.

Dean continued. "I suppose all that would depend on whether Owen—Is that his name?" She didn't wait for Liza to respond. "Whether Owen would want to move here with you."

Liza stared at the other woman, feeling violated. As far as she was aware, no one here even knew Owen existed. Which meant the detectives had been looking into her background.

If Dean sensed Liza's discomfort, she didn't let on. "It would be a big lifestyle change, no doubt. Not to mention the money. But it seems as though Mr. Graham might be willing to help you out with the financial end of things." Dean leaned closer. "Not sure Owen would like that, though, eh?" The woman winked.

Liza pursed her lips. Within five minutes, this woman had hinted at her flirtation with two different men in addition to invoking her current relationship, such that it was. "Are you accusing me of something, Inspector?"

Dean's affronted expression was exaggerated. "Of course not, Ms. Ramsay. It's none of my business what you do with your own time."

"I meant, regarding the murder of Charlie Campbell," she said through slightly gritted teeth. Her voice was firm, cold. She was too tired to play this game with these detectives. She may have been a bit nervous, given the circumstances, but she had absolutely nothing to hide. There was no way she could've remotely been involved with the boy's death or have had any knowledge of the circumstances that led up to his passing.

Dean studied Liza, then picked up her notepad again. The false camaraderie disappeared. "I know you traveled in after Charlie Campbell was found, but have you seen or heard anything suspicious since you've been here?"

Liza shook her head. "Nothing at all. Although everyone seemed surprised by the fact that you're investigating. Everyone was under the impression the death was an accident."

DCI Dean gave a terse nod. "It certainly could be an accident," she said. "But given that Charlie's uncle—Lachlan's father—is who he is, and given the theft perpetrated by the victim, we thought it best to take things just a step further."

"Lachlan's father?" Liza asked.

"James McClaren," Dean said. At Liza's blank look, she continued, "Permanent Secretary to the Scottish Government."

Liza blinked. She wasn't sure what that position was, but it sounded high-level and contradictory to what she knew of Lachlan, who had told her he'd worked at the Ramsay Estate the past eight years. Mr. Douglas had indicated that others in the family had worked here too. "I don't understand," she said. "Lachlan works *here*."

"That he does."

"His grandmother had also worked here."

Dean arched an eyebrow. "The McClarens are nearly as tied to this land as the Ramsays, as a matter of fact."

"But…why?"

The chief inspector laughed and looked up at Lawson. "I forget sometimes how different it must be in the States." Lawson let out a spasm of air that could have been a chuckle, a snort, or a sigh. "Over here, families are still tied to their names, their land, their heritage. You don't simply waltz away from your past."

Liza felt insulted, but she wasn't sure why. She didn't think it was inherently better or more noble to be immobilized in the claws of history. "Lachlan's father didn't work here, though. Why does Lachlan?"

Dean cocked her head and studied Liza. "Has Lachlan said anything about young Charlie?" she asked without acknowledging Liza's question.

Liza thought back to their conversations. He hadn't mentioned Charlie at all, but Mr. Douglas had made a comment—something about the two of them being no good. *Rotten to the core*, is what he'd said. It had been Dean herself who'd mentioned that Charlie and Lachlan had argued recently. Over the stolen Lewis chessmen, she supposed.

Liza could not reconcile the seemingly gentle man, who had shown her around the property and saved her from fainting in the dungeon, with a criminal.

"He's been nothing but lovely to me," she answered.

DCI Dean nodded.

"Is he a suspect?"

Liza wasn't sure if she should read anything into what seemed like a slight pause. "As I said, Ms. Ramsay. We don't even know if a crime has occurred."

"You said Charlie's head was bashed in."

"Did I?" she asked. Then she shrugged. "He could have slipped on a wet stone. We're simply covering all possible scenarios."

There was a long pause while Dean and Lawson stared at her, waiting. She stared back. There was a finality in the air.

"Am I free to go now?"

"You're free to go whenever you wish, Ms. Ramsay."

She nodded and rose from the chair. Even though she had napped earlier, the warmth of the space, the dim lights in the room, and the smell of old books had made her feel as if she were in a cocoon. A deep fatigue penetrated her bones.

She had to search for the door, hidden by the books. Neither Dean nor Lawson offered to help.

She had just made contact with the concealed doorknob and twisted it when Dean said, "Oh, Ms. Ramsay, just one more thing."

Liza turned around.

"Has Lachlan happened to mention Nicola to you?"

Liza frowned. "Not that I remember."

"That might be something to ask him."

Liza felt a sense of foreboding. "Who is she?"

"Probably best to ask Lachlan who she was." Dean's voice was tight and strained. She went back to her notes, effectively dismissing Liza.

The words of Mr. Douglas in Callum's sitting room came back to her. *That poor girl.*

Liza left the library, and without another word to her hosts, found her way to her room, avoiding looking at the spooky eyes of the portraits that followed her through the dark halls. When she reached her room, she locked the door behind her and didn't bother with her nightly routine. She just shed her clothes and climbed into the big bed, squeezing her eyes shut until the creaks of the old house and rush of the wind faded as she floated off to sleep.

But before unconsciousness dragged her away, she could have sworn the pale face of Catherine Ramsay leaned over her. The ghostly hair fell over Liza's face as if in blessing. Or as a curse.

Chapter 9

A piercing, otherworldly screech echoed through the air, assaulting Liza's ears and causing her heart to race in her chest. The sound seemed to linger even after it had disappeared, leaving a tense stillness in its wake.

Liza frantically scanned her surroundings, trying to pinpoint the source of the noise. Was it a bird? An animal? Or something more sinister? Each heartbeat felt like a drum pounding in her chest as she braced herself for whatever may come next.

Then there was more yelling—deeper, masculine. The sound seemed to be coming from outside.

She flung herself from the bed and ran to the window, where the early light of a Scottish summer morning was just brightening the sky.

Peering down from her towering fourth-floor window, Liza could clearly see the distinct figures below. The short, round form of Mrs. Boyle, her head buried in her hands as if consumed by despair. Lachlan McClaren, a flurry of frantic movements as he struggled with an object on the ground. But it was

Brodie Graham's swaying body that caught her attention, hanging from a sturdy branch of the great sycamore tree. His face was a sickly shade of purple, twisted and misshapen in death. The once majestic tree now served as an eerie backdrop for the gruesome scene below.

Liza stared for longer than she might have, struggling to make sense of what she witnessed. Only when her brain had processed the scene in front of her did she look away.

A wave of nausea rolled over her, and her stomach roiled. She took a few deep breaths to steady herself. She backed away from the window and threw on her dress from the night before. She didn't bother with shoes, just ran down the stairs, trying to find her way to the back side of the castle so that she could do something. What help she could possibly provide, she had no idea.

Near the foot of the stairs, she encountered Keith Morrison and Robert Douglas, both still drunk with sleep. "What was that?" Mr. Morrison demanded, and Mr. Douglas shrugged his meaty, hairy shoulders, bare where the fabric of his white undershirt ended. Their bloated faces told the tale of yesterday's whisky.

"Did you hear that sound?" Mr. Douglas asked, and Liza nodded.

"It's outside," she said pointing behind her, reluctant to verbalize what she'd seen. "Brodie Graham."

Just as the words left her mouth, another thud sounded from the backside of the hallway, toward Callum's room. The three of them hurried in that direction. A moaning was coming from inside the bedroom. Liza was the first to bound through the door, and she found Callum on the floor next to the bed, a gash on his temple.

She crouched down to help him. Outside, she heard sirens wailing, louder and louder.

Mr. Douglas was by her side a moment later, and they lifted Callum up to a seated position. The gash appeared to be a surface wound, and she directed Mr. Douglas to find some bandages.

"Callum, can you hear me?" She tried to keep the panic out of her voice.

His eyes were closed, but he was conscious.

She heard Mr. Morrison exclaim from the other room, "Dear God. He's killed the man!" Alarmed, she strained to look out of the windows next to Callum's bed, but Mr. Douglas came back quickly with the bandages, a cloth, and some disinfectant, and the scene outside the window was forgotten for the moment.

Liza dabbed at the blood on Callum's head and applied the disinfectant then the bandage. The wound was just a scrape of the skin, and she didn't think he'd done any lasting damage. There didn't appear to be a knot on his head, which was good, but she was also concerned about what else he may have damaged in the fall. His bones were already frail, and the advanced illness along with the medication for treatment would have made his bones even more fragile.

Mr. Douglas had stood, staring out the window at the manic efforts on the lawn. He was lost in the scene outside.

Callum's eyes were open now, intense on hers.

"Good morning," she said, trying to keep her voice light, despite everything happening. The purple face of Brodie Graham had imprinted itself on her mind, and she blinked it away as she looked at Callum. "You took a tumble," she said. "Can you stand?"

He didn't respond. His eyes looked haunted. "I saw them," he said, his voice barely more than a whisper.

"Who?" she asked.

He shook his head nearly imperceptibly. She couldn't be sure the movement wasn't a tremor.

Mr. Douglas and Mr. Morrison stood in the doorway, and Callum made a sound at the back of his throat.

"Elizabeth," Mr. Douglas said gravely. Liza looked over her shoulder. She realized they didn't know she'd already been a witness to the scene near the sycamore.

She shook her head and turned back to Callum. "Come on," she said brightly. "Let's see if we can get you back into bed."

She managed to work her arm and a shoulder underneath Callum's right side, and with a herculean effort, she stabilized herself and hoisted the elderly man up. She noted the lack of help from the two able-bodied men still in the room.

She had been prepared to abandon these efforts at any sign of pain, but when Callum was on his feet, he seemed to be physically intact. As she guided him back into the bed, she said to Mr. Douglas, "I believe Mrs. Boyle said his doctor would be visiting today?"

Mr. Douglas nodded, said with a shaky voice, "I'll...I'll confirm it with Margaret."

Something told Liza that Mrs. Boyle might need some recovery time. "If you can find the number, I'll make the arrangements." She remembered her useless mobile phone and cringed. She should have found an adapter to charge it the day before.

After she'd settled Callum with the promise of tea and toast, she made her way back into the anteroom, where Mr. Morrison and Mr. Douglas were now glued to the window.

Liza looked out. The inert body was now lying on the ground with two men in uniform standing over it, while another man in a black jacket squatted low, looking closely and making notes. A woman in a dark uniform walked around the body taking photos. Half of the rope still swayed in the breeze beneath the thick branch. Another wave of nausea gripped Liza, and she swallowed down hard.

Tires crunched on the gravel drive as a black sedan

pulled up and stopped near the edge of the yard beyond the emergency vehicles. DCI Dean and DI Lawson climbed out. Dean looked at the figures of Lachlan and Mrs. Boyle standing off to one side, then her eyes traveled to the window where she stood with Mr. Douglas and Mr. Morrison beside her.

Liza could have imagined it, but their eyes seemed to meet. Liza broke the contact quickly, cleared her throat and stepped back.

"Mr. Douglas, I'm going to need a phone charger or an adapter for my phone."

His eyes were still glazed, and it was Mr. Morrison who spoke. "I have one you can use." He hurried from the room as if he were grateful to have a task.

Liza glanced out the window again. The man who had been crouching over the lifeless form of Brodie Graham stood up and gestured toward Mrs. Boyle, whose hands were still on her face. Lachlan stood next to her, a protective arm around her shoulders.

The man in the black jacket crossed the length of grass to talk with the two of them. DCI Dean crouched down and peered close at the body. She said something to Inspector Lawson who nodded then joined the others.

Lawson said something to Lachlan, who pointed toward the tree and answered. Lawson nodded and walked back to Dean and the body. After a moment, the man in the black jacket moved back toward the body and had a short conversation with Dean before he gestured to the two uniformed emergency responders.

They nodded and walked to the ambulance where they retrieved a stretcher.

Liza's gaze went to Lachlan and Mrs. Boyle. Lachlan's square jaw was set as if he were clenching his teeth together. His eyes were on the lifeless body.

Mr. Morrison came rushing back to the room. "Sorry, took me a minute to find it," he said breathlessly as he handed the accessory to Liza.

Tearing her attention away from the scene on the lawn, she took a moment to look in on Callum. His eyes were shut, and his breathing was regular.

"Keep an eye on him," she directed Mr. Douglas.

After she made the journey to her room, she probed her bag for the phone, and once located, plugged it into the charger. It would take some time for the device to charge, so she left it on the bedside table and walked back downstairs, determined to be of use, if only to keep at bay the mental image of Brodie's body swaying in the sycamore.

Liza walked down the main staircase and opened a door to her right. She wandered through the labyrinth of rooms before locating the main kitchen in the area Lachlan had mentioned in passing. It was a cavernous space, filled with large, if dated, cooking appliances. An immense gas stove was positioned to the left with one oven beneath and another double oven next to it. In the middle of the floor was a large sink and preparation island over which hung dozens of pots, pans, and other cooking vessels.

To the right of the room was a deep fireplace, the arched opening nearly a quarter of the wall itself. The brick of the hearth was the same color as the outer walls of the castle, and Liza wondered if this feature was original to the building. She remembered Lachlan saying the kitchen was built atop the dungeon.

She found a large kettle, filled it with water, then placed it on the stove to boil while she searched multiple cupboards for tea, finding something called Brooke Bond. While the water boiled and the tea steeped, she toasted half a dozen pieces of bread in a large toaster oven and buttered them heavily. She had no idea where Mrs. Boyle kept the lovely fine teacups, so her tea went into the chipped mugs that she'd found in a corner cabinet.

She was working out how to get both the tray of toast and the mugs to the dining room when Lachlan entered the kitchen. His gaze was ferocious, and Liza shrank back for just a moment before announcing the obvious. "I've made some tea and toast."

Without a word, he crossed the room and opened a large dark cabinet against the back wall, revealing a series of deep shelves. He grabbed the tray of tea, placed it on one shelf, then returned for the tray of toast. Once both plates were on the shelving, he closed the door and pushed a button to the right of the cabinet. A motor sounded, and Liza realized she was looking at a modern dumbwaiter.

Then Lachlan walked out of the kitchen. Liza followed him up the stairs to the small chamber just outside the dining room on the second floor. As Lachlan took the tray of teacups, Liza grabbed the plate of toast and followed Lachlan into the sitting room where they'd gathered the night before.

Her eyes went to the table where she and Brodie had huddled in the dim light. She remembered the flirtation and her subsequent rejection. She did not flatter herself to think that her dismissal would have had much to do with the man's death, but she couldn't help but wonder if it may have been a contributing factor. A knot of emotion collected in the back of her throat.

Mrs. Boyle was sitting on a sofa against the far wall, her head resting against a cushion. Lachlan handed her a cup of tea.

She took it, sniffed. "Where are the good mugs?" she asked. She peered into the dark liquid. "No cream?"

"Drink," he instructed. She listened.

Mr. Morrison and Mr. Douglas took mugs of tea and toast offered by Liza.

"Callum took a fall this morning," Liza said to Lachlan.

Mrs. Boyle sat up. "What's that?"

Liza made a smoothing motion with her hands, patting the air. "He's fine." Then she clarified, "He seems fine. If you have the number for his doctor, I'll confirm he'll come out today and fill him in on the morning's events."

"I can get it for ye in a bit," Mrs. Boyle said. She took a sip of the tea, made a face, and then reclined her head against the cushion again.

Lachlan lifted a piece of toast, took one bite, and put it back down on the tray.

"Is my tea and toast that bad?" Liza said, her voice cautiously light.

He almost smiled before he seemed to catch himself. "Just not much of an appetite."

"Are you okay?" she asked. He looked at her, his eyes wide and disturbed.

"I did not know the fellow," Lachlan said. "But ye never want to think a man can get to that point—to take his own life. Because then ye have to admit to yerself that if someone else can find that point, so can ye."

The reflective silence that followed Lachlan's words was broken by the keening of the doorbell. Mrs. Boyle started to rise; Liza held up her hand. "I'll get it."

She hurried down the staircase, aware that she was still barefoot, her hair was unbrushed, and her teeth fuzzy from the night's sleep. Liza smoothed a hand over her frizzy waves before she pulled the door open.

DCI Dean's eyebrows raised at the sight of Liza in the doorway. As Liza had come to expect, DI Lawson was a silent looming sentinel behind her.

"Ms. Ramsay," she said. "You're becoming a fixture here."

Liza stood straighter. "Answering the door is the very least I can do after what happened this morning."

"And what is it you think happened here this morning, Ms. Ramsay?"

Liza was at a loss for just a minute. *What kind of question was that?* To Dean, she said, "I think Mr. Graham made the decision to end his life on the Ramsay Estate."

"There certainly has been a lot of tragedy on this property since you showed up." Before Liza could form a response, the inspector continued. "Might we come in for a few minutes?"

Liza didn't see that she had the option to refuse the request, so she moved to the side, closed the door behind them, then led them up the stairs to the sitting area without another word.

When they entered the room, the energy shifted palpably.

Dean's gaze swept over the occupants—Mrs. Boyle on the sofa, Lachlan staring purposefully into the distance, and Misters Douglas and Morrison looking puffy and jaundiced in their respective armchairs.

She looked at the two older men. "You both spent the night then?"

They nodded, and she perched her reading glasses on the bridge of her nose, pulled her notepad from her pocket, and made a note.

"Mrs. Boyle, you found Mr. Graham, is that right?"

"Aye." Mrs. Boyle nodded and covered her eyes with her forearm.

"Did ye see anything out of the ordinary?"

"Besides the body in the tree?" Mrs. Boyle cried. "No, nothin' t'all," she added sarcastically.

Dean didn't acknowledge the mockery. "And what were you doing out at such an early hour?"

"I'd gone around to the back garden to pick some herbs fer the morning meal. I thought the laird might like a nice quiche."

"And Mr. Graham wasn't breathing when you saw him?"

"Well, I did not climb the tree to check, if that's what ye mean."

"What did you do?"

The older woman looked perplexed. "I suppose I yelled," she said, but she didn't seem sure of herself.

"She did," offered Liza.

Dean looked over at her. "You heard her?"

"Yes, her scream woke me up."

"Did you see her scream?"

"No," Liza said. "I was in bed."

Dean nodded. "So how do you know it was Mrs. Boyle who yelled?"

Liza paused. Finally, she said, "It was a woman screaming. I'm not sure who else would it have been."

The chief inspector turned back to Mrs. Boyle. "And then what did you do after you screamed, Mrs. Boyle?"

"And then…" Her words trailed off. "Next thing I knew, Lachlan came running up the path. He got Mr. Graham down."

"How did he do that?"

Mrs. Boyle looked up. Her mouth worked, but no sound came out.

Lachlan spoke up. "I stood up the ladder and cut him down."

Dean cocked her head like she was extremely interested in what Lachlan had to say. "I noticed the ladder next to the tree," she said. "How did it get there?"

"It was there when I arrived," said Lachlan. "It looked like it had been kicked over."

Dean furrowed her brow. "So, the ladder—a stepladder—was lying next to the tree?" She turned to Mrs. Boyle as she asked this question.

Mrs. Boyle's eyes were wide. "I-I could not tell ye."

Liza sighed impatiently. "I saw the ladder."

"You saw the ladder lying on the ground?"

This question made her hesitate. "I saw Lachlan setting it up." She didn't say anything else, because thinking back, she wasn't sure exactly what she saw. The scene had been jumbled and chaotic.

"The ladder was on the ground when I got there after I heard Mrs. Boyle's scream," Lachlan said.

DCI Dean held up a hand as if she had reached her limit of patience with this point. "Alright. And whose ladder is it?"

"The estate's ladder," said Lachlan.

"The estate's ladder," repeated Dean slowly. "Who has access to the estate's ladder?"

"Everyone who lives at the estate," said Mrs. Boyle.

"Do you use the estate's ladder on a regular basis?" Lawson asked Mrs. Boyle. Everyone looked at him, surprised.

"Well, no. These old bones don't allow for much climbing."

"Would I be correct in assuming that it's Mr. McClaren who does most of the climbing?" asked Dean.

Mrs. Boyle gave a tiny nod of her head.

A muscle worked at the side of Lachlan's jaw.

"So, Mr. McClaren, where would Mr. Graham have found the ladder, assuming he put himself in that tree?"

Mr. Morrison bellowed, "Who *else* would have hung 'im?"

DCI Dean gave him a sideways glance. "We're just trying to examine the situation from all angles."

"I'm still confused why a detective chief inspector is wrapped up in this amateur business."

Dean ignored Mr. Morrison and prompted Lachlan with a stare.

"Yesterday afternoon, I'd been cleaning up branches that'd fallen from the tree in the storm," he said. "I think I put the ladder back in the bothy."

"You *think*?"

"I remember dragging the branches down to the burn pile, and I'm fairly certain I came back up and took the ladder back with me."

"And where is the bothy, Mr. McClaren?"

Liza wasn't sure what a bothy was, but she figured it must be similar to what she would call a shed.

"It's down by the cottage, near the stream."

"Close to your living quarters."

"Yes."

Dean made another note in her pad. "Is the bothy locked?"

"There's a padlock on the door, but I don't believe I locked it last evening."

"Why not?"

"I didn't want to be late for dinner."

"Why was that, Mr. McClaren?"

He shrugged. "It seemed important to be on time with the rest of the group."

"So, it didn't have anything to do with your feelings for Ms. Ramsay."

Liza looked up sharply, and noticed that Lachlan's face had reddened. He glanced at her and then glanced away quickly.

"I think that's highly inappropriate, Inspector Dean," Liza said. She didn't mention it was also silly and irrelevant.

"Is it, Ms. Ramsay?"

Something about the way the chief inspector responded caused Liza to bite back her retort.

"Mr. McClaren, did you see Mr. Graham after he left the dining room last evening?"

"No, I did not."

"Where did you go after DI Lawson and I spoke with you in the library?"

"I went to the cottage."

"Did anyone see you?"

Lachlan didn't respond.

Dean looked around. No one else responded either.

Liza thought back. She recalled scanning the room for Lachlan the evening before, but he had not returned. That information wouldn't help Lachlan's cause.

DCI Dean sighed and closed her notepad, putting it in the pocket of her black trousers. She shoved the black glasses into her hair. A look passed between Dean and Lawson. "One more question before we take our leave, Mr. McClaren."

Lachlan's face was still red. He didn't look in the

direction of the chief inspector, nor did he acknowledge her comment.

She went on anyway. "When Mrs. Boyle screamed, how did you know to bring a saw with you to cut down the rope if you hadn't already known Mr. Graham was hanging from that tree?"

Lachlan didn't answer, nor did Dean wait for a response.

Liza glanced sideways at Lachlan. She didn't think he was guilty of anything, and from her vantage point, it still seemed as though Brodie Graham had killed himself. But she had to admit—a handsome, successful man like Mr. Graham seemed to have everything to live for. She had no idea what was happening in the man's personal life, but in her brief interactions with him the day before, he had certainly not seemed like a man who was contemplating suicide.

Dean shoved her hands in her pockets as she and DI Lawson began their walk to the door. "We're going to need the lot of you to stay put here."

Mr. Morrison spoke up again. "Do ye really think that's necessary? We were here all day yesterday."

"I'm afraid I have to agree," protested Mr. Douglas. "Ye seem to have yer suspect in Mr. McClaren. The rest of us should be able to leave."

"I don't recall telling anyone that Mr. McClaren is a suspect," said DCI Dean. "He *is* a person of interest to us. As are the rest of you. You'll be seeing us soon."

DI Lawson gave the room a smile that looked foreign on his stoic face. "And if any of ye try to leave, two policemen will meet ye at the end of the lane. We'd be more than happy to continue the conversation at the station." He gave a crisp salute as they walked out the door. Mrs. Boyle sighed, and Lachlan swore loudly and strode out the side door.

Liza wanted nothing more than to go home to Boston where life was uninspiring and predictable. She'd had enough death to last her the rest of her life.

Chapter 10

Mr. Douglas put a hand to his forehead, and Mr. Morrison cleared his throat. "Ms. Ramsay," he said, his voice still phlegmy, most likely with the drink from the prior day.

She looked at Mr. Morrison, waiting for him to continue.

"I was wondering if I might have a word."

Liza hesitated. She had nothing to say to the man, and she was quite sure she wasn't interested in anything *he* might have to say.

Mrs. Boyle raised an eyebrow and stood. "Thank ye for the tea and toast, Ms. Liza. I'll prepare a proper breakfast for when ye're hungry later on."

"You don't think you should rest?" Liza asked.

"No, dear. It's not the first dead body I've seen. Just the most unexpected."

Liza nearly stopped the older woman to remind her to check on Callum, but she watched as Mrs. Boyle turned left instead of right at the main door of the sitting room, and Liza knew she was headed to Callum's quarters.

Liza looked back at the two remaining men. Mr. Douglas still had his hand over his eyes, but she thought she detected his shifting gaze under his meaty palm.

Mr. Morrison looked at her expectantly.

She nodded and followed Mr. Morrison out of the room, once again trying to keep her eyes off the table where she and Brodie Graham had shared their last conversation. She thought of the flash of his smile, the curve of his lips. It seemed impossible he'd been right in front of her, so full of life, less than twelve hours earlier.

Where had the essence of him gone? she wondered.

As she followed Mr. Morrison across the hallway, she looked around. This castle had seen so much death throughout its existence. It was amazing there weren't more spirits haunting its halls, she supposed. Perhaps they were here, just on a different frequency. Perhaps Mr. Graham would join them.

She followed Kenneth Morrison into the library, which was brighter in the rising morning light. The space was no less impressive. Her eyes sought out the chessmen; they stood proud on their checkered board, their polished eyes still staring up at her.

She looked away before Mr. Morrison could see what had caught her attention. She had no idea if the man knew the treasure this room held, but she didn't want to alert him to it. When he felt up to it, she would talk to Callum about storing the artifacts in a safe place instead of out in the open.

Instead, Liza ran her hand over the volumes of books, some leatherbound, others cloth. She saw *The Aeneid*, *The Iliad* and *The Odyssey*. She saw works by Plato and Aristotle and Socrates, so worn that they could have been first editions. She wouldn't have been surprised to find a first-edition Shakespeare somewhere among the tomes, and her heart thrummed at the thought. She wondered if anyone had an appreciation of the knowledge contained in this one room.

She pulled one slim leatherbound volumes off of a shelf and touched the embossed gold lettering printed on the cover. *The Bridal of Triermain, or The Vale of St John*. She opened the volume to the copyright page, and on a yellowed page read, *1813, Edinburgh. John Ballantyne and Co.*

She longed to explore the room alone, but Mr. Morrison cleared his throat again. She looked over at him. His cheeks were spiked with new growth, and she noticed hair growing out of both his ears. He was dressed in the black trousers and white button-down shirt he'd worn the day before, but his clothes were rumpled—she assumed he'd slept in them.

She kept in mind that she was just as disheveled in her wrinkled blue dress. She looked down at her feet, still bare, and so cold she now realized they were numb.

"Elizabeth," he began, and she held up a hand.

"It's Liza," she interrupted. Brodie Graham seemed to have been the only one who'd been able to get her name right.

Mr. Morrison nodded but did not bother to correct himself. "When I'd heard ye'd be visiting, I asked Robert if we might have a chance to talk. I realize a lot has happened over the past day, but I'd still like to have that conversation."

"I don't know what we could possibly have to discuss."

His mouth worked, and she watched a fleck of spittle form at the corner of his lips. He blinked his piggish eyes a few times, and she could feel his frustration with her. She intuited that this man didn't like women very much. At least women who questioned him too closely or disagreed with him too quickly.

"If ye're to be the new owner of the Ramsay Estate—" he began, before Liza cut him off.

"Then I would have no need for the services of a land developer."

The energy of his anger hit her like a wave, and she stopped herself from taking a step back. She'd dealt with plenty of determined executives—both men and women—in her career. She certainly wasn't going to allow this arrogant man to bully her in personal matters.

She watched him take a visible breath. He recognized that she had the upper hand.

"Ms. Ramsay," he said, clearly making an attempt to soften his tone. "Liza," he tried, getting her name right, but with condescension in his voice. "I know ye can't want to manage this old place from across the ocean. And after all that's happened, ye certainly can't want to relocate here. Now, I'm not saying we need to knock the structure down, for heaven's sake. But there are hundreds of prime acres, and the location makes this land nearly priceless. Ye could make ten times what it would cost to maintain only the acreage."

Liza folded her arms across her body, but she stood up straighter.

There were only two small windows in this room, and they faced the side of the property, overlooking what may have once been an archery range, or even farmland gone fallow. A bird wheeled and swooped low, searching for a morning meal. In the distance, the tree line curved with the Creagan River.

Though it was still early, the sun was bright, promising a pleasant summer day.

Mr. Morrison must have believed that she was considering his offer. Emboldened by her meditation, he continued, "As for the castle..." He swept his plump arm around the room revealing a discolored circle of dried sweat on his rumpled shirt. "...ye could convert the place into luxury apartments or sell it to a hotel chain and make a fortune. Ye could even turn it into a boarding school. Ye know it has been one once in the past, right? Ye'd never have to work a day in your life again," he said and laughed. His bushy eyebrows moved up and down as if they were inviting a nod of her head. An agreement.

She was at a loss. She didn't feel at all as if she needed to explain her decisions to Mr. Morrison, but the problem was, she had made no decision. She certainly didn't want Callum to exit this world without a solution, and she did not want to be the cause of Lachlan and Mrs. Boyle potentially losing their jobs at the estate. On the other hand, she still had no idea what she'd possibly do with the place. Brodie Graham had offered the most logical solution to the predicament, and now he was dead.

She supposed she could contact someone else from the Royal Kingdom Trust, and the organization would be able to offer the same benefits and agreement that Brodie had proposed. Perhaps. But Brodie had made his interest in the Ramsay Estate extremely clear. So much so that he'd been willing to pretend an attraction to Liza to get his hands on the property. So much so that perhaps the potential loss of the property had caused him to take his own life.

"Mr. Morrison, can I be honest with you?"

He took a step toward her, thinking that they'd established a bond. Again, she stopped herself from stepping back, even though he was in her personal space. She could smell his morning breath mingled with the odor of the strong black tea. She wanted to gag, and she turned her head slightly to the side.

"Not two days ago, I decided to hop on a plane, travel halfway across the world to learn more about a random letter I received. Since then, I've been questioned about the possible murder of a boy I've never met, and now will certainly be questioned about the death of a man I'd known for less than a day. I am not ready to make a decision as to whether or not I want to take on the responsibility of owning what is very likely a haunted castle on the outskirts of Edinburgh."

He opened his mouth to speak; she stopped him with a raised eyebrow and a finger pointed very close to his chest.

"But there is one thing I can tell you for certain. Under no circumstances would I ever consider entering into an agreement with you to develop this land." She didn't add that she'd rather see the castle fall into ruin before she'd see Kenneth Morrison make a penny off the Ramsay family name. The passion with which she felt this sentiment was so strong she was sure it must be coming from outside herself.

No sooner were the words spoken, than a terrible crack sounded just outside the door of the library causing both of them to jump.

Liza, who was closest to the exit, ran from the

room. On the red carpeted floor lay a large gilt-framed portrait, the glass shattered into pieces where the object had hit the opposite wall. Carefully, Liza moved toward it, doing her best in her bare feet to avoid the shards of glass. She tilted the frame up to check for further damage to the object.

It was a professionally photographed portrait of a woman with kind eyes, and in more modern dress than many of the other Ramsays that populated the walls. The woman smiled mischievously as if she had a happy secret, her eyes dancing with the knowledge. Her dark hair was arranged in elaborate ringlets, and though her skin was youthful and unblemished, she appeared to be slightly older than the women in some of the other photographs.

As the remainder of the glass fell free of the frame and the thick stock of the portrait slipped free of its compromised structure, Liza noticed a yellowed and fragile-looking parchment affixed to the backing.

Mr. Morrison emerged from the room but offered no help, even when she caught the fleshy pad beneath her thumb against a jagged piece of glass that sliced into her skin.

She immediately pressed her hand against her dress, damping the flow so she might not bleed onto the parchment.

She felt another presence close by, and looked up to find Callum shuffling toward them. He was dressed in a red sweater and khaki trousers, and looked the most put-together of the three. The bandage was still affixed to his forehead, but there was no other indication of his earlier tumble.

He looked down at the remnants of the frame and glass on the floor. "Elizabeth!" he cried.

Liza was about to assure him that she was fine, but he slowly lowered himself to his knees beside her and lifted the woman's portrait. "This is my great-grandmother," he said. "Elizabeth Cunningham Ramsay."

As Callum touched the woman's face gently, Liza laid a hand on his arm and cautioned him to be careful of the glass.

"I think Elizabeth may have been protecting something for us." She gingerly maneuvered the portrait around to reveal the parchment on the back. "It looks very old," she remarked, wiping a drop of blood from her hand. She tested the edge of the document with the tip of the finger. Despite its age, it felt durable. She slid her finger gently beneath the edge.

It broke free from the stock with a soft sucking sound, and Liza realized that it was not glued to the albumen paper of the portrait, but rather had adhered from age and temperature change over time.

With her uninjured hand, she carefully unfolded the ancient document. Its edges were worn, but otherwise the paper was in remarkably good condition.

The ink was faded and in a script that was foreign to Liza.

"The Seal of Huntingdon," Callum whispered. He held a trembling finger to the top of the paper, at what looked like an emblem depicting a ram in the sea. "This the original deed for this land." He began to translate the words that Liza thought might be Latin. "On this date, October 19 of the year of our Lord, A.D. 1124, I, David of Scotland, Earl of Huntingdon, do bequeath this land to my faithful servant and nobleman, Symon de Ramesie."

When Callum looked up, his eyes were watery. "I had no idea this existed," he said, staring intensely at Liza. "Don't you see what this means?" he asked, clutching at her hand, her blood smearing on his fingers.

Liza did not at all understand what it meant, and her confused expression must have given her away.

"You have found this document. The deed to the property, lost for many, many years."

"It's merely a coincidence. That's all."

"No, my dear. It's a sign. This place—it is now yours. All of it. It can only belong to you."

Chapter 11

After handing over the ancient parchment to Callum for preservation, Liza agreed to meet him in his living quarters after lunch to further discuss her future with the Ramsay Estate. Liza knew that Callum assumed she would be signing paperwork, but Liza was still conflicted. Callum believed in signs, but so did she. And the two deaths on the property in two days were massive red flags.

As if the bodies weren't compelling enough, the reasons for refusal that she'd outlined a million times in her mind continued to scroll across her brain. She was not in any way prepared to own a castle across the ocean from her home. She had a career; she had obligations.

The problem was, when she thought about her career, a hard pit formed in her stomach. Lately, her job seemed more like a burden than a place of excitement and growth. Add to that the disintegration of her relationship with Owen, she was having a difficult time defending the 'too many obligations' argument.

Her thoughts continued to swirl as she returned to

her room. The race against Callum's health was important, and given his fall that morning, Liza feared the end loomed ever closer each day. If she were going to walk away from this endeavor, she needed to do it soon so that another suitable owner could be identified.

As she prepared to shower the cramped bathroom, her mind unwillingly went to Lachlan McClaren. Her feelings for him were complicated, vacillating between amusement, protection, and just a touch of fear. She wasn't sure what to make of that, or what to make of him, but she knew she wasn't interested in exploring it further. Particularly after her very brief attraction to poor Brodie Graham.

After she'd washed, and dressed in a completely inappropriate brightly colored flower-print sundress, she dried her hair and applied a touch of makeup to mask the deep circles under her eyes. She sighed and readied herself to check her phone which had been charging since that morning.

She only had two new text messages from Owen—a further one demanding to know where she was, and the other more conciliatory, acknowledging her need for space and offering to talk when she was ready.

She felt her resolve to end the relationship waver. Certainly, she didn't want to be with someone who was unfaithful. But she also realized that the act of infidelity was a symptom of a much larger problem. She'd devoted years of her time and energy to their relationship. Did it really make sense to abandon what they'd built without a fight? Didn't she owe it to herself to at least try to discover the root of the problem?

If Owen was willing, they could try couples counseling. They could try to make it work.

At this resolution, she felt two things—relief and dread. She wasn't sure which one troubled her more.

She pulled open the door to the bedroom and found Mrs. Boyle standing outside. They both jumped. Liza put a hand to her heart. "Mrs. Boyle," she said, breathing heavily. "I was just coming to find you."

Mrs. Boyle nodded and held out a stack of fresh towels. "And I was just coming up to see if ye needed anything."

Liza took the towels and went back into the room, setting them on the small bench next to her suitcase. "I'm fine, thank you." When she turned back around, she asked, "And how are *you*?"

"I'm all right," the woman answered. "Still a wee bit shaken, truth be told."

Liza cocked her head toward the window. "After hearing your scream and witnessing the scene from the window, I certainly understand your emotion." A shadow passed over Mrs. Boyle's face, and Liza changed the subject quickly. "I was actually coming to find out if you'd been able to talk with Callum's doctor. Callum seemed fine earlier, but I'm still concerned about the fall he's taken."

"Dr. Patel is here now. He'd like to talk with ye when he's finished his examination, if ye have the time."

"Me?"

Mrs. Boyle shrugged. "Expect he wants to ask ye about Callum's state when ye found him."

Liza nodded.

"Probably also wants to update ye on his condition, given developments."

"Developments?"

"Callum said ye'd agreed to the inheritance. Just need to take care of the paperwork."

Liza frowned.

"Well, didn't ye?" Mrs. Boyle's question emerged as a demand, and caught Liza off guard.

"No, I…" She ran a hand through her hair. "Mrs. Boyle, you have to understand my position." She raised her hands then let them fall to her sides. "This isn't my home."

"So ye've not agreed, then?"

"No, I'm not sure it's the right decision. Truth be told," Liza added with a small smile, echoing the woman's earlier expression.

Mrs. Boyle exhaled. "Ah, I understand all about home," she said. "And sometimes, it's clear that home isn't even a place. It's where yer heart goes to rest. It's where ye can breathe." She gestured around her. "It has not been very easy to breathe around this place for the past few days."

Liza didn't have a ready response to that, other than to silently acknowledge she'd run to this place when she hadn't been able to breathe in Boston.

She inadvertently took a deep breath, and when she exhaled, she imagined all the tension leaching from her body. She couldn't say she felt completely relaxed in the castle, but she did feel lighter and alive. Like an invisible energy were buzzing through her bloodstream. She felt like she belonged. She said none of this to Mrs. Boyle, because feeling alive wasn't a good reason to leap off of a cliff into an unknown future. Especially when surrounded by so much death.

She smiled at Mrs. Boyle. "I just don't want to put you in a difficult spot."

Mrs. Boyle put a hand to her bosom. "What could yer decision possibly do with me?"

"If I were to assume ownership, I would, of course, consider your long history with the property. But if I decline Callum's offer, it's hard to tell what might happen. You could find yourself jobless. And homeless," Liza added.

Mrs. Boyle moved her plump hand from her chest and waved it in front her. "Ye can't make a decision based on what ye think other people might want ye to do. Yer heart, and maybe the spirits, will guide ye to the right path. Ye need to do what ye think is right.

And if that's headin' back to Boston, then that's what ye need to do."

"And what about Lachlan? This has become his home, too."

The darkness passed over Mrs. Boyle's face again. She glanced behind her. "Can I ask ye a question?" She lowered her voice to just over a whisper.

Liza took an inadvertent step forward.

Along with the slightly doughy smell that Mrs. Boyle carried with her, Liza noticed another scent—something sharp and slightly sour.

Mrs. Boyle ran a hand over her unruly hair that stuck out from the bun at the nape of her neck like a halo. She looked into Liza's room, and her gaze landed on the windows overlooking the back side of the estate.

"When ye looked out this morning, did ye see Lachlan run up?"

Liza paused. "By the time I got to the window, it looked as though he was struggling to set up the ladder to cut Mr. Graham down."

"So ye don't know if it was already on the ground?"

"I-I think it must have been. Lachlan was crouched down." Liza tried to picture the scene in her mind, but her memory continued to present her with Brodie's face.

"And he had the saw in his hand?"

Liza frowned as she struggled to conjure the image. Had she seen the saw in his hand? "I think so."

Mrs. Boyle's mouth had slackened.

"Are you saying you think Lachlan may have had something to do with Brodie's death?" Liza whispered the question.

"I don't *want* to think anything of the sort," she said. "But that detective woman—Dean. Some of the answers to her questions just don't seem to make any sense, when ye think about them."

"What possible reason could Lachlan have had for wanting to hurt that man?"

"I can't speak for the lad. But, as ye said, this estate is his home." Her eyes darted around the room, and Liza knew she was thinking of the best way to formulate her next words. She waited patiently while Mrs. Boyle decided what to share and how.

Finally, she wetted her lips. "I never believed anything anyone said about Nicola." But she hesitated, the rest of the thought remaining unspoken.

Liza straightened. *Nicola.* It was the name Chief Inspector Dean had spoken to her the night before. The question came tumbling out of her mouth before she could stop herself. "Who is Nicola?"

Mrs. Boyle looked at her with wide eyes. "I've said too much."

"On the contrary, you haven't said anything at all."

Mrs. Boyle turned to go, and Liza put a hand on her arm. "Please," she said.

She hesitated again, then looked around as if someone may be listening. Finally, she said, "Nicola was a young girl who died."

Liza felt the icy finger of apprehension snake its way up her spine. "How?"

The older woman didn't answer right away. Her eyes darted around like she were searching for help in coming up with the words. "She was...assaulted and strangled."

"By whom?"

"Ms. Ramsay, I should no' have said a word."

"By whom?" Liza repeated, more forcefully this time.

Mrs. Boyle threw up her hands. "They never caught her attacker. I have to go, Ms. Ramsay," she said. "The doctor will be waitin' fer ye."

Liza sighed as she watched Mrs. Boyle hurry down the hallway without looking back. Clearly there was some sort of connection between the death of this woman—Nicola—and Lachlan. Had he been suspected? Questioned? Charged, even?

She grabbed her phone, ready to perform a search. Then she stopped herself. She needed time to gather these details, and time was something she didn't have. Not with the doctor waiting for her. Not with a major life decision looming over her.

And truthfully, she had become fond of Lachlan. After all that had happened, she wasn't sure she was prepared for yet another sharp twist of her emotions.

She glanced down at the home screen of her phone, hesitated, and felt the familiar cool breeze swirl around her shoulders in the still hallway. She looked up, half expecting to actually see Lady Catherine standing next to her.

"Fine," Liza said to the air. "But I deserve to know what's actually going on here."

With a sullen look at where she thought the ghost might be standing—if ghosts did indeed exist—Liza pulled the door shut behind her and headed for the stairs.

†††

The doctor, a short, Indian man in his mid-forties with dark hair going gray, was at the front door when Liza descended the staircase. "Hello," she called out just as his hand found the doorknob.

"Elizabeth?"

Liza just pursed her lips and nodded.

"I'd been waiting," he continued, a censure in his voice. He seemed to be expecting an explanation or an apology. Liza didn't offer one.

He cleared his throat. "I need to be going, but you can walk me to my car."

She followed him out into the sunshine. The sky had developed into a brilliant blue, and the trees and grass were varying shades of vibrant green. The air smelled sweet and the sun warmed her face. In the distance she could hear the rush of water as it wended through the trees.

The doctor's dark hair ruffled in a soft breeze, but he didn't seem to notice. He stopped next to a shiny silver sports coupe and placed his briefcase in the back seat. When he straightened, he gave her an impassive once over, then spoke. "Mr. Ramsay seems fine as far as the fall goes. A shallow flesh wound as you saw."

She nodded.

"Is there anything else you'd like to share about the condition in which you found him this morning?"

The way that he asked made her think he might be fishing for some additional information. "I don't believe so. He did seem slightly confused at first, but that passed quickly."

"In what way was he confused?"

She shrugged and remembered his reference to seeing *them*. He could have been referring to the ghosts. She decided not to share this with Dr. Patel. "Just a general fog, I suppose. Nothing in particular."

Dr. Patel nodded. "Well, Mr. Ramsay doesn't appear to be concussed. When I spoke to him, he seemed lucid and sound of mind. He was quite excited about your discovery of the original deed to the property."

Liza pressed her lips together but didn't respond.

"Ms. Ramsay, I'm telling you this because even though Callum seems unaffected by the fall and is cogent and clear today, he does not have much time. His health is fast failing, and the final deterioration, when it comes, will happen quickly."

"Can you estimate when that will happen?" she asked.

"It could be a few weeks, or it could be longer. He's in a lot of pain. More than he lets on. His insulin levels are high, and he has other, more delicate, complications. But his weight continues to decrease rapidly. His ability to put on a brave face is remarkable." The doctor offered a small smile, one of the few Liza suspected he would measure out that day. "I suppose his mettle is not a surprise given his lineage." Dr. Patel gestured toward the face of the castle.

"Is there anything that we can do for him to make him more comfortable?"

The doctor hesitated for a moment, giving her a long look. "He has elected to forego treatment. I have prescribed him pain medication, and when the pain becomes too much for even that, we'll increase his pain management efforts."

"Should I be sitting with him? Reading to him?" Liza remembered those small efforts that brought comfort to her mother during the last long days of her illness. The hospice nurse had been there to administer the medication, but Liza had provided the human and spiritual support so that her mother could pass peacefully.

"From a medical perspective, spending time with Mr. Ramsay certainly won't hurt. It likely will not extend his time."

Liza nodded, thoughtful, remembering. Callum had seemed so full of vigor and vitality earlier that morning as they'd uncovered the ancient parchment. It was hard to reconcile his excitement with the seriousness of his illness.

"Ms. Ramsay," the doctor said, bringing her out of his reverie, "Callum shared his plans to bequeath the estate to you. From an objective standpoint, I'm trying to make you understand that his health is very fragile despite his good days, and those good days will become fewer and fewer as the disease rapidly progresses."

She looked at him, not sure what he was trying to tell her.

He stepped closer and lowered his voice when he spoke. "I have known Callum for quite some time. He is a good man. A trusting man. Some might say a *naive* man. There are people around him that act as a result of their own selfish intentions. I don't know you, but I don't detect that same selfishness in you." He smoothed a hand down the side of his rumpled white shirt. "If you plan to accept Callum's endowment to you, with his sound intentions and your mutual acceptance, that must happen soon." His eyes were very dark and intense on hers.

She searched those eyes, suspecting his advice was

about more than just Callum's health.

The doctor stepped back and opened the driver's side door of his car, but turned back before he climbed in. "And Ms. Ramsay, if I were you, I'd watch my back. There are likely people who would rather see you on a plane back to the United States. Or worse," he said, the advice now a warning.

Liza was stunned as the car's engine revved to life. She stepped back and watched it reverse and retreat, the tires crunching on the gravel.

A breeze disheveled her hair and swirled her colorful sundress around her legs. It also brought with it a shiver of something sinister. She felt as if someone were watching her. She glanced up at the face of the castle just in time to see a movement in one of the windows above, but when she focused her eyes, she saw nothing but the red stone and smooth glass that with a stroke of a pen could belong to her.

Chapter 12

After the doctor had left, Liza wandered the periphery of the castle, careful to avoid the back side of the estate where the blue and white police tape still fluttered around the old sycamore. It was one thing to look upon the scene from the safety of the castle walls, but quite another to come face to face with the place where a man had decided to take his own life. Or perhaps where his life *had been taken*. She shuddered.

She hadn't fully explored the grounds, and the warm weather was perfect for a walk to try and clear her head and consider her options. She could delay no longer the decision about this land. She kept feeling the pull toward Owen—the urge to call him and ask for his advice. Any advice he gave, of course, would not be pure. It would be colored by his own wants and desires. It would be tainted by the potential for money or the promise of an imagined status. It would be influenced by his hope for their relationship and whatever future he had conjured up.

Still, she was so used to him being beside her and helping to guide her path. Until a few days ago, it hadn't occurred to her that that path may be the wrong one.

She thought of the doctor's warning to her. She did not know of whom he was suspicious, but it didn't matter. Callum wanted the estate to belong to her, and somewhere throughout the past hours, she realized there was a small part of her that wanted it too. She had no plan, no path, no experience, and no ideas. It was the worst possible decision she was being forced to make.

She went to the heavy wooden door of the castle, glanced up at the indentations that once held the beams for the drawbridge mechanism. A giddiness rose in her chest, and a sudden and unexpected bubble of delight escaped her lips as she pulled open the door. Of all people, this was being offered to *her*.

A smile still lingered on her mouth when the figure of DCI Dean met her on the inside of the entrance. "Something amusing, Ms. Ramsay?"

The smile faded. "No, Chief Inspector. Nothing at all." She glanced behind her at the parking area, which was empty except for the small Peugeot that Liza assumed belonged to Mrs. Boyle.

Dean noticed the direction of her gaze. "We're parked down near the entrance to the estate. It's easier to keep an eye on the comings and goings from there."

Surveillance, then, Liza thought to herself.

"Wondering if ye had time fer a few questions."

"I was just on my way to talk with Callum, if you could give me a few minutes."

"Oh, this won't take long, I'm sure of that."

Liza sighed inwardly and followed the woman to another room on the second floor. It had a long boardroom-style table, as if it had once been a conference room. Dean looked back at her as they entered. "Amazing how much space is in this place." Dean motioned toward a chair to the right of the table's head, then took a seat in front of a laptop, notepad, and a collection of files and papers.

Liza noted the difference from the night before, when there had been an informality to their conversations. Now, Dean was all business.

"Where's DI Lawson?"

"He's taking a look around, making sure everything is in order. I will be recording this conversation," Dean informed her and clicked on a slim device, slightly smaller than a mobile phone. "Standard procedure in these types of investigations. But again, this is just a conversation. You're not a suspect."

A suspect, Liza thought. That meant they had reason to believe Mr. Graham's death was suspicious.

"How long had you known Brodie Graham?"

"I met him soon after I arrived at the Ramsay Estate for lunch yesterday afternoon. Just before I met you, actually."

"And you'd never encountered him before?"

"No."

"Ever talked with him on the phone, texted, connected through any type of social media?"

"No."

Chief Inspector Dean made a clicking sound with her tongue against her cheek and scribbled something on her notepad, squinting. Liza glanced at the glasses on the woman's head but said nothing.

"When did you find out about your inheritance, Ms. Ramsay?"

Liza thought back to the day she'd received the letter from *Douglas, Burns, and Bruce: Solicitors and Estate Agents*. It had arrived when she'd been home for a few days near to the end of her last assignment. She gave Dean the approximate date she'd received the letter. Then added, "But it wasn't notice of an inheritance. It was more of an invitation to learn more."

"But it mentioned the inheritance?"

"Yes."

"You were contacted by Mr. Douglas?"

Liza nodded, and Dean looked pointedly at the recording device.

"Yes," Liza clarified.

"And you spoke with Mr. Douglas on the phone regarding this...invitation?" Dean asked.

"Yes."

"Immediately after you'd received the letter?"

"No, I waited a few weeks."

"And why was that, Ms. Ramsay?"

Liza hesitated. How was she supposed to answer that question? She had no intention of talking with this detective about her personal struggles, her inner conflicts, her ambivalence about and bond to her job. "I wasn't sure I was interested in the Ramsay Estate."

"But you decided to come to Edinburgh anyway?"

Liza hesitated again. "I did. After reading the letter, I thought I owed it to myself and to Mr. Ramsay the benefit of a visit to make an informed decision."

"Have you made a decision yet?"

"I think I have. Yes."

Dean waited a beat, as if Liza were going to reveal what the decision was.

When Liza didn't elaborate, Dean switched gears. "Tell me about your father, Ms. Ramsay."

Liza's upper hand evaporated when the surprise weight of the question hit her. After stammering for a moment, she answered. "There's not much to tell. He left when I was a child, and I had no contact with him after that."

"Are you aware that he and Mr. Ramsay—Callum—were acquainted?"

Heat rose into Liza's cheeks. She cleared her throat. "I was not."

DCI Dean let the silence sit between them while she finally shifted her thick frames from their home in her nest of hair to the bridge of her nose. She shuffled through a file to her left. When she'd found the notes she was looking for, she studied the paperwork. Without looking at Liza, she said, "He was the beneficiary of the Ramsay Estate for a very short period of time."

Liza said nothing. So much for the expanded forensic generic testing. Callum had known exactly who she was. She wondered if her father had also known how to find her all these years and had simply chosen not to. She told herself it didn't matter, that she didn't care. But that was a lie.

"I understand that he's dead," Liza said to Dean, her words flat.

"Yes. Car accident in the city, not long after Callum named him in his will."

Liza tried to keep her face impassive, but she felt a twitch pull down the corner of her mouth.

Dean's perceptive gaze landed on the tic, and she raised an eyebrow. "It wasn't investigated at the time. Seemed to be an accident."

The detective's gaze shifted to Liza's eyes, and Liza knew what the other woman was thinking. There was an awful lot of death associated with the Ramsay Estate. It was certainly possible that some of those deaths had been tragic accidents. But so far, there had been three. Even Liza had a hard time believing there was not some connection between them.

Dean leaned over and touched the mouse pad on

the laptop. "Can you tell me a little bit about your relationship to…" She paused. "…Owen Bell?"

Owen, again. Liza bristled. "I fail to see what my relationship could have to do with your investigation. You clearly know he's my significant other. You asked about him last evening, remember?"

Dean allowed her gaze to linger on the screen. "Are you aware he called the police station in Edinburgh looking for you? He seemed to think you might be in some kind of danger. Any idea why he might have reason to be concerned with your safety?"

Liza's emotions were a carnival ride, and she was becoming exhausted from this conversation. She sighed. "I left without telling him where I was going. I have no idea how he tracked me here."

"Why didn't you tell him your destination?"

"We'd had an argument. And, frankly, this was none of his business."

Dean's face morphed into an exaggerated and horrified grimace. Liza assumed this was supposed to make Liza feel guilty or inadequate or immature. "Was the argument about the inheritance? Because that's a quite a big development to keep from someone you're supposed to be in love with."

Liza didn't intend to respond, but before she even had time to consider the question, a rapping on the door sounded. Lawson poked his head in. "Chief Inspector—a word?"

Dean glanced at Liza then at the recorder. She clicked it off, held up one finger to Liza, and went to the door.

Though they talked in low voices, Liza struggled to listen to the words. Lawson was facing her, but she could only make out snippets of the sentences in his baritone timbre.

Can't find... Seems to have disappeared... Vehicle remains...

Dean's responses were equally quiet. Her back was to Liza. *Discreet search... Unmarked car...*

Lawson nodded and turned, latching the door behind him.

When Dean returned to the table, she didn't look nearly as smug as she had before speaking to Lawson. She picked up her pen, clicked on the recorder, and immediately returned to business. "Tell me about this morning. How did ye come to be looking out your window?"

Liza was glad her relationship was no longer the subject of inquiry. She repeated what she'd offered earlier that morning: how she'd heard Mrs. Boyle scream, and that by the time she'd collected her wits and ran to the window, Lachlan was already struggling with what appeared to be the ladder on the ground.

Dean pursed her lips, and tapped the pen against the wooden table. "Anything else you may have remembered since this morning?" she asked, clearly distracted.

"No, Inspector."

She nodded. "Thank you, Ms. Ramsay." She leaned forward to switch off the recorder. Her finger paused on the button. "Just one more thing. Have you had a chance to ask Mr. McClaren about Nicola Munro?"

Liza shook her head and Dean glanced at the recorder again.

"No," Liza said firmly, though the apprehension she'd felt earlier when Mrs. Boyle had mentioned that same name crawled over her skin.

"It's an interesting story. Young Highland lassie, from a wee borough up north," Dean's soft Scottish burr became remarkably stronger. "She went to uni and met a lad. Fell in love with him for a time, then fell out of love. Story as old as time." Dean shook her head slowly. "But the lad—handsome, prominent family, plenty of money—well, he did not react well to rejection. He was an extremely jealous sort, it turns out. And poor Nicola Munro ends up dead. Sexually assaulted, strangled. The lad denies involvement, of course. And those family connections and money come in mighty handy."

The sensation drained from Liza's extremities. Her lips tingled. "Am I correct to assume you're referring to Lachlan?"

DCI Dean shrugged. "Mr. McClaren was not charged with a crime."

Liza stared at Dean. Dean stared back. "You may want to be extra watchful, Ms. Ramsay. We have an increased presence around the estate, but we can't protect everyone, especially if the danger is from within."

The click of the recorder shutting off was deafening in the silence that followed. "That'll be all, Ms. Ramsay."

Liza stood to leave, her legs shaky.

"If you happen to see Mr. McClaren, can you tell him we'd like to have a word?"

Liza nodded silently, and for the first time in the conversation Dean looked sympathetic. "Are you sure ye're interested in the inheritance after all?"

Liza didn't answer, but she could safely admit to herself that she was not sure of one damn thing.

Chapter 13

Liza wandered out of the room and floated aimlessly toward the back of the castle, glancing up at the ornate ceiling that not an hour earlier she may have been ready to admire as her own.

Had her conversation with Dean really changed anything? Did it matter that her father had been heir to the castle at one point? She wanted to tell herself it mattered little or not at all, but if that was true, then why hadn't Callum mentioned it to her? He clearly knew they'd been estranged.

She found herself at the door to Callum's living quarters. She wasn't sure if she were ready to have a conversation with him, but she figured a delay wouldn't benefit anyone. She was about to lift her hand to knock when Mr. Douglas came toward her. He gave her a stern look. "Callum is resting," he scolded, as if she'd have any way of knowing that.

"I'm happy to return later then." She turned to take her leave.

"Actually, I have something I'd like to discuss with ye."

He stepped toward her, reminding her of Mr. Morrison earlier that morning. Instinctively, Liza took a step back. She knew she was being ridiculous, but with the warnings of both DCI Dean and Dr. Patel fresh in her mind, she was on edge.

Robert Douglas wasn't a large man, but even in advanced middle age, he appeared to be sturdy. A memory materialized from her childhood; Liza was startled at its sudden appearance. Robert Douglas reminded her of the participants she'd seen years ago in a reenactment of the Highland Games. There were plenty of strong men in kilts who could throw the trunk of a tree as if it were a toothpick. She'd been surprised by the agility and strength on display, the men adorned in the tartan colors of their clans.

"What is it?" she asked, impatient.

Mr. Douglas indicated that she should follow him to one of the back rooms where they could talk privately, but Liza held her ground. She was tempted to confront him about her father's unexpected involvement in the business of her inheritance, but she resisted. She wanted an explanation from Callum himself. And she didn't want to tip her hand to someone she did not trust.

When he realized she didn't intend to follow him, he looked around to ensure no one was within earshot.

"I realize there's a lot of funny business going on here," he said. "I just want ye to know that both Callum and I understand if it's all too much for ye."

"What do you mean by that?"

"If ye want to remove yerself from these discussions." He waved his hand around him. "Two deaths, ghosts, old documents, a police presence. It's a lot for all of us. I can't imagine how it all must look to you—a guest."

Liza narrowed her eyes. "Callum said that?"

Mr. Douglas sighed. "He did. He wants ye to inherit the place—he really does. But he also understands the complications, and frankly, the danger it may pose to ye."

"Danger," she said slowly.

He filled the silence between them quickly. "I'm not saying the deaths of young Charlie Campbell and Brodie Graham are anything more than tragic accidents, despite what the police seem to think. I'm just saying if there *is* any danger, ye'd be right to be concerned."

The man's face was a mask of sincerity, and Liza felt herself falter. She had so many questions, and Mr. Douglas would at least have some of the answers she was seeking.

"What can you tell me about a woman named Nicola Munro?"

Mr. Douglas blew out a breath so that his ample cheeks puffed out then deflated. "Who told ye?"

She didn't respond, and he must have figured that

it didn't matter, because he began to talk.

"I never met the girl," he responded. "But it is a tragic story. The way she was found..." He shuddered. "No one deserves to die like that. Least of all an innocent young thing."

"Did they ever find her killer?"

"No one was arrested, though plenty of people—the police included—were sure they'd found the killer. But he walked away." He raised an eyebrow, and he didn't need to say the name of the man he suspected.

"Do you believe Lachlan McClaren is capable of murder?" Liza made her voice strong. She didn't care who may have heard her.

"I think all of us are capable of things—dark things—that live deep in our souls," he answered. "It's not my place to say if Lachlan did anything to that girl. Was he capable?" He shrugged a shoulder. "If he wasn't, why would he be hiding away in the laborers' cottage on the grounds of a castle?" he asked. "Only Lachlan knows what's in his heart."

Liza's heart sank, because she knew Mr. Douglas was right.

"I'm sorry," he continued. "I know ye liked the lad."

She looked up sharply. "I don't know him."

He held up his hands. "Of course. I didn't mean to imply anything."

She stared at him, assessing. He looked innocent

enough, and she nodded once then turned around, needing space from this castle and its suspicious inhabitants.

⁜

Liza spent the rest of the afternoon outside in the warm sunshine. She knew she couldn't roam far, and was reminded of that fact by the suspicious raise of an eyebrow of the young uniformed police officer who sat guard at the end of the lane. "Can I help ye?" he asked as she wandered in his direction.

"I'm just trying to get some fresh air."

"Aye, the American," he said. She thought she detected some fascination, along with a touch of contempt, in his voice. "Ye'll need to be gettin' yer fresh air that way." He pointed toward the direction from which she'd just walked.

She glanced back at the path, the hulking silhouette of the sycamore just over the slight rise. Still the rope dangled from the branch.

She turned back to the smooth round face of the officer. She estimated he was younger than her by a few years. His hair was a bright shade of red, but despite his boyish quality, his stare was arrogant and sure. "Don't you think you should remove that rope?" She jerked her chin toward the sycamore.

"Does it bother ye, Liza?"

Her eyebrows shot up at the use of her first name, but she quickly smoothed over her surprise. "It does. Yes." She was determined not to let him get to her.

"Maybe it bothers someone else too."

"I assume you're implying the someone who may have killed Mr. Graham."

"Might ye know who that would be?"

Liza narrowed her eyes. "I'm sorry. What rank of detective did you say you were?" The officer's smirk quickly vanished. "Maybe you should leave the crime-solving to DCI Dean and refrain from speculation."

His gaze shifted from contemptuous to detached. "Have ye seen Lachlan McClaren, Liza? I understand ye've become quite cozy with him."

They stared at each other, a visual showdown.

She backed down first, casting her gaze aside. It wouldn't give her any advantage to get into an argument with the police. "Not since this morning," she finally answered.

The young officer sucked on his prominent front teeth. "If ye happen to run into him, ye may want to tell 'im that Chief Inspector Dean is keen to ask a few questions."

The hair on the back of Liza's neck stood up. So, Lachlan's sudden absence was the reason Lawson had interrupted her discussion with—*interrogation by*—Chief Inspector Dean. Liza knew this was more than just a casual request. These officers were closing in.

"Ye're lookin' a bit ill, Liza."

She didn't answer. "I'll tell him if I see him." She turned to walk away.

"Ye have a pleasant day, Liza." His lilting Scots accent was both musical and taunting.

She didn't return the pleasantry.

After retracing her steps up the lane, she made a left through the tree line and followed a rough path along the Creagan River. The canopy of trees—cypress, oak, birch, and fir—blotted out the midday sun, and she walked silently over the path softened by pine needles. The water burbled cheerfully, unaware of the shadows on its surface.

Aside from the sound of the water, it was quiet in the trees. It should have been peaceful, but Liza couldn't help feeling as if silent hidden eyes were watching her. Every glance over her shoulder was met with nothing but green and the soft brown of the forest floor.

She came to a fork in the path that led away from the river. Following it, she eventually found herself at the top of a small hill overlooking a house made of the same red rock as the castle. The structure was small, but it was well-maintained and had a lived-in feel to it. A movement caught her eye, and she watched as another police officer roamed at the periphery of the property.

Instinctively, she stepped back, but the man didn't

seem to be looking in her direction.

He was older than the officer she'd encountered at the entrance to the property, and had a prominent stomach and a ruddy face. He peered into the window of an older model pickup truck with the word 'Warrior' displayed across the back gate of the vehicle.

This must be Lachlan's cottage. If his vehicle remained, the officers would assume he'd fled on foot.

She shifted her weight, and a twig cracked beneath her foot. She held her breath, wishing she weren't wearing the bright sundress.

The officer's head snapped around, but still he didn't look in her direction. She was barely hidden behind the slim trunk of a young maple tree. Instead, the officer turned his attention toward the drive to the cottage and called in a deep hoarse voice, "Alright, is someone there?"

It would have been easy for Liza to simply signal her presence to him, and she wasn't sure why she didn't just call out. She was doing nothing wrong, and she had nothing to hide.

Instead, she crept slowly in the opposite direction to hide herself behind the trunk of a large oak tree. She held her breath, her heart thrumming furiously in her chest.

Why she was so nervous? Shouldn't she be pleased that the officers were guarding the estate after all that had happened over the course of the last few days?

She did not move from her hiding spot.

After what felt like an eternity, she turned her head and peered out from behind the great gnarly trunk. The officer had begun his retreat in the opposite direction. Liza carefully picked her way through the trees leading away from the cottage and the castle.

She prepared herself to encounter other officers, but all she could hear were forest sounds. With fewer pine trees in this area of the woodland and with no discernable pathway, the branches crunched beneath her feet, and she trod on green grasses and ground-level purple and white blossoms. She could still hear the steady song of the river in the distance, but she seemed to be moving away from the water.

She found herself in a thicket of mature trees. The water's murmur was softer here, and the birds seemed subdued. She stopped and listened. A hush fell over the land. She closed her eyes and lifted her face to the heavens, reveling in the stillness of the moment.

Though the trees' canopy was thick, sun dappled the ground. She breathed.

Then her ears picked up another sound—a murmur in a lower register than the water. A soft low tone. A voice. Just a whisper.

Liza looked around but saw no one, and sensed no presence here. At one end of the thicket, she saw what may once have been a path. A small mound of stone that could have been the remnants of some sort of ancient wall or building.

She picked her way past the stone, deeper into the forest through lichen-covered rocks and woodland ferns. Holding her dress at her side, she prevented the fabric catching on branches and limbs. Pines grew thicker here, softening the forest floor.

The trees opened up into a forest glade, revealing a tumble of rock and stone, gray and worn and covered in moss. This had once been a building, and though the roof of the structure was gone, on one side of the remains rose what seemed to have been large arched openings. At the base of one of the arched openings was a rudimentary impression of a skull and crossbones.

The low murmuring voice was louder here. Someone—or something—was inside.

Every hair on Liza's body was standing on end, her senses silently screaming for her to turn back. She did not listen. She crept forward over archaic rock and stone.

Silently, she reached an arched stone entranceway and peered into the interior of the decayed building.

At the far end of the moss-covered stones was an ancient altar. Kneeling in front of the altar, lighting a row of small, tapered candles, knelt the figure of a man. Lachlan. He murmured words that Liza did not recognize. A language she had never heard before. It was low, throaty, and guttural.

She stood with her hand on one of the standing stones and watched him for a few moments. He moved to light the candles. Liza imagined that the words he murmured were prayers.

Her plans to confront him with the information she'd learned from both Chief Inspector Dean and Mr. Douglas fled, instead she bowed her head silently and turned to take her leave.

"Ye can come in," he said in his soft accent. Still on his knees, he twisted to look around at her. "I promise I won't hurt ye."

Chapter 14

Liza felt as if she'd been caught. "I'm sorry," she said. "I didn't mean to interrupt."

"Aye, ye did." He stood. "It's all right. I was just about finished."

Liza stared at the row of candles. Red wax had melted and pooled on the stone of the altar below, as if the candles had been lit many times before.

She stood there dumbly as he stared at her.

If he'd killed Nicola, if he'd killed Charlie Campbell, if he'd killed Brodie Graham...

She should be terrified right now. She was not.

"They're looking for you," she said finally.

He nodded. "They think I killed them."

She didn't respond.

"I didn't kill anyone."

She considered this and then said, "Tell me about Nicola Munro." She hadn't meant it as an order. Instead, it was an invitation to tell his story.

He gestured behind him toward the candles. "I light one for her every week."

"Who is she?"

He shoved his hands in his pockets and looked at the ground. "Who told ye about her?"

"Does it matter?" she asked.

"Aye. They're tryin' to turn ye against me."

"Why would they want to do that?"

"Because that's what they do. They break ye down, remove yer support. This isn't my first time in their crosshairs." He laughed, but there was no joy in it. "They couldn't get Callum to turn against me, though. He always believed me." He shook his head and turned toward the tapers burning down. He blew them out.

Abruptly, he turned back around. "She was *mo chridhe*," he said, placing his hand on his chest. "My heart."

Liza was surprised by the intensity of Lachlan's words.

He sank down on a large square rock, part of the wall of the ruined church, as if the memory had exhausted him.

Liza glanced around and sat on her own cairn of stones. "How did you know her?"

"I met her at uni in Stirling, during my second year. We were both part of the swimming program. She was belter," he said with a faraway look on his face. "A brilliant athlete. I don't think she ever realized just how good she really was."

"Did she fall in love with you and forget her potential?" Liza had known plenty of girls who'd given up gifts and talents for temporary boys. Boys who would be gone in a few months or years. She would have done it herself, if the opportunity had presented itself back then. Hadn't she done the same, to some extent, with Owen? Held herself back?

But Lachlan shook his head. "No. She was a quiet little burd at first. From a small village called Dalmally on Loch Awe. Her family didnae have much money. I think I scared her a bit when I started to show her attention." He smiled at the memory. "If anything, I tried to encourage her talent when she didn't know her own potential."

"And you were popular?" Liza asked.

"Not so much. But my father—he was well-known."

Liza remembered what Dean had told her about James McClaren, but she didn't comment.

"She was a sweet lass." Lachlan's voice thickened when he said her name. "She had this long, red mane of hair that fell to her waist." He touched his hand to his back. "Our coaches used to try to get her to cut it, even just a little bit, but she refused."

Liza thought of her own plain brown hair, and compared it to the description of the deceased Nicola's amazing tresses. She quickly pushed the thought away.

"I finally convinced her to go out on a date with me, and we were nearly inseparable after that. For two years, anyway."

He was silent for so long that Liza didn't know if he planned to continue.

When he finally spoke, he said, "It never occurred to me we wouldn't get married. But as she grew and came into her own, I wasn't what she wanted."

"Did that make you angry?"

"It made me sad. It *still* makes me sad. Because if she hadn't broken it off right then, she might still be alive."

"You might be married with a few little ones by now." Liza wasn't sure what prompted her to speak the hypothetical, especially since it was probably painful to him.

But he didn't seem offended. He laughed. "I don't know about that. We were just kids back then. It probably wouldn't have lasted." The laughter faded. "But maybe I wouldn't have to mourn her every single day."

There was another silence, longer this time.

Lachlan took a deep breath and sat up straighter. "This is the original kirk built by the Ramsay Clan back in the thirteenth century. A braw structure it must have been in its day."

Liza looked at the ruins around her. She touched the stone on which she sat and wondered what ancient hands had also made contact there.

"The burial grounds are just on the other side of the altar," said Lachlan.

"Is Lady Catherine there?" she asked.

Lachlan nodded. "Her stone is nearly worn smooth, but she's there. Sir Alexander, too."

"Do they haunt the kirk?"

"I expect they go where their energy is drawn. I've never felt them out here. But if they're here, they come here for peace. The unrest is in the castle."

"What do you think they want?"

"I think they want someone to do the right thing. Callum has been trying."

"Callum thinks I'm a descendant of Lady Catherine."

"I know. He met yer father a few years back, but he's talked of nothing but his Elizabeth since he found ye."

Liza traced a finger along the rough edge of the stone. "You met him then?" she asked, trying to keep her voice casual.

"Yer father?" He nodded. "Just once. It was right after Callum found out he was sick, and around the time of the business with Hamish. Robert Douglas, the sleekit bastard, was livid when yer father showed up."

"What was he like?"

Lachlan studied her, his lips pressed together. She expected to see pity in his eyes when she finally looked up to meet his gaze, but she only found understanding. "He seemed like a good fellow. He didnae talk much, at least around me. Callum was excited to have him here."

"Do you know if Callum found *him* or the other way around?"

"Don't know the answer to that. It was a bit of a shock for everyone when we heard the news of his accident. It hit Callum especially hard. That's when he started the search for you."

Liza nodded. "You might've thought my father would have searched for me years earlier."

"I suppose our parents do the best they can with the tools and scars they themselves have been given."

"I suppose," Liza responded cynically. She wasn't sure she was in the mood to be generous with her father. "What is your father like?" Liza asked, changing the subject.

Lachlan looked down at the ground and kicked the toe of his boot against the ancient dirt of the church's ground. "He wasnae around much when I was a lad. My mum mostly raised my sister and me. And now, he'd just as soon I didn't exist. Can't say I blame him."

Another silence.

"What happened to Nicola, Lachlan?" She asked the question gently but firmly.

The only sound in the forest was the faint rush of water and the high-pitched call of a nearby starling.

He licked his lips. Then he spoke. "I'd heard rumors she was seeing another guy. A bampot called Liam Burns. When I confronted her, she broke it off with me." His words were abrupt. Halting. "And I wasn't quite honest with ye earlier. I *was* angry, and I said some horrible things. Things that other people heard." He opened his mouth, then shut it again. "That night…I got jaked on cheap whisky, and sent some awful text messages." He shook his head. "Really terrible things." His voice was swollen and heavy.

Liza could imagine what those words may have been. She thought of the extensive string of text messages that had been sent by Owen, and he was nearly a full decade more mature than a college-aged Lachlan. Liza imagined hard and ugly words that floated in the ether of the internet, forever discoverable, forever hurtful.

Lachlan went on. "She was found the next morning in her room, strangled with her own hair. They made me look at the photos." Lachlan looked off into the distance as his words trailed off.

Liza shut her eyes for a moment. She was horrified, yet she couldn't help picturing the poor girl—the images that Lachlan had seen. "Did they arrest you?"

"Not quite. They questioned me for hours until my solicitor showed up. All the evidence was circumstantial. My fingerprints were all over the room, but there was no dispute that I'd been there earlier. She'd been violated, but no DNA was found—mine or any other. But those witness statements and text messages…" His words trailed off. "If my father hadn't been who he was, I probably would've been arrested. As it was, they knew that with my representation, they didn't have enough evidence to make the charges stick."

Lachlan was staring down at the ground as he talked. His voice changed. It became quieter, but harder, like he was reciting the lines by rote.

"Did they ever find out who did it?"

He shook his head. "I don't think they looked very hard. Most people assumed it was me, and that I'd gotten away with murder."

"And there were no similar crimes in the area?"

Lachlan looked at her then. "I don't know. I had to leave uni. I was just a kid, and I was scared. I didn't spend a lot of time trying to solve the crime on my own." All of the emotion had leached from his voice. Now his face was like stone, and his eyes were cold. "I've already been interrogated by the police."

Liza understood the implication.

Lachlan's face was illuminated by the dappled sunlight winking through the trees. Had she really known him long enough to trust him? Did she trust her own judgment? Despite his calm exterior, he could be hiding something more sinister. Her mind raced back to the warnings of danger from nearly every person she'd spoken with in the castle.

She considered her slip-on canvas shoes and her sundress, barely fit for a leisurely stroll, let alone for outrunning a former athlete in unfamiliar and uneven terrain. If her instincts about Lachlan were wrong, would she be able to protect herself?

Unconsciously, she touched an end of her own long brown hair, and imagined the terror of poor Nicola Munro.

When she spoke again, her voice came out slightly breathless and uneven. "I'm not trying to interrogate you. I guess I'm just trying to understand how you ended up…here." Though she gestured at their surroundings, her meaning was deeper.

"My father quietly removed me from our house, and Callum took me in and gave me a home."

He was watching her closely now; she felt twitchy. But she stayed still.

"I would have never hurt her, Liza. I loved her."

Unlike his earlier words, these words were impassioned. A plea. A confession. Despite the fierce logic of her mind, her heart softened. She wanted to believe him.

"What about Charlie Campbell and Brodie Graham?" Liza asked. "Can you say the same about them?"

Before he could respond, the quiet reverence of the forest was disturbed by the sound of heavy footsteps crunching through dry leaves and snapping branches.

Through the crumbling arch of the kirk, DCI Dean and DI Lawson appeared.

"Aye, Mr. McClaren, suppose ye thought you could elude us." Lawson's deep voice somehow managed to reverberate off of old stones and ancient trees.

Lachlan couldn't quite keep the disdain from his expression. "I've not been eluding anyone. I've been out here all morning."

"We cautioned everyone to stay close," Lawson argued.

"And I'm not a kilometer from my home, Detective. If ye had competent officers searching for me, I shouldn't have been that hard to find."

Lawson smiled, his expression smug and superior. "So ye acknowledge ye knew we were looking for ye," he said. "Luckily, we have Ms. Ramsay on our side. Thanks for leading us to him," he added, with a throwaway glance at Liza.

Liza opened her mouth to protest, but was interrupted by Chief Inspector Dean. "Mr. McClaren, we have some questions, and we'd like you to come down to the station."

Lachlan's eyes flashed fury as he looked at Liza, his jaw clenched tightly. She could feel his anger cutting through her like a knife, reacting to the implied betrayal. There was nothing she could say in that moment that would convince him of her innocence, nor would she even try to argue it with Dean and Lawson standing there.

Lachlan gave her one last contemptuous stare then shifted his attention to the detectives, abruptly dismissing her. "Am I under arrest, then?"

"Nah," Dean said. "Not yet."

"Then I don' believe ye can force me to go anywhere."

"That's very true, Mr. McClaren. But I likely have enough to get a warrant for your cottage. And wouldn't it be a shame if the press found out that the son of the Permanent Secretary was connected to two new suspicious deaths. They'd likely start digging around, and Nicola Munro would be resurrected, so to speak. Do you think your father would want that, Lachlan?"

Liza tensed in the silence that followed, waiting to see what Lachlan would say.

In the end, he said nothing. He simply rose from the rock on which he sat and walked to the other end of the kirk, past Liza without a glance in her direction. "Alright then," he said calmly. "Let's go."

The three of them walked away, leaving Liza alone, as if she didn't exist. She sat there with her thoughts for some time. She wasn't sure how long. She only knew that when she stood, her muscles were tight, and the light had begun to dim.

She walked around the old sanctuary and found the moss-covered headstones that guarded the resting place of generations of the Ramsay family. There were silent residents from as late as the mid-twentieth century, including the woman who may or may not have been her namesake. Elizabeth Ramsay's headstone was a smooth marble tablet elaborately sculptured with vines, blooms, and an image of praying hands. Her inscription, in its flowery script, read:

> *Elizabeth Cunningham Ramsay*
> *Beloved wife of Dougal Ramsay*
> *Born 1837 Died 1877*
> *If there's another world, she lives in bliss;*
> *If there is none, she made the best of this.*

Liza smiled at the words. They sounded familiar to her, but she couldn't place the source. Nonetheless, she appreciated the sentiment, supposing that might be the best that anyone could either live for or hope for.

She placed a flat palm against the stone, wishing her ancestor eternal peace, then she wandered through the graveyard, noting the names of the inhabitants. The men's names were sturdy and solid: Alexander, James, David, Robert, William, Charles, Bernard. The women included Agnes, Elspeth, Mary, Wilhelmina, Grace, Flora, Sophia, and Jane. There were various other birth surnames inscribed for the women, but every one of the headstones included the name Ramsay. Though Liza had always felt rather ambivalent about her last name, mostly because of her father's absence, she now felt a curious sense of pride walking through her family's resting place.

She came upon one memorial stone, separate from and much older than the rest. The stone looked to have been made of the same red rock as the castle. The letters and carvings at the top of the tomb were heavily worn and illegible. But something was drawing her here. She knelt on the grass and placed both hands against the rock. In contrast to the smooth marble of Elizabeth Ramsay's, this surface was rough and rather crudely carved.

As she sat there, the energy around her seemed to shift and move, almost as if the earth was spinning faster. She could have sworn she heard music, bagpipes in the distance playing slightly out of tune. Her body felt heavy and impossibly light at the same time. Strange words entered her mind—the throaty and guttural sounds that Lachlan had been muttering. She breathed in earth and wind and sky and sweet decay. She breathed out all she knew of her old life. She could have sworn she felt herself fall, and yet she was on solid ground. She could have been sitting there for minutes, hours, or an eternity, but she had no inclination to move. In fact, she felt as if she'd come home.

Chapter 15

"Ms. Ramsay...Liza, dear? Are ye all right?"

Liza, still kneeling in front of the strange old tombstone, drew in a sharp breath. She looked up to find Mrs. Boyle standing over her. She blinked.

"I'd been callin' for ye." Mrs. Boyle narrowed her eyes and peered into Liza's face. "Ye look a little peely-wally."

"I don't know what that means."

"Pale. 'Green around the gills'. That's what the sailors used to say, did they no'?"

Liza took the hand offered to her by the older woman. When she stood, she tested her wobbly legs. She felt a bit fuzzy, but she supposed she felt well enough to make the hike back to the castle.

Mrs. Boyle was staring down at the marker. "I see ye found Lady Catherine."

That sent a jolt of energy through Liza. "This is her grave?"

When Mrs. Boyle nodded, Liza added, "Lachlan told me it was marked." She stared down at the plain stone. "I would have thought her memorial would be more elaborate."

"At one time, there was a family crypt fer the centuries-old members of the Ramsay Clan." She waved her hand vaguely to her right. "A tree fell on it, and it deteriorated. Instead of spendin' the money to rebuild it, the original inhabitants were reinterred over there, around the large white memorial."

Liza noted that off in the distance, a white obelisk stood watch over what looked like a circular pattern of stones.

"But Lady Catherine was never with the rest of them," Mrs. Boyle continued. "With the illegitimate child, she'd have brought them shame, so she was exiled over here. At least, that's the story."

Liza couldn't help thinking of that tree. "She was safe over here."

"Suppose so," Mrs. Boyle said. "I came to fetch ye. Lachlan was worried ye didn't know yer way back."

Liza looked up sharply. "They took him—Dean and Lawson. They made him go to the station for questioning."

Mrs. Boyle nodded her head. "Aye, I know. He asked me to check on ye before they took him away."

Liza was surprised to find tears fill her eyes and a lump form in the back of her throat. "But it's not fair, is it? Just because something happened in his past." Liza was still conflicted—not convinced of his innocence and yet quick to defend him.

Mrs. Boyle stared at her. "We've all been questioned," she said.

"He's the only one they've taken to the station."

Mrs. Boyle took her gently by the arm. "Come, dear. Let's get ye back and get a bite to eat."

"You don't truly think he could have done this, do you?" Yesterday, Lachlan had saved her from the odd occurrence in the dungeon. Today, despite his belief she'd betrayed him, he'd sent Mrs. Boyle to find her. Could this man, whom she felt so drawn to, really be capable of murder?

Mrs. Boyle was quiet as they walked. The golden rays of the sun shone in beams through the tree canopy, creating geometric patterns of brilliance on the forest floor.

Finally, the older woman spoke. "I've been thinkin' a lot about Lachlan today. I've known the boy since he was a wee lad. I've watched him grow up, and I've seen him fall down. I don't want to believe he could have done the things he's accused of. But, Liza..." She paused again. "...Lachlan has got some demons he's fighting. And ye can be a good person—a kind person—and still lose some of those battles."

"But what motive would he have had for killing his cousin?"

Mrs. Boyle sighed. The water rushed louder here; Liza could see the river over the rise.

"Charlie Campbell had been helping out around

the grounds. Lachlan caught him stealing. He made Charlie apologize to Callum and then Lachlan fired the lad. But I wonder if it may have gone farther than that."

Liza's head snapped toward Mrs. Boyle. "You actually think he could have done it." Liza said this with an air of finality.

"I honestly don't know," Mrs. Boyle said. "And of course, I didn't share that theory with the chief inspector," she added hastily.

"What about Brodie Graham?"

Mrs. Boyle shrugged again. "As I said earlier, this is Lachlan's home. I know he wasn't keen on the idea of the Royal Kingdom Trust getting its hands on the estate. And Brodie did seem to be sweet on ye, even if it was because he thought you might be the next owner. Lachlan wouldnae have liked that."

Liza winced. But she certainly didn't believe *she* was the reason Lachlan would have killed Brodie. She wasn't romantically involved with either of them, and she said as much to Mrs. Boyle. Then she said, quietly, "Lachlan told me about her. Nicola. And what happened."

Mrs. Boyle leaned closer to Liza with the air of a confidant. Now that Liza knew the secret, the older woman was more than happy to indulge in the tale that went along with it. "There are a lot of people who think Lachlan killed her in a jealous rage."

"Callum didn't think that."

Mrs. Boyle shook her head. "No, he did nae."

"But you do."

"I didn't say whether I did or I did nae. I'm just saying I think the potential is there. And combine that with his reaction after I found Mr. Graham's body…" As if on cue, they came through the trees and the pathway opened onto the grounds of the castle. Out in front of the grand home, the sycamore tree was still defiled by the swinging rope.

They stopped and stared up at the majestic castle bathed in the fading golden light.

"Ye do not have to stay here," Mrs. Boyle said quietly. "This disnae have to be yer burden."

"But what about Callum?" she asked. "What about *you*?"

She scoffed, a throaty barking sound. "Eh, I'll be just fine."

"You've been here for so long." Liza knew that Mrs. Boyle didn't want her to make a decision based on other people's wants and needs. But Liza couldn't help thinking about the time and energy that had been invested in this place.

"Nearly forty years," Mrs. Boyle answered, then made a face. "Can ye believe it?" She shook her head. "This was never supposed to be a permanent life for me," she said, a little sadly. "When I was young, I was going to be a dancer. And I was good at it."

Her definitive tone made Liza think the woman spoke the truth, though Liza couldn't quite see it now. The woman had to have been close to sixty or even older, and was pleasantly plump.

"I loved the stage," Mrs. Boyle continued, her voice far away.

"What happened?" Liza asked.

"I tore something in my knee. I was young and stupid, and ignored it until I couldn't dance anymore." She fluttered her hand in front of her. "I tried my hand at the theater, but I wasn't a good enough singer or actress to compensate. Too many girls who were prettier and better than me." She lifted a shoulder. "When the opportunities dried up, I started working here. I was sure I'd go back to the stage at some point, but I never did." She looked up at the castle. "And then I never left."

"No husband or boyfriend?" Liza asked.

"There was a bloke or two, including *Mister* Boyle," Mrs. Boyle said chuckling. "But none of them stayed, and he didn't stick around either."

"What happened?"

"He wanted me to leave and take care of him. But I couldn't do it. I was too busy takin' care of this place—managing a staff and looking after the laird. And up until just a few years ago, Callum was quite the socialite. The castle was always filled with people—nobles, royals, the rich and famous. It was a scene."

Should Liza assume ownership, she would never be able to replicate what Callum had managed to do for the estate. And she certainly didn't want to try without the sure hand and support of Mrs. Boyle.

Mrs. Boyle seemed to sense the direction of her thoughts. "It may just be time for the place to rest. Give up the ghosts, so to speak."

A gentle breeze kicked up, carrying with it the smell of sweetgrass, wildflowers, and the slightly earthy scent of the river.

They left their post at the edge of the trees and walked across the grounds toward the building. "I need to talk with Callum this evening," Liza said. "It's important I tell him my decision as soon as I can." There was a finality in her words that made her sad. This place—its history, majesty, and beauty—had become a part of her, too. Just like the rest of them. But despite Callum's insistence, none of this *belonged* to her. And the more she thought about the prodding of the castle's ghosts, the more she thought they were warning her away from this place.

Mrs. Boyle nodded approvingly. "I think ye're making the right decision," she said and placed a hand on Liza's arm. "But Callum's been having a bit of an off day after this morning. Might be best for ye to wait till the morrow."

Liza nodded. A few more hours wouldn't hurt anything.

She took her leave of Mrs. Boyle, spending what was left of the day on her own in the library pouring over the ancient volumes that had been collected by the Ramsays throughout the years. The more she explored, the more she became lost in thoughts of what could have been and what the future might have held.

Despite everything—the overwhelming knowledge that she needed to leave Owen and re-evaluate her career—she knew the Ramsay Castle could not be hers. And when the shadows lengthened in the room and darkness finally fell, the soft flickering of the candles she had lit on the small tables told her that the ghosts of the castle agreed with her.

† † †

She'd gone to bed far too late, and after just a few short hours, Liza woke to the rustling sound of fabric or cloth sliding against a solid surface. She sat up, her back resting against the mound of soft pillows stacked behind her. The room smelled of lavender and linen, cotton and dust.

Darkness blanketed the room, making it hard to see. Thin slivers of moonlight seeped through the curtains, providing a soft glow that settled like a mist over the furniture. Shapes were otherworldly, chairs became surrealistic objects, and the air was heavy with the thoughts, hopes, dreams, fears, and emotions of

PERILS PAST

guests past. Despite the hour and the stillness, the air buzzed with energy.

The rustling continued very near to her, but Liza could see no movement. She held her breath for a moment. Closed her eyes to listen. Every hair stood at attention, electrified. Gooseflesh rippled over her body and chills whispered down her spine like the fingers of a ghost.

She opened her eyes again; immediately her gaze fell to the portrait of Lady Catherine. Was it her imagination or did the face seem illuminated and animated? The inanimate eyes were coaxing, almost eager. Liza had the strange sense that the woman wanted something.

The rustling stopped, but the room still seemed to be occupied, spirited. Liza doubted very much that she was alone.

"What do you want?" she asked aloud.

She didn't expect an answer, but what she heard was the slightest whisper, so very hushed that she may well have imagined it.

Come.

Liza's heart leapt into her throat. She listened intently, and caught the sound again. "What did you say?"

The rustling started again, this time more persistent. Liza could hear a voice now.

It continued to repeat the same words in a hushed

tone. *Come.* She heard it again, not just one whisper, but many, all at once. A rush of words. She held her breath as the hushed sound overwhelmed her.

Then, as quickly as it started, it was gone. There was silence.

Her eyes wide, she looked around the room, waiting for something to happen.

Where, just a few moments earlier, the room felt energized, it was now empty and still. Lady Catherine's portrait had returned to its inanimate state, and the only sound was the thundering of Liza's heartbeat in her own ears.

She swore aloud, under her breath, just so she didn't feel so alone and isolated. She needed to get out of this place.

She switched on the lamp next to the bed, but the illumination only succeeded in making the objects in the corner of the room look more ethereal.

With a burst of movement, she pushed the blanket off of her body, and went into the bathroom. She splashed cold water on her face. Her reflection was pale and drawn, exhausted.

That's what a few murder investigations and some ghosts will do for you, she thought to herself.

She crept slowly back into the bedroom. Everything was in order, the room quiet and peaceful. Liza wondered if she'd imagined the sounds, emotions, and voices. She climbed back under the covers, and was about to switch off the light when she heard another faint rustle, then the lightest of dips in the mattress, as if someone very small had sat on the edge of the bed.

Her hand close to the bedside lamp, she paused. An intense smell of lavender and something else—softer and sweeter—wafted toward her.

The ghost was here, so close to her. Liza's heart was racing. She took a deep breath.

"Lady Catherine," she whispered. "I know you need something from me, but I don't think I'm the person who can give you what you want."

The bedding shifted and the pressure on the mattress lifted. There was another rustling and the creak of floorboards. The sound and movement continued toward the door of the room. The ghost was walking away from her.

Liza barely breathed. Her eyes following the imagined path of the young mother's spirit.

There was silence. Then, clearly, from the door, another single word.

Come.

The door creaked slowly open.

Liza wanted to bury her head under the covers. But as inconceivable as it seemed, she was afraid the spirit wouldn't rest until she'd complied.

Liza steeled herself, then slid out of bed and padded across the room, slipped a long silk robe over her shoulders, and carefully pushed the bedroom door the rest of the way open.

The hallway was illuminated with the same spectral glow, though there were few windows to light the way as Liza followed her spirit companion. The soft fabric of her robe made a similar swishing sound against the wooden floors to the ghost's transparent garments.

Each time Liza's better sense caused her to turn back and abandon this foolish mission, she would catch the flash of mist, just in front of her: a nearly transparent petite figure in a long dress with billowing sleeves. The figure seemed to glance over its shoulder; the area where a face should be was hazy and unfocused.

They descended the isolated stone stairs at the end of the hallway instead of the primary staircase. When they emerged onto the main floor, Liza stepped out into the open hallway. The mural of the great battle stared down at her from just above the castle's entrance. Her eyes rested on the placard beneath the scene, which read, *I seize the tales as they pass, and pour them forth in song.*

As if on cue, Liza heard music. A distant drone of discordant notes, similar to the sound she'd heard the day before in the forest. She turned from the mural and found herself outside Callum's great wooden door.

She touched the cool cast-metal knob and twisted it slowly. The latch gave way, and she pushed open the door. It swung silently on its hinges. All other sounds ceased. There was no music. There were no ghosts. There was only Liza.

She stepped inside the room, surprised and yet prepared, to see Callum waiting for her. He was wearing a light-colored sweater, and a smile stretched across his face making him look years younger. His white hair was neatly brushed, and he appeared to be lucid and well-rested despite the early hour.

He stretched his hands toward her. "My dear," he exclaimed. "I've been waitin' for ye for so long."

Chapter 16

Liza wasn't sure if Callum were talking to her or if he had again confused her with Lady Catherine. And though it was completely crazy, a part of her felt as if Lady Catherine was within her, inhabiting her body. She felt as if she'd become one with her ancient ancestor who had endured so much to get them to this point, and which had culminated in Liza standing here in her home of centuries earlier.

Perhaps to make herself feel better—steadier—she said to Callum, "It's Liza, my laird."

"Of course, of course." He brushed her words away. "Come, I have everything ready fer you." He motioned her toward the small table where she'd taken tea two days earlier. A folder filled with paperwork was laid out, two dark pens on each side of the documents.

She looked from the papers to Callum. "Has this been prepared by Mr. Douglas?"

He gave a dismissive wave of his hand then motioned her forward again.

Liza sat down on the sofa and stared at the folder.

Callum handed her a pen. Liza stared at it without

taking it from him. "Why didn't you tell me about my father?"

Callum's bright eyes dimmed just a bit, and he sat back in the chair.

"I even asked about him," Liza said.

"I didn't mean to keep it from ye. I wasn't sure ye'd understand."

"I don't," she responded flatly. "After what he did to me. Did to my mother."

"I didn't realize any of that immediately. And even afterward, I'm not sure that I completely understood. The timing was perfect, right after Hamish had betrayed the estate. It seemed like the perfect solution."

"Did he tell you about me?"

"He did. In fact, he wanted to bequeath the estate to ye anyway. He wanted to make up for everything all those years ago."

Nothing would have made up for what he'd done. She was sorry he was dead, only because she couldn't tell him as much.

"Did he tell you why he left?"

Callum shook his head. "He was a quiet man, Liza. Intense. He seemed to be looking for something he might never find. Not that that's an excuse, but some people are just born that way. They're wanderers."

Callum was right—it wasn't an excuse.

"And the accident that killed him?" she asked.

"It was along Lothian Road. Another car came up

on his, and he lost control and overturned somehow. Freak accident."

"Who was in the other car?"

Callum looked up at her, shrugged. "I'm not sure. It was Mr. Douglas who handled the details. It was close to his office. Yer father had been heading to Mr. Douglas's office to sign the paperwork. I'm surprised ye weren't informed. Ye'd have been his next o' kin."

This had puzzled Liza, too. But she supposed it didn't matter. She didn't want anything from her father—neither his property nor his debts.

"And the genetic testing, the forensic investigation—that was all a lie?"

"Oh, no. We did all of that. Ye've always been a direct descendant of this family. Everything else we told ye was the truth." He put a gnarled hand to his heart. "We just left out that one part."

Liza bit the inside of her cheek, considering this new information.

Callum leaned forward. "Ye can hate him all ye want. It doesn't change the fact that ye are his kin, and this place belongs to ye. But, Liza, it may make yer heart a lot lighter if ye can forgive him. He may have been doing the best he could for ye at the time. Maybe he thought ye'd be better off without him."

Hot tears sprang into her eyes. She quickly dashed them away with the back of her hand. She had no intention of forgiving the man.

"He said he'd written to ye. Do ye still have his letters?"

Her head snapped up. "Letters?"

"He said he'd been tryin' to contact ye for years."

"I've never received any letters from him."

Callum gave her a kind smile. "Maybe he had yer address wrong, then. The point is, he wanted ye to know that he loved ye."

Liza really could have used someone to love her, especially after she'd lost her mother.

She exhaled and rubbed her eyes with the heels of her hand. "How am I supposed to maintain this place?" she asked, looking around. "What am I supposed to do with it?"

"What do ye mean? Ye live in it."

"With what money?"

He looked perplexed. She remembered Lachlan telling her about Callum's inheritance and trust from his mother. He'd always just had the means to pay for whatever he may have needed. Working for a living was likely a foreign concept to him.

She leaned forward. "And that's why I can't take you up on your offer, Chief Ramsay," she said, reverting back to his formal and official title. "I don't have the resources that you do."

He stared at her. "Liza, ye have all the resources that ye need right here." He tapped the slim stack of documents with the tip of his pen.

"This estate isn't self-sustaining. The castle isn't enough," said Liza. She opened her mouth and shut it again, trying to figure out a way to make him understand her dilemma. "I have to work for a living, and my salary, while substantial, is not enough to preserve this amazing location as it should be." She leaned forward, placing a hand on his knee. "I can't move here, Callum. I have a life somewhere else. I'd have to sell this place, and I know that's not what you want. I'm sure one of the other Ramsay family members, while maybe not a direct descendant of Lady Catherine, would be a more appropriate benefactor. I'm sorry."

Callum continued to stare at her. "Liza, I thought Robert had explained this all to ye. I'm a very wealthy man. My mother left me a nice inheritance, and I've invested it wisely over the years. Ye'll have plenty of resources to maintain this place, even if ye have to stay in the States fer a while. Ye can hire all the help ye'll need. Ye can also rely on Lachlan, God willing."

Liza shook her head. "I don't know if I understand." She paused, trying to come up with the best words to ask the question. "Are you telling me that the inheritance includes your personal wealth?"

"Of course it does." He leaned forward and flipped through the paperwork, pulling out one of the documents. He tapped on one printed line.

Liza leaned forward, staring at the line of zeros after the number 36. The blood drained from her face and the feeling left her extremities. "That can't be right," she whispered.

"I can assure you it is," Callum responded, still seeming confused.

"But I can't accept that."

"Why not?"

"I didn't earn it," she said simply.

"My dear, I was lucky enough to be born into a family of great wealth. And even if ye didn't know it, so were ye. Ye earned it simply because ye exist."

Liza stared at the paperwork, then looked up at Callum. "Are you sure?" she asked, her voice barely more than a whisper.

He leaned forward and took her hands in his. "I've never been so sure of anything in my life."

Liza stared at the pages for a moment longer. This was the wrong decision, she was sure of it. But as if she were outside her own body, she watched as her shaking hand picked up the pen and began signing each of the pages.

When she finished, Callum did the same, then they repeated the process on an identical stack of documents.

When they'd finished, Callum looked at her. "Congratulations, Lady Ramsay. This now officially belongs to you."

Her breath came out in a whoosh. "Don't you have to file this paperwork with the government or some other entity?"

"Aye, I've already made the arrangements for that to be done first thing in the morning. And the property and assets will officially transfer to you upon my death, so don't wish the time away too quickly." He laughed. "But it will be here soon enough." He sounded tired. "I imagine ye have some of yer own affairs to organize, in the meantime."

An image of Owen popped into her mind, dimming the levity of the moment. She needed to figure out what she was going to do about him. About their relationship.

Callum gestured toward the second stack of paperwork. "Keep that in a safe place. If something were to happen to me before everything is notarized and filed, this is yer proof of my intentions while I am sound of mind. It might not hold up in court, but it'll help."

He hugged her, and Liza again noticed how thin Callum was. She felt if she squeezed too hard, she might crush him.

They broke apart. Since she'd been in the room, dawn had broken. A ghostly mist blanketed the lawn at the rear of the castle. It was just about this time the previous morning that the body of Brodie Graham had been discovered.

"Is there anything we can do for Lachlan?" she asked, staring at the sycamore. At some point the previous evening, the rope had finally been removed, and the tree had subsumed the secret of Brodie's death.

"He didnae do it."

"Do you know who did?"

His brow furrowed. He looked as if he were concentrating, trying to catch a memory. Finally, he shook his head and sighed. "Lachlan is a good lad. Luck has dealt him a bad hand."

Liza felt awful, especially having just encountered such an unexpected stroke of luck. Now she just needed to figure out what it all meant.

↓↓↓

Upon leaving Callum's quarters, Liza heard movement and voices from the lower floor of the building. Mrs. Boyle, she suspected, but who could she be talking to? Perhaps Lachlan had returned. She realized that of everyone in her life right now, Lachlan was the one person with whom she wanted to share her decision regarding the inheritance. She wasn't sure what that meant, and she didn't want to examine it. She was done second-guessing and examining her feelings. That had gotten her exactly nowhere over the past decade or so.

She walked down the stairs, closer to the entrance to the kitchen, stopping when she heard Mrs. Boyle's words. "I'm telling ye, she disnae want it. She's plannin' to go back to Boston."

The other voice, male, responded, but Liza couldn't

make out the words.

"She told me herself. As soon as this bloody investigation is over."

Another low rumble of words.

"I don't think they suspect anyone but Lachlan, and why would they?"

Some pots or pans clanged, drowning out the next part of the conversation. Then the words from Mrs. Boyle, "I don't think that's necessary at all. Lachlan isn't here anymore."

Mrs. Boyle was talking about her, and it wasn't Lachlan in the kitchen. She frowned, trying to decide if she should risk getting closer to the doorway to get a look at the other speaker.

"I'm just sayin', it's a risk I don't think we need to take," Mrs. Boyle continued. "Not yet. We still have some time."

A loud knock on the door sounded, and Liza jumped then dashed up the stairs, not wanting to alert the kitchen's occupants to her presence. Instead, she ducked into a hallway to the right, peering out so she could see the activity below.

Mrs. Boyle appeared, her apron covered in what looked like flour. Even though it was just after dawn, the older woman's hair was already disheveled. She looked harried. Muttering something under her breath, she dusted her hands on the apron, creating a small puffy cloud of flour. Then she opened the heavy door.

Dr. Patel stood at the door with another man by his side.

"Dr. Patel," Mrs. Boyle exclaimed. "I wasn't aware ye were comin' this morning. And so early! The sun is barely up."

The doctor stepped through the door, and his acquaintance followed. "I told Mr. Ramsay I'd be by this morning," he said. He introduced the other man as his associate with no further explanation.

"He seemed just fine last night. Ate all his supper and wasn't complainin' of aches, pains, or other ailments. I don't think he needs an examination this morning." She stood in the doorway like a guard.

But Dr. Patel didn't let her stop him. "Excuse me, Mrs. Boyle."

She stood her ground. "I think Callum should be restin' this early. No need for ye to wake him."

"Mrs. Boyle, my *patient* asked me to come." He didn't wait for Mrs. Boyle to move. Instead, he and the other man squeezed past, leaving her no choice but to get out of the way. They climbed the main stairs, passing right by Liza's hiding place. She flattened herself against the wall.

The older woman hurried after them. "I'm just looking out for Callum's best interests."

Neither the doctor nor the other man responded.

Once they'd passed her hiding spot, Liza could no longer see them, but she heard Mrs. Boyle rap on

Callum's door. The door opened, and seconds later, shut again. Mrs. Boyle bustled back toward the stairs. She muttered angrily under her breath, eyes straight in front of her.

Liza waited until the other woman had returned to the kitchen, then hastened toward the side stairs, holding her signed papers against her chest. She ran up the four flights of stairs and down the passageway, closing and locking the door behind her.

She looked around the room, searching for a safe place to keep the documents. Her eye was drawn to the bureau. Callum had mentioned he'd found Lady Catherine's memento mori necklace hidden there. She pulled open an empty drawer, working it completely off of its wooden runners. Folding the papers twice, she placed the documents against the backside of the bureau and replaced the drawer. She wasn't sure whether hiding the documents was necessary, but the warnings of danger were still fresh in her mind. Dr. Patel's caution that there were those who would rather see her on a plane back to Boston. This prudence seemed somehow necessary.

When the task was finished, Liza sat on the bench at the foot of the bed and allowed herself to consider the momentous decision she had just allowed herself to make. It was almost too much to fathom, but she refused to second-guess it. It was over and done with, and now it was time to think about the next steps in this new life rather than reflect on whether or not she'd made the right decision.

She showered and dressed, and when she was finally presentable in a pair of jeans and a light sweater, she heard the crunch of gravel and looked out the window in time to see Dr. Patel's shiny car heading down the drive. With Lachlan safely questioned at the station and the perceived danger neutralized, the police presence had vanished from the property.

Liza should have asked for Dr. Patel's card or saved his contact information on her phone. She realized Mrs. Boyle hadn't shared that with her when she'd asked the day before. She would need to get it so she could keep apprised of Callum's health after she'd returned home. Somehow, she didn't trust that Mrs. Boyle or Mr. Douglas would be willing sources of information.

She pulled out her laptop, which had lain untouched for days, so she could research return flights. She paused, unsure if Chief Inspector Dean would agree to her departure. She resented feeling like a prisoner in this castle to which she now had a legal claim.

Of course, that was absolutely nothing compared to the feeling of helplessness that Lachlan must have been going through.

On a whim, Liza typed into the browser search bar: 'Nicola Munro death'.

The first result was the obituary she was searching for.

Nicola Louise Munro, daughter of James Munro and Andrea Dean Munro, died with her life unfinished before her at the age of nineteen. She was an athlete, having competed in her beloved sport of swimming since a child of five years old. She was studying Economics and Business and, while her future plans had yet to be laid out, she was a role model for her young sister Emma and her brother Thomas. Also survived by aunts, uncles, and cousins.

In the list of results following the death notice, Liza found plenty of articles that featured a beautiful red-headed girl, with a brilliant smile and full of life. Many of the news stories used the same photo: Nicola's head thrown back in laughter, exposing her smooth white neck. It was hard for Liza to tear her eyes from the unblemished skin of her throat.

Many of the stories also featured accompanying and unflattering photos of Lachlan McClaren looking tired and rageful. There were just as many photos of Lachlan's father, James McClaren, stern-looking and unsmiling in both his official headshots and the candid photos of him entering and leaving various government buildings.

According to the articles, Nicola's body had been discovered by her roommate just after seven in the morning. She was lying on her back, naked from the waist down. There were visible injuries to lower body, indicating severe brutality and anger. One of the articles even published a crime scene photo of Nicola's pale and lifeless face, eyes open in terror. Liza quickly clicked away.

The case had clearly received heightened attention from the media, all blame pointing toward Lachlan, with heavy mention of his father. After eight years, the evidence remained.

Liza thought back to the conversation with Lachlan in the old church. What was the name of the other boy he'd mentioned—the one for whom Nicola had ended her relationship with Lachlan?

With a sudden flash of memory, she typed in 'Liam Burns'. Hundreds of results popped up, and after scrolling for a minute, Liza returned to the search field and typed in the boy's name along with the name of the university. A few hits resulted, but when she clicked on the links, she discovered that these students had attended in the wrong timeframe.

Perhaps she'd misremembered the name. She was about to give up, and then, on a whim, she typed in 'William Burns' with the university's name.

A number of images of a muscular and intense-looking young man with deep-set eyes and black hair appeared on a website that was not associated with the school's rugby team, but that listed standout players. Liza clicked through and found that the timeframe coincided with that during which Lachlan and Nicola would have also attended. In most of the photos he was on a rugby field, but she found one headshot with his hands clasped behind his back, scowling at the camera. Underneath that photo was some basic information—height, weight, age, and hometown, Fort Augustus.

She returned to the search box and typed in 'William Burns, Fort Augustus'.

Three obituaries appeared, all for older men named William Burns who had died over the past two decades. One result featured a news story about a middle-aged business owner of the same name who lived in a place called Invermoriston. She discovered a number of articles outlining the success of the same William "Liam" Burns on the rugby field throughout his teenage years and university career. And then, at the bottom of the page, she found a lone article from one year before from a local newspaper about a man named Willam Burns who'd been charged with stalking, assault, and harassment of his ex-wife.

She clicked on the link, and sure enough, the mug shot was the same intense face with a few more pounds and a lot more anger. After reading the article, it was clear to Liza that the woman was lucky to be alive. It told a tale of emotional and physical abuse, manipulation, and violence.

There was no mention of Liam Burns's connection to Nicola Munro.

Had the police investigating Nicola's death even interviewed this man, or had they instead immediately decided Lachlan McClaren was the guilty party?

Liza stared into Liam's cruel eyes. A chill ran through her. Was this the last image Nicola Munro had seen before her time in this earthly realm ended? She clicked the share icon at the top of the article and sent the article to her own email address.

Chapter 17

When Liza entered the dining room for breakfast, she found Mrs. Boyle, Mr. Douglas, and Mr. Morrison sitting at the table.

"And then there were four," she quipped, a reference to one of her favorite mystery authors.

Mrs. Boyle ignored the reference and tilted her head toward the dishes on the sideboard. "Scotch woodcock, black pudding, and haggis," she said. "I would've come to fetch ye, but I figured ye could use the rest."

Liza peered at the unfamiliar dishes, and noticed that Mrs. Boyle was watching her out of the corner of her eye.

Liza took healthy portions of each and sat down next to Mr. Morrison who grunted and shifted away from her. She supposed he was still affronted about her lack of enthusiasm regarding the development of the estate.

For a few long minutes, the only sound at the table was silverware scraping against the china. Liza pushed the food around on her plate, tasting each dish tentatively.

She looked at Mr. Douglas, opening her mouth to let him know that she and Callum had come to a written agreement. When he noticed that she seemed about to speak, he held up his hand. "I'm afraid Callum still isn't feeling well, Elizabeth. You're going to need to wait to talk with him."

She frowned, and nearly told him that she'd already spoken with Callum earlier that morning. A faint rush of air—*shhhhh*—stopped her. Instead, she said, "I could have sworn I saw the doctor leaving from my window."

"Aye, that's right," Mrs. Boyle interjected. "I called him to check on the laird. I'm afraid Callum's taken a turn for the worse."

Liza frowned and looked down at her plate. They were lying, and she didn't know why. "Well," she said, choosing her next words carefully, "I'm going to need the number for Dr. Patel so that I can keep in touch with him after I return to Boston."

"Why would ye need to do that?" Mrs. Boyle asked.

Liza cleared her throat. "I've decided I'm going to take Callum up on his offer, after all." Though her heart was pounding furiously, she managed to keep her voice steady. "I've agreed to become the new, eventual, owner of the Ramsay Estate."

A long, heavy silence followed.

Mr. Douglas and Mrs. Ramsay exchanged a glance,

and Mr. Morrison blustered. "Robert," he bellowed. "We had a deal." He threw his napkin on the table. "This is unacceptable." He pushed his chair back, nearly knocking it over, and stormed out of the room.

Liza stared at Mr. Douglas. "A deal?"

He ignored her question and instead turned to Mrs. Boyle. "Margaret, did ye hear that? Elizabeth has come to a decision."

Mrs. Boyle waved her napkin in front of her face like a fan. "I thought ye said yesterday ye were goin' to go back to the States."

"I don't recall saying anything of the sort."

"Yesterday mornin'. Ye said this wasn't yer home. And last evenin', ye said you had to talk with Callum to tell him yer decision."

"I hadn't actually made my decision yesterday."

"I'm curious. What changed yer mind?" Mr. Douglas's voice was even enough, but when he took a sip of tea, Liza could have sworn his hand was trembling.

She did not share that the ghost of Lady Catherine had led her to her decision. "I've decided that a Ramsay ancestor should be the person making decisions about the fate of the estate. Aside from Callum…" She looked around the room pointedly. "…it appears I'm the only other Ramsay in residence."

"I'm sure that when Callum is well enough, he'll be happy to know yer decision." Mrs. Boyle stood up abruptly and began to clear the plates. They clinked together noisily.

"Would you mind giving me Dr. Patel's contact information, Mrs. Boyle?" Liza repeated her request.

"I'll just need to find it for ye."

One of the plates clattered to the floor, and bits of food scattered in all directions.

Liza stood and hurried to the other side of the table. "Let me help you," she said bending down.

"I've got it," Mrs. Boyle yelled. Her breath escaped her lips in short puffs. She patted the air with a free hand. "I've got it," she said more calmly, but still visibly agitated.

Liza nodded, stood, and backed away slowly. She returned to her seat.

Mr. Douglas watched Mrs. Boyle clean up the mess, then he turned to Liza. "Why don't ye join me in Callum's chambers in about an hour's time? If he's up to it, we'll get all of the paperwork settled."

Maybe this wasn't going to be as difficult as she'd feared. If Mr. Douglas planned to talk with Callum, Liza didn't even need to mention she'd already signed the paperwork. Callum would do that for her. And surely Mr. Douglas would not go against Callum's wishes.

Mrs. Boyle dropped another plate, and Liza stood up to peer over the table. "Are you all right?" she asked. "Maybe you ought to get some rest."

"I'm quite all right, Ms. Ramsay," Mrs. Boyle said.

But her voice was strained, and if Liza didn't know better, she would have thought the woman had been about to cry.

Mr. Douglas made no move to help Mrs. Boyle, or even acknowledge there might have been a problem. He took a big bite of the scotch woodcock, and one of the anchovies slipped away just as he was about to fork it into his mouth. It made a greasy splotch on his white shirt. He picked it off his lap and ate it.

Mrs. Boyle finished gathering up the plates and flatware and walked into the other room. Liza heard the whir of the dumbwaiter before the sound of the woman's retreating steps.

Liza was left alone with Mr. Douglas. Tension filled the air. Something thick and threatening. She wanted to leave the room as well, but her manners and upbringing kept her rooted to the chair. She had been trained to stay seated at the table until everyone was finished eating. The times she'd left in anger or frustration had seemed like the greatest act of rebellion, and punishable by grounding or loss of some other precious privilege. She wasn't sure what the punishment might be in this house, but she thought of Brodie Graham and determined that it might be somewhat worse than not being allowed to attend the spring dance.

She filled the silence with a question. "Have you heard any news about Lachlan?"

"They likely arrested 'im." Mr. Douglas responded. "Hopefully this time, they got it right."

He spoke with a vitriol that nearly stunned her into silence. Before she could stop herself, she asked, "Have you heard of a man named Liam Burns?"

He frowned. "Liam Burns? Not that I'm aware of."

She pushed the food around on her plate and considered his response. If the police had looked into this man, then Mr. Douglas would likely recognize the name. His ignorance seemed sincere, and she concluded that Lachlan had indeed been the only suspect in Nicola's death. They simply figured that he had gotten away with murder.

"Who is he?" Mr. Douglas followed up, looking at her with suspicion in his gaze.

"Just someone Lachlan mentioned in passing."

"You'd do well to ignore anythin' that boy tells ye. I told ye, he's bad news."

"He's hardly a boy, Mr. Douglas. He's over thirty years old."

Mr. Douglas shook his head. "Callum has a blind spot for him too. For the life of me, I can't understand it. He killed that girl," he said. "Then he just waltzed away, as if it never happened. His father hired some good lawyers, and that was all it took."

"I assume you tried to talk Callum out of allowing him to stay and work at the estate?"

Mr. Douglas shook his head and his cheeks wobbled. "I wasn't Callum's solicitor at the time."

This surprised Liza. She had thought Callum and Mr. Douglas were old friends. She said as much, and Mr. Douglas shook his head again. "I was representing Hamish Ramsay. I discovered Hamish's intentions for the property and alerted Callum. I've worked for Callum ever since."

Liza turned this over in her mind, trying to work out the implications. She still did not understand nor trust the presence of Kenneth Morrison, a developer, who had apparently been brought by Mr. Douglas to meet her.

In the end, it didn't matter. She had no intention of developing the property or doing anything to destroy the historical significance of the building or the land. Still, she couldn't work out Mr. Douglas's motives.

Mr. Douglas took one final bite and washed it down with a slosh of tea. "If you'll excuse me, Elizabeth. I'll need to attend to some…" He cleared his throat. "…personal matters before we meet with Callum in a bit." He gave her a little bow before he left the room.

Liza sat by herself at the table, sipping her tea. She had clearly shocked her breakfast companions with her announcement, and while she knew they might be surprised, she was taken aback by their poorly concealed disappointment.

She sighed and pushed the remnants of the breakfast around her plate, and instead reached for a scone that sat on a dish in the middle of the table. She took a bite of the moist pastry, barely tasting it.

The table was littered with dirty dishes and half-eaten plates of food and cups of tea. After she'd swallowed a few bites of the scone, she began to gather up the dishes and took an armful to the dumbwaiter cabinet in the other room. When she opened the cabinet door, she heard a voice from below.

"It's not how it was supposed to be. This was never part of the plan."

It was clearly part of a longer statement. One of the teacups slipped and rolled onto the floor of the dumbwaiter, sloshing tea everywhere.

"Is someone there?" the same voice asked. Liza recognized it as Mrs. Boyle, who had opened the kitchen's entrance to the chamber and whose voice reached her as if they were standing right next to each other.

"It's Liza," she said into the cabinet. "Just gathering up what's left of the dishes."

There was a long pause. Liza began to think the woman hadn't heard her when Mrs. Boyle called back, "Ye don't need to do that, dear. I'll clean up."

Liza set the rest of the dishes into the cabinet. "Okay, I'll just be up in my room then."

Again, no response. After another pause, she pressed the button concealed just inside the panel. The motor whirred into life and the elevator descended.

⸸⸸⸸

Liza entered her room, and immediately felt a disturbance in the energy. She looked around the space, the morning light streaming through the window. Everything appeared to be as she'd left it, but she couldn't help feel like something had shifted. "Hello?" she called out tentatively, her hand on the doorknob.

She walked over to the bed, the comforter still in a disarray where she'd slept earlier. Her laptop seemed to be in the same place, but it was closed. Had she closed it before she'd gone down for breakfast? She couldn't remember.

Her suitcase sat open on the bench at the foot of the bed, and the clothes within were rumpled. She hadn't bothered to unpack because she hadn't planned to stay long. But had she rifled through her suitcase so carelessly?

Her phone was plugged into the charger on the nightstand.

She was being ridiculous, she thought. And paranoid.

Still, she shut the door to the room and opened the drawer where she'd hidden the paperwork earlier—the agreement to assume ownership of the Ramsay Estate. She slid the heavy wooden compartment off its sliders, and touched the stack of folded papers still in its hidden recess. She was about to replace the drawer, but stopped. Instead, she grabbed the papers and tucked them into the back pocket of her pants, letting the long hem of her sweater fall back into place. She replaced the drawer.

She expected she'd return to the United States within the next few days, as soon as she was able to talk with Chief Inspector Dean. She may even be able to leave later that evening. There was a flight from Edinburgh directly into Boston leaving at eight.

The thought of returning filled her with a giddy dread. An anticipation. She would need to talk with Owen. And what about Raj? She supposed she could continue working until the estate came into her possession. But maybe it would make more sense to return to Edinburgh and live at the Ramsay Estate while she had the benefit of Callum's knowledge. She had no idea if Mrs. Boyle would want to stay on. Given the few comments she'd overheard that morning, combined with her thoughts from the night before, something told Liza she might need to find new staff.

And Lachlan. Her heart gave a little lurch for the boy he'd been and the man he had become, living under the shadow of suspicion and a family he couldn't escape. She had no reason to trust him or believe him, and yet she did.

She sighed and finished folding and repacking her

clothes. She remade the bed neatly even though she knew Mrs. Boyle would probably strip it bare after she'd left. She realized she didn't know where the laundry was. There was so much history she was still missing, but there were modern amenities, too, that she would need to learn.

She glanced at the time on her phone. It was nearly time to meet with Mr. Douglas and Callum. Still no new messages from Owen; she felt relief, but it was an uneasy relief.

There was, however, a new message from Raj.

Liza, call me. We need to talk.

It would have been early in Boston, and she struggled to remember what day of the week it was. Time had ceased to matter here.

She pocketed the phone and took a look around the room before heading to meet with Callum and Mr. Douglas.

Halfway down the stairs, she heard a commotion and raised voices.

"Call 999!" came Mrs. Boyle's frantic voice. Followed by Mr. Douglas bellowing, "What in the bloody hell is happening here?"

"There's no time!" Mrs. Boyle yelled, her voice desperate, breathless.

"Should we move him or leave him where he is?" yelled Mr. Morrison.

By the time Liza had followed the voices to Callum's living quarters, Mr. Douglas was attempting to perform CPR on the prone figure of Callum stretched out in front of the chair where he'd been sitting only a few hours earlier with Liza.

Chapter 18

Callum wasn't moving. He was very pale, except for his mouth and the tips of his fingers, which were a gray-blue color.

Liza stared aghast at the scene. Mr. Morrison was speaking into his phone, telling an operator on the other end their location; Mrs. Boyle was kneeling on the other side of Mr. Douglas who was frantically working to revive the body beneath him.

"Yer goin' tae crack his ribs," Mrs. Boyle yelled, her fingers threaded through her hair.

Mr. Douglas ignored her. He pressed down at regular intervals on Callum's concave chest, still clothed in the pale sweater he'd been wearing earlier. One of Mrs. Boyle's fine chinaware teacups and a half-eaten piece of toast lay discarded on the floor beside Callum.

Standing there watching the scene, Liza couldn't ever remember feeling more useless than she did at that moment.

After what seemed like an eternity, but was likely only minutes, the wail of sirens pierced the air followed by the heavy crunch of tires on the gravel outside. Liza ran down the stairs to pull open the door, and men in dark green uniforms hurried in past her. She directed them to the top of the stairs.

There had been no response from Callum, and Liza didn't need to fear the worst. She already knew the elderly gentleman was gone. In one of the recesses in the wall overlooking the intricate mural of the battle for Scotland's freedom was a banister-back side chair, carved with an intricate crest and upholstered with a cane seat. It clearly wasn't meant for sitting, but Liza sat anyway, her forehead resting in her hands.

The three men eventually emerged, subdued, accompanied by Mr. Douglas. "Ye'll want to call his doctor," the tallest and oldest of the three men was saying. "He'll be able to formally pronounce him and help with the arrangements."

"Ye won't be takin' him with ye, then?" Mr. Douglas said.

The tall man shook his head and responded, but Liza didn't hear the words. Their voices sounded like they were underwater—slow, distorted, and unfocused. It wasn't until one of the uniformed men was kneeling in front of her that she realized her breath was coming in quick greedy gulps. She couldn't seem to get enough air into her lungs.

The man had his hand on her arm and was telling her to try to relax. Liza clawed at her chest, struggling to control the pace of her breath. Another man rushed forward and placed something over her face. It was a clear mask from which fresh, cold oxygen flowed into her nose and mouth.

She felt better almost immediately. The first man had one of his fingers against her neck, checking her pulse.

It was during this scene that DCI Dean and DI Lawson walked in, both looking tired and grim. They looked over at her as they climbed the stairs and then kept going toward Callum's room.

Liza pulled the mask off.

"Do ye want us to take ye in to be examined? Just in case?" the medic said.

"No, it's fine. I'm fine."

"Are ye sure? If something else happens, I would need to report the fact that ye refused treatment."

"Nothing else is going to happen," she said and stood up, brushing past him to follow after Dean and Lawson.

Mrs. Boyle was sobbing in one corner. In another, Mr. Douglas talked in low tones to the detectives. Liza could see the lower half of Callum's body prostrate on the floor. She interrupted the conversation between the detectives and Mr. Douglas. "Can we move him into his bed, at least?"

Dean glanced at her. "We're going to have a forensics team process the place first."

Mr. Douglas added, "Dr. Patel is on his way."

Liza turned to Chief Inspector Dean. "Do you think a crime has been committed?"

"Ms. Ramsay, I'm sure I don't have to remind you that this is the third death here in the past three days."

Liza wandered away, still dazed. She looked around. Did she own the castle now? She had no idea. There had been no time to file any paperwork. The only documentation she had of Callum's wishes were the signed copies of the paperwork in her back pocket. She glanced over at the coffee table where she'd earlier signed the stack of papers. She saw no sign of Callum's documentation.

The detectives moved to talk with Mrs. Boyle, who was still crying but seemed to be forming coherent sentences. Mr. Douglas pulled out a handkerchief and wiped the sweat off his forehead and spittle from around the corners of his mouth.

He watched her approach. "This week has been a lot for ye. If I'd known all of this would happen, I would never have sent ye the letter in the first place."

She'd never met Charlie Campbell, and she barely knew Brodie Graham, though that didn't make their deaths any less traumatic. But the loss of Callum hurt.

"I think we were all prepared for Callum's death, but none of us expected him to pass like this." Mr. Douglas wiped his mouth again. "I expect his heart just gave out. Likely all the stress of the past few days."

Liza hadn't thought Callum seemed anxious, but

she supposed you couldn't tell what was going on in someone's heart.

"I'm sorry it didn't work out for ye," Mr. Douglas continued. "I know Callum wanted the place to stay in the Ramsay family, but the estate will likely go into probate now."

"What do you mean?"

"We never had a chance to sign the documents. Callum elected not to change his will until he'd met ye and ye'd decided it was something ye wanted. I know ye made the decision to accept his offer, but without the signatures…" His words trailed off and he shrugged. "There's not much ye can do from a legal standpoint."

Liza stared at him. "Mr. Douglas, I certainly was not wishing death on Callum, but his intent was for me to inherit this estate."

The other man nodded and gave her a pitying look, his thick wet lips downturned in a grotesque pout. "Of course, Ms. Ramsay. But unfortunately, Callum's intentions won't hold up in a court of law."

She glanced over at Dean and Lawson. They were listening to Mrs. Boyle who was gesticulating wildly, her hair completely undone from her chignon.

Liza took the paperwork from her back pocket and handed it to Mr. Douglas. He stared at it without touching it. "What's that?"

She pushed it forward. "Read it."

He glanced at her for a moment before snatching the papers and unfolding them. His mouth moved as he read over the words, but no sound came out. He rifled through the last few pages and refolded them. "Where did ye get these?" he asked.

"Callum gave them to me, of course."

"When?"

"Early this morning."

He glanced up sharply as he handed the stack of documents back to her. "Ye saw Callum this morning? Ye didn't mention that earlier."

"I didn't think it was any of your business."

"None of my business?" The volume of his voice increased, and Lawson glanced in their direction. "I'm his solicitor."

"I had planned to tell you when I met with you and Callum. Callum has his own copy of this paperwork."

"None that I've seen," responded Mr. Douglas. "I'm sorry, Elizabeth, but yer signature isn't worth the paper it's written on. Those documents haven't been notarized nor have they been witnessed. Additionally," he raised his voice again, "I have serious concerns about the fact that ye met with Callum just a short time before his death. Ye, more than anyone, would have had a lot to gain from his passing."

Liza's mouth fell open. Unsurprisingly, DCI Dean walked toward them. "How about if we move this conversation into the sitting room?" Her question was general, but she was looking directly at Liza.

As they walked out of the room, Dr. Patel had arrived, alone this time. "What happened?" he demanded.

It was Mrs. Boyle who answered. "Oh, Doctor, it was just awful. I walked in, and his tea and toast were on the floor, and he was blue. Mr. Douglas tried to save him, but we were gone."

Chief Inspector Dean turned to the doctor. "I know Mr. Ramsay was ill, but I still think it might be a good idea to have an autopsy done."

"As the executor of his estate, I don't think that will be necessary," Mr. Douglas interjected. "Callum was well aware his days were few."

"Mr. Douglas, I just examined Callum this morning. It's true he didn't have much time, but I couldn't be more shocked that he has passed this quickly."

"So, you think the death could be suspicious?" Dean asked.

"It's certainly possible."

Mrs. Boyle made a sound of protest. "This is not what Mr. Ramsay would have wanted," she said. "He had made his peace. I dinnae think we should disturb that."

Dean looked from Mr. Douglas to Mrs. Boyle. "Which one of you was the last to see Mr. Ramsay alive?"

Mrs. Boyle put a hand to her head. "I took him his

tea and toast this morning after Dr. Patel left, but I didnae see him. I just called to him through his bedroom door."

Dean looked at Mr. Douglas. "And you saw him?"

"Actually, I didn't. I had planned to meet with Mr. Ramsay and Elizabeth together, but he was gone before we had a chance to meet. Elizabeth, though, apparently met with him this morning."

Liza nodded and folded her arms across her stomach. "That's true, but it was before Dr. Patel arrived."

"Can anyone confirm that?" asked Dean.

Liza opened her mouth then shut it. She didn't speak, just gave a small shake of her head.

"She's got some useless papers that you'll probably want to take a look at." Mr. Douglas nodded his head at Liza. "They mean nothing, but apparently, she convinced Callum to sign some paperwork turning over the castle and estate to her."

Dean raised her eyebrows. Liza pulled the papers from her back pocket and handed them over.

Dean slipped on her thick back reading glasses and studied the small print and signatures. "This looks pretty official to me." She refolded the paperwork and tucked it into the folder that she was carrying. "I thought that was Mr. Ramsay's intent all along," she said to Mr. Douglas.

"Does not matter what his intent was," repeated Mr. Douglas. "The paperwork has not been properly witnessed or filed."

"So, what happens now?" asked Dean, looking at him over her glasses.

"You, of all people, know the answer to that, Chief Inspector," said Mr. Douglas. "Probate."

Dean winced in an overly exaggerated manner. "That's a long and complicated process, Ms. Ramsay. But I suppose you'll have as good a chance as the other family members. Or a judge could break up the property between the petitioning relatives. That would be a shame."

They seemed to be waiting for a response from Liza, who was frankly at a loss. Her emotions had been on a roller coaster the past four days, and she was exhausted. At this point, she just wanted to go home and forget she'd ever met this group of people or had nearly inherited this property. None of this was worth her mental or physical health.

She was about to say as much when Dr. Patel spoke up. "Actually, I can confirm Ms. Ramsay's visit to Callum—at least the visit before I arrived this morning."

All eyes shifted to the doctor, and he cleared his throat. "This isn't exactly the ideal time for this conversation to take place, but I suppose it's necessary to have it now." He shifted from one foot to the other. "It's true that I performed a brief examination on Mr. Ramsay this morning, but the examination wasn't the primary purpose of my visit." He cleared his throat again and straightened the cuff of his button-down shirt.

He continued. "Mr. Ramsay called me last night and asked me to visit him early this morning. He asked me to bring an associate and old friend of mine, Niall Murphy, who handles estate law. Callum had asked Niall to draft a new bequest, and we were both on hand to witness his signature this morning. There are two sets of original documents. The ones that Mr. Ramsay kept are in a locked safe in his room, and the others will be filed today, if they haven't already, with the Scottish Courts and Tribunals Service."

Mr. Douglas's face turned a turnip shade of red. "This is preposterous," he said. "I demand to see this purported paperwork." Spittle flew from his mouth as the words flew from his mouth.

Mrs. Boyle put a hand on his arm.

"I'd also like to have a look at them," said the chief inspector.

"I'm sure Niall will be happy to provide you both with copies. Otherwise, you can request them from the courts."

"What did this so-called will and testament say?" Mr. Douglas demanded.

"It bequeathed the Ramsay Estate to Ms. Liza Ramsay, along with all of Mr. Ramsay's monetary assets, upon his death." Dr. Patel looked at Liza. "I also have

Callum's copy of the documents that *Liza* signed, acknowledging her acceptance of the inheritance, and her good faith efforts to keep the building and grounds *intact.*" He looked back to Mr. Douglas. "Those documents may not be legally binding, but I have a feeling that any judge would take them under serious consideration, in light of the circumstances."

"This is outrageous!" Mr. Douglas's whole body was shaking now. "I'm still the executor of his estate, and as such, I demand a full review of these highly unorthodox practices. We all know that Callum Ramsay had been ill for quite some time, and was not in his right mind. I will challenge the validity of this alleged document!"

"You can demand and challenge whatever you'd like," Dr. Patel said evenly. "As his doctor, I can testify as to Mr. Ramsay's sound state of mind, which is why I suspect he asked me to be a part of this process. I think you'll find that everything is in order. But I should let you know—you are no longer the executor of Mr. Ramsay's estate. That responsibility has also been granted to Ms. Ramsay." He turned to Liza. "So, Liza, the question of Callum's body is left to you. Would you like the medical examiner to perform an autopsy?"

Liza looked around this group of people who were staring back at her, all as shocked as she herself by this turn of events. She turned to Dr. Patel. "The last time I saw Callum, he was fully alert and in relatively good health, despite his diagnosis." She turned to DCI Dean. "The answer is, yes. I would like an autopsy to be performed. I don't believe for a second that someone didn't help his death along."

Chapter 19

Liza spent the next hour being interrogated by Dean, detailing the previous sixteen hours, up to the discovery of Callum's body. The detective grilled her about what she knew regarding the inheritance and when she'd learnt it, but at no point did Liza feel as if she was under suspicion of any wrongdoing. And in fact, she couldn't be sure any wrongdoing had actually occurred. As far as she could tell, no one but Liza herself had anything to gain from Callum's immediate death. And the fact remained—Callum would likely have passed before the end of the year, if not sooner.

What could possibly have been the purpose of helping him along?

The more questions Liza was asked, the more she wondered if all the deaths were just tragic occurrences that happened to take place at roughly the same time and in proximity to one another. She expressed this theory to Chief Inspector Dean.

Dean, her laptop open in front of her, looked over her glasses at Liza. "You don't think Mr. Ramsay's death was intentional?"

Liza shrugged. "None of this makes any sense. If I wasn't the one to inherit the Ramsay Castle, then the property would go into probate. Why take the risk for that outcome?"

Dean removed her reading glasses and rubbed her eyes with the heels of her hands. "You know, I've always been fascinated by this place. There are plenty of castles in Scotland, and being from up north, I've visited a lot of ruins over the years. But this place—a castle still inhabited by a private family. There's a sort of fairy-tale quality to it." She put her glasses back on. "But after the last few days, I never want to come back here again."

"Imagine how I feel. A month ago, I didn't know this place existed. Now, I seem to own it."

"Let's talk about your ownership, Ms. Ramsay. Before this morning, Callum had given you no indication he was going to leave you his entire estate, including the monetary assets?"

"No, none at all. I knew he wished me to inherit the castle, but he seemed to think I already knew about the money."

"The news of the money is what changed your mind about agreeing to assume ownership upon his death?"

"The money was a factor, yes. Without the funds, I wouldn't have had the means to sustain the estate in the manner it deserved."

"So you would have had to have partnered with an organization like the Royal Kingdom Trust, or you may have had to develop the property."

"Callum didn't want any of that to happen."

"No, he didn't." Dean looked as if she were working something out deep in the recesses of her mind.

Whatever it was, Liza couldn't see it. "Look," Liza said, laying her hands on the table in front of her. "I'm sure Mr. Douglas is going to challenge the legality of all of this, and given his purported connections, I don't expect it will be resolved quickly. Do you have any objections to me returning to Boston? There are some things I need to resolve. I can ask Mrs. Boyle to continue on for the time being, longer if she wants. And maybe Lachlan would be willing to continue to work here—"

"Lachlan?" the inspector interrupted.

Liza nodded. "I don't see why not. He hasn't been arrested. And since he hadn't even been released when Callum died, he can't be considered a suspect in that death too."

"Who said he *hadn't* been released?" Dean asked.

The two women stared at each other.

Finally, Liza asked, "So he wasn't with the police at the time of Callum's death?"

"He left the station around ten last night when his lawyer finally showed up."

Liza considered the implications of this. Callum's

death would have been of no benefit to Lachlan. Quite the opposite, in fact. Callum was Lachlan's protector. Surely, the police weren't looking at him for this potential crime as well.

"Lachlan wasn't here," Liza said aloud.

"Do you know that for a fact?"

Liza didn't know anything for a fact.

Dean gestured around her. "This place has no security cameras, which is just...*bonkers* to me. Who's to say he didn't let himself in, hide in one of the many rooms, and slip into Mr. Ramsay's room without anyone the wiser?"

Liza had remained silent for too long. She knew deep in her heart that Lachlan had not done this, and she was tired of keeping her mouth shut for the benefit of the investigation. "You could say the same thing about anyone!" Liza cried. "Who's to say a serial killer didn't do the same? You're spending a lot of time and effort trying to shoehorn Lachlan McClaren into these crimes, even when the motive isn't there. Why?"

"Because, Ms. Ramsay, I don't *like* it when someone gets away with murder. I don't think it's *fair* when a young girl loses her life because a privileged young man didn't get the outcome he wanted or thought he deserved. And I don't think it's *right* that the man in question gets to keep doing whatever he wants just because of his last name." Dean sat back and looked away, disgusted.

Liza's voice was quiet when she spoke again. "Are you saying Lachlan is a suspect in these deaths in order to right the wrongs of another murder investigation nearly a decade ago?"

"No, Ms. Ramsay." Inspector Dean sounded tired. "We're looking at Mr. McClaren so he cannot *continue* to get away with murder. Frankly, an attractive woman such as yourself, living on the same property—I'd certainly think ye'd have concerns similar to those of the police."

Something caught the edge of Liza's mind. Something she'd read about Nicola Munro. That name—*Dean*.

"Where did you say you were from, Chief Inspector?"

"I'm sure I didn't."

"You did though. Yesterday, you said the name of the place. And today, you mentioned you were from up north." Liza realized that she may be on slippery ground here, but she had a hunch.

Dean sighed. "Ms. Ramsay, I can't see how my hometown is of any relevance."

"Just curious," she said. "I may want to explore a bit."

Dean barked out a laugh. "Other than the remnants of a few castles, there's not much to see in Dalmally. It's more of thoroughfare, not a destination."

Liza's skin tingled. Dalmally was also where Nicola

had grown up. There was something else niggling at the back of her mind. Something she couldn't quite pinpoint. "You mentioned Nicola Munro to me yesterday, and I had the chance to ask Lachlan about her."

A shadow passed over Dean's face. "I'm sure he told you he had nothing to do with her murder."

"He did. He also said the police never even looked at anyone else."

"Because they didn't have to. They had their guy, and he walked."

"Does the name Liam Burns mean anything to you?"

"No, it doesn't." Dean's voice was tight and stretched thin like a rubber band about to snap.

Liza wetted her lips, took a breath. "Lachlan told me that Liam Burns was the reason Nicola ended the relationship with him. I just thought maybe—"

The chief inspector held up her hand. "I'm going to stop ye before you say something you might regret, Ms. Ramsay. I've looked over the files in that case, and the police did their job. It was the legal system that failed Nicola."

Liza pulled out her phone and opened the link to the article she'd sent herself earlier. The mugshot of William Burns stared up at her. She pushed the phone toward Dean, who glanced down reluctantly. She scrolled up on the article with a disinterested flick of her finger. "What is this?"

"Liam Burns has a record. I'm not saying that Lachlan didn't do it," Liza added in a rush. "But if she really was dating this other guy, and no one even considered him—"

"Ms. Ramsay." Dean's voice was hard. "I appreciate the due diligence, but I don't need your help."

"It's not that I think anyone did anything wrong—"

"Stop!" The word was a command, just shy of a shout. DCI Dean exhaled, cocked her head, and patted the air with the palm of her hand. She took a few deep breaths. "Nicola Munro was my niece, Ms. Ramsay. Her murder—" She stopped, corrected herself. "Lachlan McClaren…destroyed a family. Nicola's parents are now divorced. Nicola's brother is now an addict. I am not interested in alternate theories. I am only interested in justice."

As Chief Inspector Dean spoke, Liza remembered the name 'Dean' from Nicola's obituary. She thought that this woman was more interested in revenge than justice, but she didn't say anything else. She just nodded.

"As for this investigation," Dean continued, "you're free to go. In fact, I encourage you to leave. I'll just need contact information—mobile number, email addresses, next of kin." She slid a piece of paper across the table to Liza.

Liza provided the requisite information. She hesitated when she came to the emergency contact section. Then she wrote down the landline number for her grandparents.

When the chief inspector said nothing further, Liza grabbed her mobile phone, stood, and pushed her chair away from the table. Before she left, Dean raised her head. "And congratulations, Ms. Ramsay."

Liza pressed her lips together. This was no celebration and Dean knew it. Liza felt withered and old, filled with sorrow and regret. Callum Ramsay had been a kind man, a well-respected man, who deserved better than the passing he had received. She knew there would be a funeral and that his memory would be appropriately honored, but it had been tainted with a stink of scandal. It wasn't fair to him. Hot tears pricked at her eyes, and she turned abruptly so that Dean couldn't see them.

When she got to the door, Dean cautioned, "Watch yourself, Liza."

↓↓↓

In a room behind the library, a glass-paneled sunroom that overlooked the meadow leading to the Creagan River, Liza stood with her hands clasped behind her back. She watched as the breeze riffled some white, yellow, and purple wildflowers, the species of which she couldn't begin to define. Butterflies fluttered across the plain, and birds wheeled and dove toward unseen prey.

Liza hadn't yet properly mourned Callum. The deformed face of Brodie Graham still appeared in her thoughts. As far as she knew, the report from the medical examiner had not been returned, and she was left to wonder if his self-harm had anything to do with her last conversation with him. And Charlie Campbell. A boy she didn't know, but whose presence was surely still felt in these rooms.

By now Callum's body had been removed. He'd be lying naked and exposed on a stainless-steel table, or in a cold, dark drawer somewhere. Liza hoped she had made the right decision by ordering the autopsy. She wondered if she'd be expected to plan a funeral service as well. She had no idea what the process might be for that.

But for now, she was leaving; her flight booked, and her bag packed. She herself had been like a disrupting phantom, arriving to wreak havoc, then slipping away again with all the spoils and without a word.

Out the window, she looked to her left, craning her neck to see if she could catch a glimpse of Lachlan's cottage. Had he returned? Did he know she had been willed the estate? Would she ever see him again?

She was unsure of the future that stretched out in front of her, but whatever it held, she would have to face it alone. Any sense of adventure she should have felt instead seemed like a dim and hazy path, filled with pitfalls for every decision and booby traps at every turn.

She heard a noise behind her. She turned to find Mrs. Boyle in the doorway with a tray of tea and biscuits.

"I brought ye some tea and shortbread," she said tentatively, as if she were asking permission to enter.

Liza waved her in, glad for the company. "Thank you, Mrs. Boyle," she said. "I'll be taking my leave of you for a while. I'm heading back to Boston, as you suggested."

"But ye'll be returnin'."

It wasn't quite a question, but Liza nodded anyway.

Mrs. Boyle went to a small wicker table and laid out two small teacups and matching saucers with tiny pink rosebuds and gold trim. A corresponding vessel held sugar cubes ready to be served, with spoons decorated in a matching pattern. She poured a steaming cup of the fragrant liquid, and on individual plates served the shortbread.

"I'm sorry yer visit wasn't all it should have been," the older woman said, mirroring the direction of Liza's thoughts. Liza could see that Mrs. Boyle's eyes and face were red and mottled. She'd been crying.

"I'm sorry, too. When you said you were ready to move on, I'm sure it wasn't how you expected everything to end."

Quickly, Mrs. Boyle pulled a damp handkerchief from the pocket of her apron and dabbed at the corners of her eyes. "Certainly not," she said in a wobbly voice.

Liza wondered if she should embrace the woman, but decided she hadn't earned that right, so she just stared down at her tea while the older woman pulled herself together.

Mrs. Boyle managed to stem the flow of tears, and blew her nose noisily into the cloth. "Oh, goodness me," she said, with a pathetic laugh. "I'm a mess."

Liza picked at the edge of the shortbread. She had no appetite, and couldn't imagine ever being hungry again. But the cookie was buttery, crumbly, sweet, and salty, and it melted on her tongue. She took another bite.

"I want you to know that you're welcome to stay on here for as long as you like," Liza said when she'd swallowed the bite of pastry. "It won't be the same as working for Callum, and to tell you the truth, I have no idea where to begin with any of this." She fluttered her hand around her. "I haven't even seen the whole building yet. This is my first time in this room."

"Ye'll get there," Mrs. Boyle answered.

"What I'm saying is that there's an opportunity here for you. You may not have Callum to look after, but you'll have free rein over this place—cooking, interior decorating, landscaping. And it's early, but I've been thinking about some ways we might be able to share the history of the Ramsay Castle and lands with the public. Maybe we can offer tours or think about a bed and breakfast type establishment."

Mrs. Boyle raised her eyebrows. "That's certainly an interestin' idea. The laird talked of that a few years ago, before his illness."

Liza smiled and felt some sense of relief. She wouldn't want to do anything that Callum might disapprove of. "We could hire a staff again, and you could manage it. Maybe an up-and-coming chef that would work under your guidance. We could re-plant the original kitchen gardens and grow our own herbs, fruits, and vegetables. We could reconfigure some of the rooms into luxury suites and provide transportation into Edinburgh and beyond. I haven't even explored the country myself," said Liza, reminding herself that she didn't have any clue what she was talking about. "I know that Brodie Graham is gone, but we could partner with the Royal Kingdom Trust to offer tours, and clear out the meadow for outdoor weddings. Offer indoor winter weddings and holiday parties," she exclaimed, her words coming out in a rush.

Mrs. Boyle had gone silent, her face sullen as she stared at Liza.

"Maybe that's all too much," Liza said quickly. "I'm happy to have your input. It's all up for discussion."

"There won't be any discussion." Mrs. Boyle's voice was devoid of emotion, which startled Liza more than anger or tears would have.

"Oh," she said quickly. "Well…" Her words trailed off.

"I won't be stayin' here, Ms. Ramsay. I told ye last night, it's time to move on from this place."

Any enthusiasm Liza had started to feel was dashed once again. She nodded once. "Can I trouble you to stay on long enough to help out with Mr. Ramsay's funeral?" Her voice was tight. "He deserves that, at least."

"Aye, he does. But I took care of him nearly all of his life. I'm afraid someone else will need to take care of him in death."

Liza's breath was constricted as the weight of responsibility rested on her shoulders. She and her grandmother had planned a very small service for her mother, and the amount of detail that needed to be considered in the midst of grief had been overwhelming. She took a sip of tea.

Callum Ramsay had known the royal family and nobility. How on earth was she going to navigate that process alone? She assumed Mr. Douglas would be unwilling to provide support given this morning's developments.

"I'm going to need that number for Dr. Patel." Liza tried to keep her voice even despite her disappointment. She hadn't even thought to collect the information for his solicitor—Niall something—the man Callum trusted enough to assume responsibility for his last moments.

"I'm afraid I can't help with that either," said Mrs. Boyle. She folded her hands in her lap.

"I'm sorry?" Liza asked. She was first surprised. And then she became angry. Her emotions sat heavily between them.

"I said I can't help ye with that." Mrs. Boyle's voice was calm. She lifted her teacup to her lips then put it down and looked at Liza levelly.

Liza stared at her; in addition to her anger, she was confused by the sudden change in demeanor. Gone were the tears, the flighty hand motions, the grandmotherly bustling. This woman was calm and cold, as if all the emotion had leached out of her like air from a balloon.

She understood Mrs. Boyle's frustration with her situation, but how dare she leave Callum in this position? Had she no heart?

Instead of speaking, Liza picked up her cup and took a long swallow of the tea, which was incredibly sweet and had started to go cold. "I'll find Dr. Patel's number myself and make arrangements to return in a few days. When will you be vacating the premises?" She wasn't sure if she should allow Mrs. Boyle to stay in the castle alone. With Lachlan gone, there was no one left. Perhaps Chief Inspector Dean might be able to advise her on security procedures in these situations.

Mrs. Boyle didn't respond. She stared at Liza.

Liza stared back and repeated her question.

Still Mrs. Boyle remained quiet. Liza thought she saw a tic in the woman's face—a slight twitch of her eye.

Liza squinted. Her vision blurred slightly, and she blinked.

"Is somethin' wrong, Ms. Ramsay?" Mrs. Boyle asked.

Liza heard the words in slow motion. She put a hand to her head. She had made it through three deaths in the last three days. She would not let the stress of some logistics get to her.

She exhaled and found that it was difficult to inhale fully. Her breath began to come in short rapid bursts.

Determined not to allow Mrs. Boyle to see her anxiety, Liza attempted to repeat her question, but the words came out slurred and muddled. She couldn't get her mind to cooperate with her mouth in forming the right words. Her lips moved slowly like they had when she was a child and she'd stayed out in the snow and icy temperatures too long. Her face and extremities began to tingle.

She tried to take another breath, but it caught in her chest. Her heartbeat thundered in her ears.

The form of Mrs. Boyle disappeared and reappeared as a blurred blob across from her. Liza reached forward, but the other woman seemed very far away through a hazy veil of reality. In Liza's mind, she was screaming for help, but if any words emerged, she couldn't hear them.

She had a vague sense of shivering, then she was thrust backward into a velvety blackness. The last thing she remembered was the sense of someone bending over her—a man, she thought. She heard a low voice in the distance, before she felt the sensation of pulling, pulling, pulling.

And then, nothing.

Chapter 20

The darkness was absolute—an impenetrable, all-consuming, inescapable abyss. Whether her eyes were open or shut, the blackness consumed her.

If it weren't for the hard surface beneath her and the soul-crushing pain in her head and on the left side of her body, she would have sworn she'd entered a void of nothingness. She couldn't be sure that wasn't the case. She was certainly conscious, but maybe that's what death was like. The thought terrified her, and she broke out in a cold sweat.

The air was cold and damp in this void. It smelled of earth and mold.

She opened her mouth to scream, but instead of sound escaping, she vomited down the front of her clothes, retching painfully until it felt as if her insides were turning out. The act of breathing felt like being stabbed in her belly.

Despite the excruciating agony of movement, and the headache that threatened to split her face in two, she managed to push herself onto her knees. "Help!" she yelled feebly, but the voice was weak and the pain in her head throbbed until she retched again. Nothing came out but a thin trickle of bile.

She lay back down on the hard floor, closed her eyes, trying to catch her breath. She managed to inch the fingers of her right hand around her. All she could feel was stone and dirt, gritty beneath her fingertips.

She groaned and tried to cry out again; nothing but a whimper escaped her lips.

There was no sound at all, except for her heartbeat which thrummed steadily.

Da-DUM, Da-DUM, Da-DUM...

She felt another blackness slipping around her shoulders, like a cloak bestowed by a demon. *Come*, it seemed to whisper. *Let me clothe you, protect you. Let me take you away from all of this...*

She fought against it despite the pain. But in the end, the silky blackness that eased the agony, that offered oblivion, was too inviting. Too tempting. She gave over to the demon, who smiled with the face of her mother and whispered sweet nothings in her ears.

↓↓↓

When she next opened her eyes, the blackness was the same. The pain was still in her head, but now it was a dull ache behind useless eyes. She wondered if she were blind. How was she to know?

She brought her right hand in front of her face,

feeling the cavities of her eyes, her nose, her mouth. She seemed intact. She pressed her fingertips into her eye sockets, watching phantom shapes appear, morph into objects, then disappear when she tried to look directly at them.

Her entire body throbbed as if she'd been beaten all over, but her left side must have taken the worst of whatever battering she'd received. Her arm, her side, her hips...she was sure that bones were broken. Even that pain, though, seemed dulled slightly.

With a stiff movement, she touched her throbbing shoulder. She probed gently and winced sharply when she felt the spot where the upper part of her arm connected to the shoulder socket. It must be dislocated, she realized.

A wave of nausea caught her on its crest, but she breathed through it, and eventually her roiling stomach settled.

Where am I? she thought. *And how did I get here?*

She tried to remember. She pictured herself in the drawing room, at a table, talking to Chief Inspector Dean. She was supposed to go home, she remembered. To Boston.

Had her plane crashed? But...no. If there had been a crash she'd be dead, and certainly not in a black hole feeling pain all over her body.

Oh God, she thought. She had not made it out of Scotland, had she? Had she told anyone she'd planned to leave and when? She couldn't remember.

She had another vague memory. Standing in front of a window, talking to someone. *Who had it been?*

She groaned and tried to push herself up onto her knees again. This time, her weight held, and after a few minutes, she raised herself to her feet, favoring her right leg. It was hard to breathe, and she had no use of her left arm, but her legs still worked.

She remembered her phone, and with some effort, she reached around to her back pocket to see if by some miracle her phone was still on her. She wasn't surprised that her pocket was empty, but a new hollow feeling entered her soul.

She slumped back down for what could have been seconds or hours. Time had no meaning in this space.

Eventually, with her left arm tucked into her stomach, she reached her right hand out in front of her and carefully limped forward, fighting through the pain. Despite her slow movements, she was still startled when her fingers made contact with solid rock, the same gritty texture as the floor she'd been lying on.

The silence was deafening, and the blackness sweeping grave, horrific, and terrifying. Liza wanted to cry, but a voice in the back of her brain told her to save her energy. Tears flowed hot down her face, but she breathed through them and continued a slow trek around the space, shuffling her feet and feeling the walls. She counted each step that she took, estimating that it took her about fifty short steps around the space. It took about twenty-five to make her way across.

She had not encountered any other objects as she moved, which was a comfort. Part of her was convinced there may be another body down here with her, but that didn't seem to be the case. At least, she hadn't kicked anything as she'd shuffled along.

In the passing hours, she came to understand she was in the dungeon, the one Lachlan had shown her during her sleep-deprived, jet-lagged first day in the castle. The realization didn't come all at once. It was as if her mind had forgotten, and slowly, like a seeping of liquid under a door, it was filled with the knowledge.

How long ago had it been since she'd visited this location? How long had she been unconscious?

At the time, the lights along the walls had been illuminated, and Lachlan had shown her the grooves in the rock where the prisoners had been lowered. Whoever had consigned her to the dungeon had not lowered her at all. Instead, she must have been hefted over, discarded like garbage.

The knowledge of those last moments had also seeped back into her mind gradually.

It was Mrs. Boyle who'd approached her in the bright sunroom overlooking the meadow. It was Mrs. Boyle who had served her buttery shortbread and sweet, sweet tea. It was Mrs. Boyle who'd refused to answer her questions. It was Mrs. Boyle who must have laced her food or her drink with something toxic. Was she intended to die, her corpse to rot and be forgotten?

As soon as the thought had passed, she thought she heard something skitter high above. A rat, maybe? Smelling the stench of her odor, and vomit? Sensing her impending death?

The thought of unseen rodents made her want to stay on her feet, but eventually, she slumped back against a wall, her sense of time, direction, and space nonexistent. She could already have been down here for hours or days. There was nothing to measure her senses against, the only sound to keep her company the *Da-DUM, Da-DUM, Da-DUM* of her heartbeat.

One thing she did know, was that Mrs. Boyle would not have been able to drag her body down here and heft her over the wall alone. The woman may have been stronger than she looked, but Liza was taller, and even though she was slim, she was healthy. At her size, a dead weight would have been nearly impossible for Mrs. Boyle to handle alone.

Liza thought of Lachlan McClaren. Lachlan would have had no trouble lifting her.

Then she remembered Mrs. Boyle's conversation with the unknown person in the kitchen after she'd met with Callum to sign the papers. Lachlan had been released from police custody. Had he been the other voice she'd heard? Had Mrs. Boyle and Lachlan been co-conspirators, working together toward some goal known only to themselves?

She thought of Brodie Graham's body, of Lachlan cutting it down, of Callum's reference to seeing *them*. Is that why Callum was gone as well?

No, she thought vehemently. She refused to believe Lachlan had done this to her. He may have been many things, but he was no murderer. She was sure of it.

She was depleted by pain—dehydrated, exhausted, and hopeless. It was cool in the dungeon, but not freezing, and in her jeans and sweater, she was warm enough for now. But did that really even matter? She clumsily tucked her long hair into the neck of her sweater, absurdly afraid that rats would make a nest of her hair while she slept…or when she died, since she wasn't sure if she'd wake again.

⸸⸸⸸

Then something *did* wake her…by tugging at her hair. Liza scampered to her feet despite the pain in her body and the heaviness of her limbs.

Her heart thrumming in her chest, she frantically searched in the inky blackness. Still no light, still no sound. No scurrying of little claws against the stone.

There was, however, a smell. Her nostrils quivered, and she recognized the acrid scent of smoke and the charred odor of burnt wood and fire. The odor hung heavy in the air.

Liza froze as she realized what that meant.

Her throat was parched and sore, but she screamed as loud and as long as she could. She screamed with the hope there was someone fighting the fire and that someone might hear her.

She'd thought she would die of exposure or dehydration. Now she realized she might burn alive.

She screamed until her pharynx felt ripped apart, like the vibration of her vocal cords had carved her throat raw and bloody.

There wasn't much hope. No one here would be looking for her if they thought she'd boarded a flight home. No one at home expected her, so there was no one to alert the authorities here that she was missing.

She was alive in a limbo, and in that limbo she would die. From starvation, dehydration, exposure, smoke, fire. It didn't matter at all. *She* didn't matter at all.

She let herself cry then, and even though the sobs wracked her body, her body didn't contain enough fluid for tears to fall.

Her head bent forward; something tugged hard at her hair. It was startling enough to cause the tears to immediately cease, and she whipped her head around though she knew she couldn't see anything.

She inched away from the area where she sat.

Was the smell of smoke getting stronger?

She coughed, a raspy, thin sound. When she inhaled, smoke filled her lungs, causing her to cough more intensely. Every spasm bruised her head, her body, her bones.

She was going to suffocate. That's how this would end. She would suffocate in the dungeon of a castle that she owned, in the same place where an ancient ancestor had perished. It was a curse, she realized. The Ramsays were cursed, and she was only the latest victim in a long line of tragedy.

A fresh coughing fit overtook her, and she thought of the ghosts whom she'd failed. She thought of Callum and Lachlan and Owen. The face of Mrs. Boyle floated in front of her, and she realized that all this time the woman had been her nemesis, without her even knowing it. She'd been such a fool.

On her hands and knees, pain shooting through her shoulder as she gasped, something pulled her hair hard enough that her head snapped back. This was no phantom, no figment of her imagination. There was someone, or something, in this dungeon with her.

Terror coursed through her veins, and she was more petrified of the thing she could not see than she was of suffocating to death. She skittered back again, praying that the invisible ropes of smoke would strangle her before the creature in the pitch black could touch her again.

She heard a low growl—a man's voice—and she thrust herself backward, ignoring the pain in her left shoulder as she moved frantically away from the noise.

Her hand touched something on the floor and she jerked her arm away.

She paused, and the world went very still. Whatever she'd felt was small, smooth, and solid.

Her phone…

She immediately moved to her knees, searching the ground with her fingertips. Another fit of coughing shook her. Her eyes stung. She fought through the slow asphyxiation of the smoke.

Finally, her fingers closed around the object. She felt the webbing of cracks on the glass screen, but when she pressed the button along its slim side, the face lit up, and through a thick haze, she made out the photo background: her standing with Owen in Provincetown that spring. They were bundled in sweatshirts and jeans, smiling broadly as the wind from the ocean whipped at their faces.

Between the sudden light and the smoke, her eyes felt as if they were on fire. She squinted.

There was no service this far underground, but she awkwardly pressed the buttons on either side of her phone until finally the SOS slider appeared and activated the emergency service. She had very little hope the feature would work.

But she felt a surge of electricity so strong that her fingers tingled against the phone. Her molecules seemed to be vibrating rapidly, and her body felt as if it would break apart into a million pieces.

She heard a voice through the speaker: *What is your emergency?*

She could only make a wheezing sound as the smoke thickened around her, but she managed one final cough before pricks of light appeared at the periphery of her vision then burst open like a sudden flash of Independence Day fireworks.

Then, everything faded, faded, and she thought she dreamed that someone called, *She's down here! Follow me this way!*

Chapter 21

Liza sat up, struggling to sip slowly from the paper cup. A nasal cannula connected her to a steady stream of oxygen, and her right arm was connected to an IV bag of clear liquids.

A cheery-looking nurse around the same age as Liza bustled into the room.

"And how are we feeling?"

"I'm okay," Liza whispered. Her throat was sore, but she was parched, and her lips were cracked and peeling. She had to force herself not to gulp down the water.

The nurse's nametag read 'Eden Ritchie, R.N'.

"You'll be out of here in a jiffy. Are you hungry yet?"

Liza shook her head, and Eden Ritchie patted her arm. "No rush on that." She pointed to the IV bag. "You're getting all the nutrients you need into you, and you're young and healthy. You'll heal up right as rain. I don't expect you'll have any significant effects from the fall once that shoulder heals. But your doctor at home will need to check you out."

Liza's left arm was secured in a sling across her stomach. Another wire tethered to a monitor was tracking her vital signs and heartbeat.

"What about the poison?" Liza asked, testing it out.

Eden shook her head. "You'll have to ask the doctor about that. My guess is that you ingested just enough to knock you out. Lucky, lucky," she said as she plumped the pillows behind Liza's head; she smelled faintly of sugar and roses.

"Ye've got some people waiting to talk with you when you feel up to it."

Liza took one last sip of water and placed the cup on the tray beside her. She wasn't sure what day it was or how long she'd been in this bright white hospital room. When she'd woken, she had vague memories of events before she got here: strong arms hefting her into an embrace, the sensation of being pulled up and up, pressure tugging at her body. A hazy face bending over her on the ground, and rain or water hitting her cheeks. Bright lights, blurry faces, indistinct voices.

"Some handsome men keeping watch for you out there," Eden continued to smile. "If I weren't married, I might ask to borrow one of them." Her lips pulled into a smile.

When Liza didn't smile back, Eden said, "I'm just teasing' you."

Liza looked toward the door, but the only person she could see was a figure in a dark uniform sitting in a chair just outside. "Is that a cop?" she whispered, placing her fingers to her throat.

Eden's smile faded. "They just wanted to make sure you're extra secure. Nothing to worry about. Not on my watch," she said ominously. "There are two other coppers who want to talk with you, too. Detectives, I think. I told them I'd call when you gave me the word."

Liza must have made a face because Eden Ritchie said, "Take all the time you need." The nurse made a notation in a chart that was affixed to the top of the frame of her bed. "As I said, you're a lucky woman," she repeated.

Liza didn't feel very lucky, though she knew she was fortunate to be alive. She vaguely wondered what else was known about her situation—the deaths, her name, her inheritance. Her gaze shifted back to the police officer outside.

"So, how about it?" Eden Ritchey said, smiling. "Ready for some company?"

Liza took a deep breath, but it hurt her chest and she coughed as the oxygen pumped into her lungs. Eden had mentioned a handsome man, and the only one she could think of was Lachlan. But she doubted very much he would have been there to see her. And if he was, was she ready to talk to him? The answer to that was *no*, but she didn't think there would ever be a time she'd be quite ready for that. The explanations and excuses. The questions and defense.

To Eden Ritchey, she just shrugged weakly.

The nurse smiled and winked. "I promise it'll make you feel better."

But that was a promise Eden Ritchey couldn't keep, because a few minutes after she'd left, Owen walked into the room.

Liza's eyes widened, and a million emotions surged through her all at the same time. The monitor next to her beeped loudly.

"Hey babe," he said, sidling up to the bedside. He tried to smile, but his face pulled into more of a grimace. Liza noticed how white his teeth were on his unshaven face which was dark with stubble, something that was quite unlike him.

"You look like hell," he said, taking her right hand carefully and holding it like it were a wet fish.

She knew she shouldn't be offended. She had reason to look like hell, after all, and she was certain he was right. But she felt defensiveness rising in her chest, and she pulled her hand away.

"That didn't come out right," he said. "I meant that it's good to see you."

She didn't bother pointing out that those were two very different sentences and messages.

"I have so many questions," he said. "What the hell happened?"

Liza stared up at him. Eden Ritchie had been right about one thing. Owen was an exceedingly handsome man: dark wavy hair, sea green eyes with unusually dark rings around the irises. His jaw was strong, and his face chiseled. After spending so much time in the gym, his physique was toned and sleek. She felt the pull of familiarity when she looked at him.

She gestured toward her throat and whispered, "It's hard to talk."

He mimed hitting himself in the forehead with the heel of his hand. "Sorry, babe. Well, I know some of it." He pointed toward the door. "Everyone is talking about it out there. They tried to *murder* you," he said in a stage whisper. "And that old guy left you millions and a freaking castle? In Scotland!" He laughed, his white teeth gleaming. "I was pissed when Raj told me you'd basically abandoned your job, but this more than makes up for it."

Liza frowned. "How did you know I was here?"

His expression shifted from gleeful to sheepish. "I had a friend run a trace on your phone, so I knew you were near Edinburgh. I headed over here without your exact location. Then some guy tracked me down to let me know you were in the hospital. You were unconscious for a few days, and they've let me hang out here. The nurses have been great."

Liza thought of Nurse Ritchie's reaction to him and bristled.

Then, all at once, she remembered his betrayal—the reason she'd made this trip in the first place. She wanted to hurl words and accusations at him. She wanted to yell and make demands and scream her frustrations. But her voice and lungs wouldn't allow that. And her body and soul were so tired. "You cheated on me," she said simply.

Owen brought his hands in front of his chest, his palms up. A plea. "No, babe. Those messages. They weren't what they seemed."

Liza blinked at him.

"Look, there was—It was nothing," he said, stammering. "Nothing more than a flirtation."

"Did you sleep with her?" Liza was amazed at the utter calmness in her voice. Then again, after having nearly died—first from poison, then from a fall, and finally from a fire—Owen's dalliance had lost some of its power over her emotions.

Owen grabbed her hand again. "Liza, I love *you*. There's never been anyone else but you."

The lack of a straight answer gave Liza her answer.

"I'll make it up to you," he said. "Whatever you need from me." His words came out in a rush, intense and desperate. "Hold on," he said, dropping her hand and holding up a finger. "Just one minute. Just one." He backed toward the door, eyes on hers, still holding up that finger.

Liza thought she should want to cry, but she didn't. She only felt the vaguest sense of disappointment, a bittersweet nostalgia for the lost years.

As she turned her head, her hair caught on the pillow, tugging at her scalp. She brought her good hand to her head quickly. Remembering…something. A chill snaked down her spine.

Then Owen was back with something in his hand. Something small.

She noticed the gathering crowd of hospital staff just outside the door. The police officer twisted to look inside the room.

No…

Owen dropped to one knee beside the hospital bed, flipping open the box to reveal a solitaire diamond—a huge, ostentatious thing that winked at her obscenely.

"Elizabeth Catherine Ramsay," he began.

"Owen," she whispered, interrupting, trying to stop him before he could get the words out.

He ignored her. "Would you do me the honor of becoming my wife?"

He beamed up at her, his eyes shining. A group of nurses, including Eden Ritchie, were watching expectantly from outside the door.

"Owen," she said again quietly. "We have to talk about this."

"We can talk about anything, babe. We can get through anything together."

Liza stared at the ring. What was she supposed to say? She opened her mouth and shut it again, no words coming out. She was fully aware that she still smelled faintly of vomit through the antiseptic, despite whatever efforts they'd made to clean her up while she was unconscious.

Should she agree for the crowd and allow him to save face?

Maybe they could even work it out. Maybe she wouldn't have to travel this strange new adventure alone. She and Owen had been together a long time. She knew his habits, knew his quirks. They were mostly compatible, except for the infidelity.

She looked into his face—open, eager, and boyish. This was the man she'd fallen in love with. But there was something she needed to know first.

"Owen…did my father ever write to me?"

His smile faltered. "What?"

"Did I ever receive any letters from my father?"

His arms fell a few inches, but the ring remained outstretched toward her. "I'm not sure what that has to do with anything."

"I just need to know," she said.

"You hated your father. You told me that over and over again."

She noted the use of the past tense. And she waited.

Finally, he said, "You may have received a few letters with his name on them."

Liza's heart sank. "And you kept them from me?"

"Babe, you got so agitated every time you mentioned him. I was trying to protect you."

She went very still. "Did you know he was dead?"

Owen sighed. "Come on, babe. Let's not do this now."

"Did you know?"

"A letter came about six months ago. I accidentally opened it. You were out of town. I thought they probably would have contacted you by email too. When you got home, you didn't mention it, and it didn't seem important."

Didn't seem important.

She wanted to scream at him that the importance was not his determination to make. But she didn't scream. She felt numb.

Owen thrust the ring toward her again. "Babe, none of that is important. The only important thing right now is you and me and making a commitment to stay together forever. Because I love you."

A movement outside caught her attention. The gaggle of nurses had parted, and a man stood in the doorway. Lachlan McClaren.

Relief surged through her. He had not been arrested, was not in handcuffs. The police officer in the doorway made no move to restrict Lachlan's movements. Which meant that he was free.

He *was* frowning, though, at the image of Owen kneeling in front of the hospital bed.

He looked up and met Liza's eyes. His gaze softened and something passed between them.

Then he turned and walked away. She wanted to call after him, but she couldn't. Her voice wouldn't allow that. She watched him go.

Eden Ritchie watched him too.

"Liza?" Owen said, the first hint of doubt creeping into his voice.

Liza looked back down. "No, Owen," she said. Her voice stronger. "I will not marry you."

Chapter 22

Liza nearly apologized but stopped herself. She hadn't forced Owen to be unfaithful. She hadn't asked him to find her in Scotland. And she certainly hadn't asked him to propose in front of a group of strangers. She was not sorry.

The group outside the door, sensing the direction of this conversation, started to awkwardly disperse, murmuring quietly to each other. Eden Ritchie gave her a look she wasn't able to interpret then walked away.

Still, Owen did not get up from his knees.

"Please stand up," she said.

He complied and stood, flipping closed the little velvet box. "This was too much." He slipped the box into the pocket of his jeans, where it bulged unnaturally. "You're exhausted and not in your right mind. I should have waited until you felt better—"

Liza held up her hand. "Owen."

He went silent and looked at her.

"I am not going to marry you."

She saw the nearly imperceptible flair of his nostrils. "Liza." His tone was calm, patient, condescending. "You've been through a lot."

She knew he planned to say more, but she broke in before he could continue. "You're right. I *have* been through a lot. I've been through more than enough to know that this relationship is not what I need right now."

"*Right now*," he repeated. "It might take some time. But don't throw away what we've built together. Take a few days—a week even—and let's see how you feel after you've had a chance to get your bearings."

She exhaled, wishing that the cannula were out of her nose and that she were free of her wires and tethers. She felt claustrophobic. Owen had planted his feet, and didn't look like he planned to budge. Liza just wanted to close her eyes and sink back into her pillows. She'd nearly agreed with him simply to get him to leave, when Nurse Ritchie strode confidently into the room.

"Sorry to interrupt," she said briskly. "I need to check Ms. Ramsay's vital signs."

"We're in the middle of something." Owen's response was abrupt and dismissive.

"It was not a request." The nurse stood facing him, her hands on her hips.

Owen looked from Eden to Liza and back again. "Fine," he conceded. "But this conversation isn't over, Liza. I'm not going to let you make a mistake this big without a fight."

He stared at her a second longer, waiting for a reply, but Liza shut her eyes.

When she could sense he'd left the room, Liza opened her eyes, waiting for Eden to come to her bedside, but the nurse stood closer to the door, making sure Owen had walked down the hall.

"He's gone," she said to Liza. She turned back around. "I'm so sorry about that. I thought he'd be a comfort to you. He made it well known at the reception station that he was your boyfriend."

"He is. *Was*," Liza corrected herself. "It's a long story."

"It's not as if you won't have other options given your circumstances." She approached Liza with her stethoscope, placing it on her chest, and asked her to inhale and exhale. It hurt to breathe deeply, and Liza winced.

"The cracked ribs are nothing but a nuisance," Eden said. "But they're all taped up. As soon as the doctor has had a chance to take a quick look at you, we can get this oxygen out of your nose. Your lungs sound clear and your oxygen levels are normal. A near miracle, all things considered." She took the chart from Liza's bedframe and scribbled something.

"Does everyone know about the inheritance?" Liza asked.

Eden looked up from the chart, then hitched her

chin toward the door. "Why do you think the police are out there?"

"To guard against the person who tried to murder me."

Eden slid the chart back into his holder and patted Liza's hand. "Maybe it's time we get the chief inspector in here to talk to you."

Liza shut her eyes. "Can it be after I sleep?"

"Of course," Eden said. Liza thought she might have added something else, but she sank into a comfortable darkness, free from people, decisions, money, and murder.

⸸⸸⸸

She woke up to voices. Eden Ritchie and a doctor in a crisp white lab coat were standing at the foot of her bed. After a brief examination and a few questions from the doctor, who looked disengaged at best, he directed Eden to remove the cannula from her nose.

"We'll keep the IV in for one more day," said the nurse, "and once you seem stable enough, we'll get you on your way."

Liza nodded. She tried not to show the burst of panic that resulted from those words. Where was she supposed to go? Back to Boston with taped-up ribs and her arm in a sling? She had no clothes. And where was her passport if the castle had burned down? *Had* it burned down? The question hadn't occurred to her until just that minute.

"DCI Dean is waiting outside if you feel up to a conversation with her now," Eden said, the statement a question.

Liza nodded.

Dean appeared in the doorway a few minutes later. "Ms. Ramsay?"

Liza pushed herself up awkwardly in the bed with her right arm.

Dean walked in and pulled a chair close to the bedside.

"Where's Lawson?" Liza asked.

"He's taking care of the investigation at the station. How are you feeling?"

Liza shrugged. Did it even matter?

Dean pursed her lips. "You're one lucky lady."

"That's what everyone keeps telling me." She knew she sounded cynical, but she couldn't help it.

Dean seemed to ignore that. "How much do you remember?"

Liza let out a breath. "I remember having tea and shortbread with Mrs. Boyle, but everything is hazy after that. I remember waking up in darkness. I remember pain. I remember smoke. I remember something pulling my hair." She inadvertently touched her hair and shivered.

Dean narrowed her eyes at that. "She poisoned

you," the inspector said. "With cyanide. You didn't drink enough to kill you, only to knock you out for a while."

Eden Ritchie had confirmed as much, though Liza felt nauseous with the knowledge that if she'd taken a healthier swallow of the sweet tea then she wouldn't be having this conversation right now.

"She couldn't have done it alone," Liza said. "There must be someone still out there." She prayed the detective wouldn't say Lachlan's name.

"She didn't do it alone," Dean confirmed. "Kenneth Morrison is in custody along with Margaret Boyle."

Liza's eyes widened. "Mr. Morrison? But…why?"

Dean rubbed her temples. "Boyle and Morrison had been in a relationship for some time. And Morrison and Douglas had a deal to develop the Ramsay land. But Callum kept foiling that. First by disinheriting Hamish Ramsay, then by finding your father. It was Morrison that ran him off the road, by the way. He claims he was just trying to scare him off."

Liza tried to process that information. "What about Charlie Campbell?"

"The kid was in the wrong place at the wrong time. He overheard Boyle and Morrison discussing the land and tried to blackmail them." She shook her head. "Mrs. Boyle gave him the two chessmen from the library to keep him quiet. But his mother found them and asked Lachlan about it. Lachlan thought he'd stolen them, so he returned them, made Charlie apologize to Callum and fired the boy. Charlie went back to Mrs. Boyle to demand repayment, and we think it was Mr. Morrison who hit Charlie in the head. That's according to Mrs. Boyle, anyway. We don't know if he meant to kill the child. But it's likely, since they were probably planning to make millions of pounds off the sale of the set themselves. Couldn't have other people knowing about the treasure they held."

Liza hesitated to even ask about Brodie Graham, but Dean told her anyway. Explained that his drink had been laced with cyanide, and it was Mr. Morrison and Mrs. Boyle working together that had managed to get him in the tree. They knew it would cast suspicion on Lachlan, given the use of the ladder and tools and Brodie's flirtation with Liza.

Liza blushed at that. "But why?"

"Because Brodie nearly talked you into partnering with the Royal Kingdom Trust. And it was easier to kill him than it was to kill you. Then when you told Mr. Morrison you had no interest in working with him, Mrs. Boyle tried to talk you into going home."

"I nearly did," said Liza. They both sat in silence for a minute. Liza listened to the muted sounds of the hospital outside the door, lost in her own thoughts. After a few minutes, she said, "I don't understand why they killed Callum."

"Because they didn't know you'd agreed to accept

the inheritance or that Mr. Ramsay had changed his will legally. If he'd died without changing the will, the estate would have gone into probate."

"That wouldn't have helped them."

Dean shrugged. "Mr. Douglas has friends in high places. From what we can gather, he figured his chances for a payout were better if the estate had to be split up among various distant relatives."

"Mr. Douglas was in on it?"

"Lawson is trying to figure out the level of his involvement. We don't think he had anything to do directly with the murders, but we're holding him on other charges having to do with Callum's business dealings."

Liza was quiet for a minute, trying to understand all of this. It seemed so ill-advised. "So, getting rid of me was the last piece of the puzzle?"

"Mrs. Boyle has been quiet about that, probably because you can implicate her. For everything else, she's blamed Mr. Morrison."

"So much for true love," said Liza, thinking about Mrs. Boyle's reaction to Brodie's body in the tree. Her acting abilities had really come in handy. She remembered the conversation she'd overheard through the dumbwaiter, lamenting the way it had to be. They must have been talking about killing Callum. "I can implicate her in Callum's murder," said Liza, and told Dean what she'd heard.

Dean thrust her glasses onto her nose and made some notes in her notepad. "We'll take an official statement when you're out of here, if you can find some time to come down to the station." Liza nodded, though she wasn't sure how she was meant to get around.

"And Lachlan?" Liza finally asked quietly.

"Lachlan is the reason you're still alive, Ms. Ramsay," Dean said quietly.

Liza waited.

"After they threw you in the dungeon, Mrs. Boyle told everyone you'd left. We didn't have any reason to think otherwise. I'd told you to go, and I didn't expect you'd stick around to say goodbye." She continued. "Lachlan is the one who was suspicious. He actually drove to the airport and convinced someone to let him know if you'd boarded your flight."

Liza didn't have to mention that Dean and Lawson could have uncovered that information with one phone call.

"When Mrs. Boyle realized he might discover your body, she started a fire in the kitchen, which is just above the dungeon. I guess she figured if the debris collapsed into the vaults, ye might never be discovered." Dean shrugged. "It wasn't the best plan, but she was getting desperate. Logic seemed to have gone out the window by that point."

Liza felt like a fool for trusting Mrs. Boyle, for discounting Mr. Morrison. And she felt even worse about ever suspecting Lachlan McClaren.

"We couldn't believe it when your phone pinged. There is absolutely no service that far underground."

Liza remembered the tugging at her hair, the flow of electricity she'd felt. She had a feeling she'd had a little extra help from someone far, far in the past, in alerting the living, present-day world to her location. Or maybe not so far in the past. Maybe that someone had always been just a breath away.

Liza took a sip from the cup of water that sat on the tray table beside the bed. All at once, she felt famished.

Dean went on. "We're searching for your clothes and passport, but you may have to stay here—in Scotland—a while longer if we can't locate your documents. You'll need to meet with your solicitor to identify next steps. Without your identification, that'll be problematic, but you'll figure it all out. In addition to the formal statement, once the trial begins, ye'll have to testify against the defendants."

Dean kept talking, but Liza had stopped listening. She could do absolutely nothing about any of this in her current state, and she was more concerned with the fact that she may be released without one item of clothing left to her. She assumed her phone had been found, but she had no idea where it was. Perhaps Eden Ritchie may be able to help her with all of that.

"Did you hear me, Liza?"

Liza looked over at Dean, not even pretending to be interested in whatever question Dean must have asked.

"Lachlan McClaren isn't a suspect in any of this?" she asked.

Dean pressed her hands together. "No. He is not."

Liza wanted to ask about Nicola Munro, but she wasn't sure how to bring up the tragedy of this woman's niece without sounding insensitive.

She didn't have to.

Dean cleared her throat. "I wanted to let you know, too..." Her words disappeared on her breath, and she paused. "That man that you told me about—Liam Burns. I visited him in Shotts Prison, where he's currently serving fifteen years for assault." She looked down, unclasped, and reclasped her hands. "He confessed to Nicola's murder."

Liza felt her insides unclench. Finally, Lachlan could be free of the cloud of suspicion that had hung over his head for the past eight years. He no longer had to hide in the Ramsay cottage, skulking away from the guarded eyes of a public who believed him to be a cold-blooded killer. She wanted to weep in mourning for his lost years and in joy for the clear path ahead of him.

"We didn't even know she'd been dating someone else," Dean said, swallowing hard.

Liza wondered if Dean had apologized to Lachlan. She didn't ask.

Dean sat there a moment longer, then she rose.

"Do you have any additional questions before I let you rest for the night?"

Liza started to shake her head, then she pointed to the policeman—the officer—in the chair outside the door. "Is that a permanent fixture?"

"You're about to be a very wealthy woman, Ms. Ramsay. And your name has been in the press for a few days. Until you can address your own security, we'll be providing an officer. It's the least we can do," she added softly.

Liza nodded her thanks, and Dean thrust out her hand. Liza shook it, and for the first time, she felt like she and Dean were on equal ground.

Chapter 23

When evening arrived, Liza found herself alone. Eden Ritchie's shift had ended, and without a phone or an old castle to wander, the only thing Liza had to do was flip through channels on an outdated television affixed to the ceiling opposite her bed.

Characters with British accents overacted while a canned laughter track cackled and rang out with loud applause. Liza stared at the flickering images without really seeing them. Instead, she was thinking about Callum and his viewing and funeral, wondering again how she was going to manage to plan that memorial, given the arrest of Mrs. Boyle and Mr. Douglas.

Once her mind began racing, it didn't stop. She puzzled over her lost passport and ID, and chewed the inside of her lip while she considered the process for replacing those documents. She also needed to contact Dr. Patel and Mr. Murphy as soon as she was released to understand the next steps for the estate.

On the television, spontaneous laughter rang out as a portly man burst into a house filled with unsuspecting party guests.

She supposed she'd need to find a place to stay as well. She wished she'd thought to ask Chief Inspector Dean about fire damage to the castle. The detective hadn't seemed overly concerned, so Liza doubted the entire place had burned down. Could a stone castle even burn to the ground?

Her stomach growled, and despite the assurance of nutrients pumped into her via IV, she wished she had something more substantial to eat than the dinner offering—a bland chicken and leek pie with wilted cauliflower, and a wobbly and flavorless vanilla pudding for dessert.

She still had some of the ginger ale left, and she distractedly sucked soda out of the small green can.

The light-blocking curtains hanging over the window had been shut, and the hushed sounds of the hallways made it seem much later than it really was. According to the guide displayed at the bottom of the television screen, it was only a little past eight in the evening. If she drifted off to sleep now, she suspected she'd be awake in the wee hours of the morning. Liza sighed.

Owen had not returned, though she figured he would. It wasn't that she wanted him to come back, but she found herself looking toward the door more than once when she heard the shuffling of feet in the hallway.

At half past nine, a new nurse, younger and bored,

came in to listen to her lungs and monitor her vital signs. She distractedly asked Liza if she needed anything. Liza could have used some company, but the nurse barely made eye contact. Liza didn't keep the girl any longer than the girl was willing to be kept.

At ten, Liza switched off the murmur of the television and sat for a few minutes in silence. She prepared herself for a restless night of intermittent dozing mingled with paralyzing uncertainty and soul-crushing loneliness, punctuated with questions about why the spirits had seen fit to spare her life when she felt so utterly useless.

A button on the railing of the hospital bed controlled the room's lights, and she was just about to turn them off when she saw a shadow in the doorway and heard a soft knock.

She looked up; the bottom fell out of her heart.

Lachlan McClaren stood silhouetted by the stark bright light of the hospital's hallway.

"Hi," she said, lamely. There was so much to say to him, and yet no words to say it.

"Hi," he responded. He did not move from the doorway.

She was suddenly conscious of her unwashed hair, her sponge-bathed body, her thin hospital gown. She pulled the bedsheet up higher on her torso.

"Can I come in?" He was holding a large cloth bag in his hand.

She gestured him in and he shuffled closer.

"How did you get past the reception desk and the cop? It must be far past visiting hours."

He stood halfway between the door and the bed, unsure of how close he should approach. "The nurse was so engrossed watching videos on her phone that she didn't look up. The cop," he pointed toward the door, "is a friend of mine from school."

"So much for security, I guess," Liza quipped. Then saw the look on Lachlan's face. "I just meant, generally," she clarified.

He glanced back at the door. "I can come back tomorrow."

"Stay. Please."

Lachlan looked as if he were debating it, and Liza was prepared to plead, then he held up the bag by its handle and stepped forward. "Eden told me ye might be released as early as tomorrow. That's a miracle, ye know. I brought ye some clothes and some toiletries."

She took the bag and glanced inside: a burgundy-colored dress, a pair of tan ankle boots, and jean jacket all with the tags still affixed. Amazingly, they were all her size. At the bottom of the bag was her own hairbrush, a toothbrush and toothpaste, and her makeup.

She glanced up at him, about to ask where he'd gotten them. He answered before she could get the words out. "Yer suitcase and clothes are gone, but they didn't bother to clean out your washroom at the castle."

"The castle hasn't burned down then?" Liza asked, cradling the bag on her lap with her good hand.

"The Ramsays and their home have withstood far more than the lame attempts of a couple of amateur villains." The half smile on Lachlan's face faded quickly. "But I hope they rot in hell for what they did to poor Charlie and Callum. What they tried to do to you."

Liza looked down.

"The kitchen is a loss, though," Lachlan said. "It'll need to be completely rebuilt."

Liza nodded. Another awkward silence fell between them.

She looked down at the clothes. "How did you know my size?"

"Eden still had the ruined outfit ye were wearing when ye came in. She was able to check the tags."

"You'll have to tell her thank you for me," Liza said. She knew her voice was tight, and a little bit of petulance had crept in.

Lachlan seemed amused. "I doubt I'll see her again, but if I do, I'll be sure to pass along yer appreciation."

Another silence.

Liza scrambled for something to say to cut the tension. "I wasn't sure what I was going to do without any clothes," she said, then realized that those weren't the words for which she was searching.

But Lachlan didn't seem to hear her. Instead, he was looking at the fingers of her left hand peeking out from the dark blue sling across her body.

She swallowed, wondering how to address the proposal he'd witnessed earlier.

"Will ye be staying at the castle then? Or will ye be staying in Edinburgh with Owen?"

She glanced up sharply. "Owen's still in Edinburgh?"

"That's what he said when he left earlier." At the look on Liza's face, he shrugged. "Owen and I got to know each other pretty well in the waiting room." He said this was just the slightest hint of sarcasm. Or amusement. She couldn't tell which.

"You knew he planned to propose?"

"The whole hospital knew. We'd even seen the ring."

There was a long pause. "I said no," she stated flatly.

"I figured as much, given the speed of his departure. He said he was going to Edinburgh to figure out 'next steps'." He made air quotes with his fingers. "Still, I wasn't sure if maybe ye hadn't changed yer mind. Ye've been through a lot, and he's familiar and comfortable."

She wanted to offer a retort to that. An argument. But she was quiet, not wanting to admit the amount of times her mind had veered in that direction. "I can't imagine how he knew where to find me," she said instead.

"I called him."

"*You?*" The word was much louder than she'd intended, and she glanced at the door in case she'd roused attention from observant hospital staff. But no one seemed to be in the hallway, let alone looking in their direction.

"Ye were in pure bad shape, Liza. He deserved to know ye'd almost died."

"How did you know how to reach him?" she asked instead.

He shoved his hand in his pocket and pulled out her phone. Cracks spiderwebbed one side of the screen, but when she reached for it and held it up to her face, it came to life with the image of her and Owen on the beach in Cape Cod.

Liza quickly dimmed the image, but looked up at Lachlan. "Thank you," she said. She'd at least be able to call for a taxi, figure out how to apply for emergency travel documents, and locate Dr. Patel. It was a start.

She turned the phone over in her hand and ran her thumb across the rough screen. "Lachlan—" she began at the same time Lachlan said, "I'd like to say—"

They looked at each other with awkward smiles, and Lachlan gestured, signaling her to speak first.

She moved the bag to one side and set the phone

on the table beside her. Then she swallowed. "I owe you an apology," she said. "Mrs. Boyle and Mr. Douglas both cast suspicion in your direction, and I fell into their trap. If I'd trusted my instincts, they would have never taken you down to the police station, and Callum might still be alive."

"Are ye kidding me?" Lachlan asked.

Liza opened her mouth, but she wasn't sure how to respond, so she shut it again.

"Liza, ye were the one who told DCI Dean about Liam Burns. They arrested him for Nicola's murder." He stepped forward and then abruptly stopped. "I'm finally free."

Liza was glad for that. He deserved to be free. He deserved to have a life. But if she were honest, she was sorry it was going to be a life away from Ramsay Castle. He seemed to belong there just as much as the ghosts of Lady Catherine and Sir Alexander.

She opened her mouth, and what came out surprised her. "'So, now, the danger dared at last, look back, and smile at perils past'."

Lachlan grinned. "Sir Walter Scott. Did ye ken he stayed at the castle often in his youth? He was a friend of Sir George Ramsay."

Liza thought of the volume in the library to which she'd been drawn and had subsequently borrowed. "Somehow, I'm not surprised." But her smile faded, and she sighed. "Look, Lachlan. I know you're probably anxious to leave the Ramsay Estate and make up for the last eight years of your life. I have no right to ask you any favors, but do you think you might be willing to stay on for a bit longer, just until I can figure things out?"

He stared at her, his eyes unblinking and intense.

She studied her hands. "I know it's a lot to ask, but I promise, I'll figure things out quickly. It's just that you have so much knowledge, and so many thoughts, and I want to make sure I do things right and make Callum proud, and I can't think of a better way to do that than to have your advice and guidance." She was rambling, she knew, but she couldn't seem to stop herself.

He was still staring at her. She gulped. "You can tell me to go to hell," she said. "It won't hurt my feelings."

He held up his hands and let them drop to his sides again. "Of course not," he said. He shuffled from one foot to the other, and seemed to be considering her words, and choosing his own, carefully.

Liza nearly retracted her request before Lachlan finally spoke. "Honestly, Liza. I'd like nothing better than to stay on. For as long as ye'll have me."

She stared at him, waiting for the 'but'. None came. "You would?"

"I would," he affirmed, nodding vigorously.

"Because you can go anywhere, you know. You can finally put your degree to use. You can move to the city, start your own business, work wherever you want."

"Are ye tryin' to talk me out of helpin' ye?" he asked, laughing.

She shook her head. Relief, like a wave released, rolled through her. She felt very close to tears. "And one more thing…Can you help me give Callum a proper sendoff to the next part of his journey, wherever he is?"

She thought she saw an extra shine in his eyes. "I would be humbled and honored. Though he loved the Ramsay Castle so dearly, I have a feeling his ghost won't stray too far from the grounds."

"His spirit is always welcome as long as he's at peace."

Lachlan bowed his head, and Liza took a moment to watch him and consider the breadth of his shoulders, the cut of his jaw, and the gentleness of his soul.

"One last request," she said, and Lachlan brought his head up.

She cleared her throat. "There is an old Chinese proverb that says, 'When you save someone's life, you're responsible for what that person does with it'. I don't intend to hold you to that forever, but since you're kind of responsible for me, it would be really great if you could move out of the laborers' cottage and into the main part of the castle."

He was quiet for a moment. Then he said quietly,

"Ye saved my life too, Liza. I expect we might need to be lookin' after each other."

Their eyes met, and Liza was glad the monitors had been unhooked, because she was fairly certain her heartbeat was so fast and loud that it may have sent the diagnostics off the charts.

Lachlan stepped forward so that he was right next to the bed. He gently picked up her right hand. "Can I kiss ye now?"

Liza nodded. Lachlan leaned in, and their lips met. Somewhere, far in the distance, she could have sworn a bagpipe played just slightly out of tune. Lady Catherine, she knew, approved.

Epilogue

For the second time in her life, Liza looked out the window of the jet descending into Edinburgh International Airport as the pilot announced their final descent. Now she was going home. The thought both thrilled her and filled her with trepidation.

It had been nearly two months since she'd departed Scotland for Boston to clean out and list her Back Bay apartment, give her official resignation to her employer, and say goodbyes to family and friends. Each task she'd completed felt surreal, as if she were playacting her own life.

She'd had a particularly bizarre encounter with Owen, who she found living in the apartment as if their breakup had not occurred. He'd seemed bemused, first by her confusion about his continued residence there, and then her anger. After attempting a half-hearted proposal again, at which she could only laugh, he had responded with his own rage, which had dwarfed hers.

She had to remind him multiple times that his name was not on the deed; then she threatened legal action. He'd finally left, though not before one of their neighbors called the Boston PD. He'd agreed to fully vacate when she wasn't at home, then knowingly took the living-room furniture and bedroom suite she'd purchased.

The breakup with her boss Raj was only slightly less uncomfortable. He was disinterested in the events that had occurred in Scotland, even her near-death experience, and was in denial that she might actually leave the firm, after making partner, no less. When she finally delivered her resignation in writing, he'd been appalled, but at least he accepted that her decision was non-negotiable. Then he'd demanded two months' notice for 'knowledge transfer', prompting Liza to work with a human resources business partner and member of the legal team. They'd reached an agreement on three-weeks' notice, during which Liza communicated directly with Raj a sum total of zero times. He'd refused to talk to her, forcing awkward interactions using his assistant as an intermediary.

The apartment sold with a cash offer in days, and because she'd bought the place before the worldwide pandemic and exponential growth of the real estate market, she profited handsomely from the deal. After agreeing to a closing date with the buyers, she visited her grandparents in Pennsylvania for two weeks where she used the income from the apartment sale to pay down their living expenses for the foreseeable future.

Her grandparents had been much more interested

in and concerned about the events that had transpired at Ramsay Castle, though she'd glossed over some of the scarier and more dangerous occurrences. They sighed over the death of young Charlie Campbell, gasped over the demise of Brodie Graham, and cried over the death of Callum Ramsay. As Liza recounted the treachery of Mrs. Boyle and the villainy of Misters Morrison and Douglas, it occurred to her that she might well have been spinning a madcap story. And yet, she'd lived through it. And survived it.

Her grandparents hadn't been able to offer much additional information about her father, who'd always been a standoffish man. But after all the pain he'd caused, they were glad to know that his involvement in their daughter's life had resulted in not only Liza but an impressive inheritance. "The man was good for *something*, I suppose," her grandfather had grudgingly said. Her grandmother had been more generous. "I'll always be thankful for Simon Ramsay, because he gave us you."

But the person they were most interested in was Lachlan McClaren. The first time Liza had said his name, her grandmother had said, "You're in love. I hear it on your breath, and it shines through your eyes." And that had made Liza extremely happy, but it had also made her worried. Because her interactions with Lachlan had been so fraught with drama, danger, secrets, and scandal, she wasn't sure what would happen between them when she returned to Scotland and circumstances were much calmer.

She'd spoken to Lachlan often on the phone, and as the cloud of suspicion surrounding Nicola's death had cleared from around him, she could hear him becoming more confident and surer of himself. Some of the moody intensity that had clung to him also seemed to dissipate, and there was often a smile in his voice that hadn't been there before. He and his father were working to mend their relationship while he took up management of the castle and renovations to the fire-damaged kitchen and first floor.

As the jet descended through the misty clouds above Edinburgh and the bonny hills outside the city came into view, Liza couldn't help but wonder if this new version of Lachlan would be as interested in her as he'd been when she'd kissed him goodbye two months earlier.

He had insisted on coming himself to pick her up, and she suspected he was just as nervous about seeing her again. She thought she'd heard it in his voice and seen it in his expression the last time they'd chatted by video call.

She was wearing an ivory cashmere summer sweater and a soft brown corduroy pant with a black Karter ankle boot. She had splurged on Newbury Street before she'd left Boston for good, and her carry-on was filled with similar expensive purchases that had made her feel frivolous and slightly giddy. The rest of her clothes and possessions had been shipped to the Ramsay Estate weeks earlier, and Lachlan had confirmed that all had arrived safely.

The temperature in Edinburgh was cool, and after the humid heat of late August in the mid-Atlantic, she welcomed the damp mist that awaited her.

She passed through customs quickly; her heart thudded in her chest as she exited the secure area and surveyed the crowd.

And there he was, smiling, waiting. His green eyes flashed, and they rushed toward each other. She dropped the carry-on case when he picked her up and twirled her around.

She noted a few passengers laughing at their obvious delight in each other, and a few others looking annoyed by their spectacle, but she didn't care. He kissed her and put her down, and she steadied herself in his solid arms.

It struck her how much nattier he looked compared to the first time she'd seen him, then she remembered the first time he'd laid eyes on her, she'd been naked. The memory still made her blush.

She felt more secure as he picked up her suitcase and led her to the car park outside, where they approached a white Audi coupe. "I was expecting the truck," she said with a note of surprise and delight.

"This was my father's car," he explained. "He was

in the market for something new, and I'd saved up a few quid, so I figured, why not? Can't be drivin' the estate truck around all over the countryside, now, can I?"

Liza nodded in agreement, delighting in his familiar voice with its lilting brogue. She'd missed the musicality of his words while she'd been in Boston where the drawl was harsher and more jarring to her ear, even though she'd lived with it for years.

"So, the contractors have been delayed a wee bit in finishing up work on the castle," Lachlan said. There was hesitation in his voice.

Liza looked over at him as he maneuvered around a second roundabout, expertly steering into the flow of traffic. "It's not habitable?" she asked.

"Aye, it is. I just thought, if ye're up fer it, we might spend a few days exploring the countryside instead."

Liza hesitated, but not because she was displeased with the idea. In fact, after the heaviness of her release from the hospital, and the solemnness of Callum's funeral and wake which had been held at the castle, spending a few days in preparation for the next part of their journey seemed like a grand idea. It was more that she had steeled herself for this homecoming, and now she needed to mentally readjust.

Lachlan took her hesitation as a rebuff. "But if ye'd like to get back to the castle and plunge right in, I understand that too. We can go there straightaway."

"No," she said quickly. "I'm up for an adventure. What did you have in mind?"

He told her of a seaside village called Oban, where he'd vacationed as a child with his family. "It's a charming little place with good food, fine shops, and access to the Isles."

"It sounds lovely, but will we be able to make reservations to stay on such short notice?"

He looked at her sheepishly, and there was a glimpse of the old Lachlan. It made her heart ache. He was just so dear. "I've already done it," he said. "I figured we could cancel if ye didn't wannae go."

Her heart ached even more. Because Owen never planned one thing the entire time they'd been together. He'd waited for her to make arrangements, then complained about them later for days on end.

She reached over and cupped his cheek in her hand. "I'd be delighted," she said, and in that moment, if any reservations had been left at all, they vanished.

Lachlan was all hers, and she was all his.

⸸

After three days of exploring, strolling through the village and gorging on good seafood, ferrying out to the Inner and Outer Hebrides, and venturing around the magnificent Scottish Highlands, they returned to Ramsay Castle with no question of their connection or their bond. Liza felt a deeper familiarity with the country, though she knew her intimacy with the country would only deepen.

Walking into the castle—her castle—was a strange and mystical experience, and she held onto Lachlan's hand as they entered the building. The familiar smell hit her first. It was a rich, ancient smell that she hadn't detected since she first entered with Mr. Douglas and Mrs. Boyle. Two of the people who had tried to kill her. It would take time to come to terms with that.

She could also smell the sweet scent of newly cut wood and fresh paint from the kitchen. While the previous kitchen had been beautiful, this updated kitchen was beyond what her imagination could have conjured—it was a true commercial-grade chef's kitchen, fit for the most elaborate of five-star restaurants. The new appliances gleamed, and paired well with warm cabinetry. The original brick fireplace had been repointed, but looked much the same as it had before.

As she explored and re-familiarized herself with the castle in her new role, Lachlan kept checking in with her to make sure she was okay. And she was. After everything that had happened here, it felt like home. That was a relief.

That evening, they were sitting in the dining room, listing off all the legal proceedings Liza needed to complete for the inheritance to move forward. She had a meeting with the solicitor Niall Murphy the next morning. Lachlan had done quite a bit of research over the past two months so that she felt more prepared than she had previously. James McClaren had even offered the services of some of his contacts in the government, so she felt certain the process would advance smoothly.

Interrupting their meticulous preparations for the future, the rich, melodic, ominous chime of a doorbell reverberated through the room.

Liza's head snapped up. "Are you expecting anyone?" she asked.

Lachlan shook his head. They both hesitated before descending the stairs together, keenly aware that they were the only two living souls in the entire castle.

But when they pulled open the door, Detective Chief Inspector Marion Dean turned around. She smiled at Liza. "Hello there. I'd heard you were back in town."

She nodded to Lachlan, who nodded back.

"Inspector Dean," Liza said, her eyebrows raised. "To what do we owe this pleasure?"

Dean's smile dimmed ever so slightly. She hesitated. Liza's mind immediately came to its own conclusions. "Is it Boyle and Morrison? Has something gone wrong with the case?"

"Oh, no," Dean said. "It's nothing like that. It's just that, well…may as well get right to the point. I've a small favor to ask ye."

Liza and Lachlan exchanged a glance.

"I've got two American girls down at the station who'd come over for a visit before their semester started back at home. Unfortunately, they are witnesses to a...*crime* involving someone of influence in Edinburgh. It's a delicate situation."

Dean paused, perhaps waiting for them to ask questions. But Liza didn't even know where to begin.

When Liza and Lachlan remained silent, Dean continued. "We have the girls secured in a hotel room for the time being, and they're quite fine. But I think they might feel more comfortable and more secure in a home." She paused again. "We can install a constable at the end of the drive to guard the property."

"You want them to stay *here*?" Liza asked as Dean's request finally dawned on her.

"If it wouldn't be too much trouble for you both. Yes."

Liza furrowed her brow. "But why?"

Dean shifted from one foot to the other. "After everything that's happened, I've come to trust you. Both of you," she clarified, looking at Lachlan. "The girls' parents won't arrive for a few days, and I want to make sure they're both safe and comfortable." She leaned forward. "We need their testimony," she added quietly. "And with you being an American new to the United Kingdom, and Lachlan being from an established family, it seemed like it might be the solution we've been searching for."

Liza nodded slowly. She certainly knew what it felt like to feel lost and alone in a strange place with murder happening all around. But she looked at Lachlan. "What do you think?"

He shrugged. "We have plenty of room." She caught the flicker of a question in his eye, and she gave him a slight nod. They were in this together.

Liza turned back to Dean. "Seeing how the danger has passed here, I don't see any reason not to invite them in."

Dean let out the breath she had obviously been holding. "Thank you, Ms. Ramsay, Mr. McClaren. I promise, I'll make it up to ye."

"We're going to hold you to that," Liza answered with a laugh.

They shook hands. Dean winked. "I'll be back straightaway with the lovely young ladies."

When they shut the door behind Dean, Liza and Lachlan looked at each other.

"The guests are arriving," he said.

"That they are," Liza responded, and a familiar sense of anticipation fluttered over her, along with the slightest of chills. Something told her that living in the castle would bring many visitors, both living and otherworldly. In the Ramsay Castle, all were welcome.

THE END

Acknowledgements

So many people to thank, not only for helping to make this book possible, but just for believing in me as a writer. To my mom, Janey Cunningham, who never fails to ask about my writing and my books, and is my biggest cheerleader. Thank you; I love you.

Perils Past wouldn't exist without Jim, my travel partner and Scottish adventurer. Thanks for listening to all of my potential plots, settings, and characters and humoring me as this story worked itself out. Also, thanks for putting up with my mood swings as these characters took on lives of their own.

To Sue, who reads my books even though she hates reading. Someday, I'll name a character after you. As soon as I find a character who can rise to your level of awesomeness.

To Nate who doesn't read my books, and to Mary, who does.

To Rachel, Noah, and Adam, my amazing children, who sometimes think I'm a pretty okay mom. I think you're all the best of the best, the cream of the crop, the greatest of all time. I'm so humbled to have had anything to do with the fabulous people you turned out to be. Thanks for taking care of yourselves so that I can create all of these make-believe characters and give them their own problems to solve.

To Natalie, my sometimes-writing partner and spooky soul sister who loves a good ghost story and mystery as much as I do. Here's to lots more writing in our futures.

Thank you to James and Sarah, the elders, who love to share their amazing adventures. I can only hope we amass half as many amazing adventures as you've had over the years. And a huge thank you to James Boswell who opened up his home at Auchinleck to us, and showed us all around Ayrshire. This book was greatly inspired by the day that we spent together in the Scottish countryside.

Paul Carson at Seminal Edits expertly whipped Liza and Lachlan into shape and smoothed out all of the rough edges of the Ramsay Castle's first story. I'm so happy that I found you, and look forward to connecting with you once again in the Ramsay Castle.

To the Dalhousie Castle, upon which much of the Ramsay Castle was based. It's impossible to visit this fabulous location and not be moved by the history of the castle. I hope that I've crafted a story that might have amused Sir Alexander and Lady Catherine. Their memories are certainly alive and well within those walls.

Finally, thank you to anyone who picked up or downloaded a copy of *Perils Past* and read to the end.

This story was a joy to write and a labor of love. If you've spent some time with Liza and Lachlan in the Ramsay Castle, I am greatly indebted to you for your time and attention. I hope you enjoyed this wild and ghostly mystery.

There are plenty of others to thank, but I'll catch you all in the sequel. Love to you all!

S.J. Cunningham

Made in United States
Orlando, FL
10 December 2024